A LOVE AS WILD AS THEIR LIFE

Wild
LIFE

A STEAM-Y NOVEL

BESTSELLING AUTHOR
VICTORIA WOODS

Copyright

Cover Design:
Sam Palencia, https://www.inkandlaurel.com/

Interior Formatting and Illustrations:
Brian Ladlee, https://www.brianladlee.com/

Editing:
Paisley Prophet, https://www.instagram.com/paisleyprophetedits/

Proofreading:
Chinah Mercer, https://editorandquill.com/
Nisha Ladlee, https://nishasbooksandcoffeepr.com/

For mature audiences only.

Table of Contents

Dedication

To all the animals that love us humans unconditionally, even when we aren't capable of loving ourselves.

And to my own first dogs, Moru and Ayoki, I will spend every life after this one looking for you.

Foreword

...and some Trigger Warnings:

Firstly, I need to mention that your reading comfort is important to me. *Wild Life* is a contemporary romance with feel-good humor and lots of steam. However, there are a few trigger warnings to be aware of before diving into this book. The major one involves the death and a reincarnation of a beloved pet. This subject matter is isolated to the two epilogue chapters at the end of the book and can be skipped. If you are particularly sensitive to this topic, I strongly urge you to exercise caution before reading those two chapters. A happily-ever-after is guaranteed before and after the two epi-logue chapters.

The complete trigger warning list is as follows:

-death of parents in childhood

-allusions to hunting – not graphic in nature

-mental health representation – anxiety

-speech impediments/stutter

-death and reincarnation of a beloved pet (only in the 2 epilogue chapters and can be skipped)

-childbirth (epilogue chapters only and can be skipped)

Wild Life is the second book of the *STEAM-y Series* and can be read as a standalone. This series is centered around science, technology, engineering, arts, and mathematics.

Sign up for Victoria's newsletter to receive news about future releases and giveaways:

The Island

Bat Caves

Waterfall

Mango Tree

Brook

Graves

Thicket

Pond

The Beach

Tick Mark Trees

Hibiscus Hedge

Camp

PACIFIC OCEAN

Chapter 1

Breaking Up and Breaking Habits

Maris

"You're so fucking big. I'm gonna come."

False. And, false. Eli was on the smaller side of average, and although size didn't really matter, according to that old adage, he didn't know what to do with it. *It's not the size of the boat, but the motion of the ocean...*

Orgasm was yet another distant dream, like dark-chocolate-chip ice cream on a waffle cone in the dead of night, or getting a seventh season of that show based on the British monarchy. And why exactly couldn't they continue the show? There were a hell of a lot of royals still alive and causing enough drama to fill at least another twelve episodes.

With lids squeezed shut, Eli rolled his neck from side to side as if he were in some deep trance. "God, Maris. It's like my fat cock was made for your pussy. I could do this all night."

Oh God. Please, no. My labia could only tolerate about three more minutes of his drilling before I'd need some ointment from all the chaffing. His scratchy pubes were abrasive as a steel-wool sponge.

Think about bats. It might seem a little weird—okay, *very weird*—to distract oneself from intercourse by thinking about bats, but that was the level of obscurity a scientist's brain achieved when searching for their next hit of dopamine. Besides, bats were never too far from my mind anyway. In a few hours, I'd get to hightail it off the boat and begin my research on my favorite species of bat, the Pacific sheath-tailed bat. Once rampant in the islands of the South Pacific, the tiny creatures now faced extinction throughout the region, with less than an estimated one hundred individuals left in the world.

I had the privilege of studying a known colony based in a cave in Fiji. My project was part of a larger one with a team consisting of myself, not-so-fat-cock Eli, and two other members who were to evaluate the effects of agriculture on the natural wildlife in the region. We'd paid multiple visits to nearby islands to investigate in the same manner, yet never before had I had the opportunity to study the largest known colony of Pacific sheath-tailed bats in the world.

But first, I needed to put an end to the jackhammering between my legs.

I arched my back, jutting my B-sized tits out, and unleashed my most seductive moan—the kind that only a woman could fake. *A porn moan.* "Babe, fuck me harder! You give me the best dick of my life!" I grabbed his ass, urging him on. It was safe to say that I would not be on Santa's *nice* list this year with the number of lies that had easily rolled off my tongue. *Good.* Maybe Krampus would come get me for being *naughty* and finally give me the orgasm I had yet again been robbed of. I'd heard he had a huge monster cock…or at least, that was what my romance novels said.

My praise worked because Eli's hips moved faster, his shaft daggered into me at lightning speed. Since there wasn't enough suction between us, I could feel his length dragging against my lower wall with each stroke. I mean, he had to be fully erect if he was able to move without it slipping completely out, right? I assumed I wasn't particularly stretched down there. My gynecologist had even noted in my charts that my vagina was *unremarkable*, as mundane as that sounded, during my last checkup when she'd inserted an IUD. So, then, why didn't we fit together properly?

A cramp seized my shoulder from playing *dodge the bullet* as I tried to avoid the sweat that dripped from Eli's bushy brow. The temperature on the boat was certainly warm, but the South Pacific air was too much for his sweat glands to handle.

The coils in the mattress creaked under the repetitive motion, which—coupled with the rocking of the cabin on the water—was beginning to churn my belly. Thank Jesus for the scopolamine patch behind my ear, or else I'd have been puking my guts out from the commotion. Then again, maybe a little vomit would have stopped the hammering.

I studied my colleague hovering over me as he pressed on. *Eli Ross, B.S., M.S., Ph.D.* Associate Professor of Entomological Conservation. Expert in the proliferation of the Fijian Megachilid bee. He was brilliant on paper. And while his thick black hair contrasted with his pale skin, making him almost ghostly under the shine of the night-light, he wasn't terrible looking either. If I saw past the Victorian-apparition exterior, I could see the faint outline of abs and vivid green eyes, the color of a Rustic Sphinx caterpillar. He would be a catch for any woman…with an extra-petite vagina.

My attention wandered from Eli to the fire-detection sensor on the ceiling, then to the blaring white display of my phone. *3 a.m.* I had to be up in four hours to prepare for landfall. It was time to employ my trusted technique, guaranteed to wrap this little tryst up. I swirled my tongue around the tip of my index finger, then guided my palm around his ass cheek creating some space to work.

Eli groaned out his appreciation. "Christ, this is like heaven."

"Mmm," I coaxed, slyly inching my finger upward. His breathing picked up, and I knew it was time to act. I quickly slid my wet finger into his asshole, eliciting a sharp grunt from him.

"Fuck!" His thrusts turned erratic, and he wheezed as the orgasm overtook his body. I squeezed my thighs around his hips and shouted out my fake release without regard for our teammates, Fran and Malcom, asleep next door. The men who had blessed my bed…or cursed it…always fell for over-the-top theatrics during sex. It boggled my mind that society deemed them more apt to rule countries when some of them were so fucking gullible.

Eli collapsed onto my chest, his weight crushing me. His warm breath blowing on my neck was as enjoyable as a turtleneck in the dead of summer. I shoved him off so that he was on his back next to me.

He hummed out a heavy sigh. "That was amazing."

I turned to him. "Mmm," was all I could manage again, proving that I was capable of…not exactly honesty, but not lying, for a change.

The last bits of his lust-filled haze cleared, and he eyed me eagerly. "Was it good for you, too? You sounded like you were really enjoying it."

I brushed my slick hair out of my face. "*Enjoy* doesn't quite sum it up." I offered a gentle smile.

His smooth fingers caressed my cheek, and I leaned into his touch. *This* was what I craved—my reason for enduring lackluster coitus. Fucking was the gateway to cuddling, and if I closed my eyes, I could bask in the ephemeral sense of being cherished for precious seconds in the afterglow of orgasm.

Don't get me wrong, sex could be enjoyable—when performed correctly—but it was the closeness I desired. I longed to belong.

Freud would say that my need for intimacy was derived from losing my parents at the age of eight in a car accident and spending my formative years being raised by my mother's sister, who had the emotional range of drywall. The only time I could remember being hugged by Aunt Sherri was the day of my parents' funeral, when I was forced to see their stone-cold corpses lying in polished wooden boxes. For the briefest moment, Aunt Sherri had let down her stern exterior to mourn her sister, and I had been the beneficiary of those rare emotions, the likes of which I knew I would never witness again.

However, it wasn't my aunt's fault. My grandparents had raised their daughters to fulfill predetermined roles. Mom had been the youngest and more outgoing of the two, so they had expected her to marry someone well-off like my father, the doctor, and give them grandchildren. Aunt Sherri had been more reserved—a thinker—so her paved route had led to a career.

Science ran in my blood, not only from my cardiologist father, but from Aunt Sherri, too. She had worked her way through college to become a biochemist. Having earned her Ph.D. at the age of twenty-five, the woman was a force to be reckoned with.

If Freud were still in the chat, he would also say that my desire to become a scientist, and to have a Ph.D. of my own at age thirty-two, was more than the critical-thinking genes and problem-solving skills I had inherited from both sides of my family. Maybe a part of me had always hoped if I became a scientist, too, then Aunt Sherri would finally wrap an arm around me and tell me how proud she was of me. That day had yet to come, so it was lucky for me that I at least enjoyed being a wildlife biologist.

"You're wearing me out, Maris." Eli stretched his arms over his head. "We've fucked every night since we left port."

I burrowed into his side, absorbing his warmth like it was a drug. "And that's a bad thing?" I replied lazily, my words already sluggish and slurring from sleepiness.

He pulled on a tendril of my chestnut-colored hair. "What kind of man would I be to look a gift horse in the mouth?"

I drew back. "Did you just call me a horse?"

"Well, I did ride you to exhaustion, didn't I?" His smile was too proud to match the tacky words that exited through it.

I grimaced—not at his poor humor, but at my desperation for intimacy from a chauvinist. In my search for affection, I had lowered my standards for men so much that I didn't know what I deserved anymore.

I rolled away from his touch, suddenly repulsed by cuddling, and myself. "We should get some sleep. We need to be up soon."

His hand remained on my hip oblivious to my self-loathing. "I'm so damn thankful for our relationship."

My spine stiffened and I shot up in the bed like he had dumped ice water on me. *Relationship?*

"Eli." I strained to keep my voice steady, though I was shaking inside. "We've been over this. We aren't in a *relationship*."

He sat up next to me and reached out for me, but I shrank away. "Maris, relax. It's not a bad thing. Give us a chance."

Us? "We're not dating. We agreed that this was only sex." The calmness I had been grasping so tightly began to slip as he twisted his mouth to bite his inner cheek. "Eli," I warned.

"Maris, we've been hooking up on these work trips for nearly two years now. We always share the same room and sleep in the same bunk every night. Don't you think we're past the friends-with-benefits stage? We don't sleep with other people, for Christ's sake."

I clutched the sheets to my chest. "You can fuck other people. I've already told you that. I'm fine with it." Really, I was. This was in no way intended to be a monogamous arrangement, and I had been very clear about that from the beginning with Eli—and every other man I had been with. Nothing about us was exclusive.

Apparently, Eli wanted what I was terrified to give—a commitment.

The corners of his eyes fell with disappointment. "I just want to be with you."

His words were clear, but all I could register was the pounding in my chest. "Please. Stop. We've talked about this. I don't want to be in a relationship."

"With me?"

"With anyone." My skin tingled as imaginary ants marched up the back of my neck. No amount of itching or slapping would stop the familiar sensation. They would only spread, suffocating me until everything went black. Until my brain shut off to escape the panic.

Eli let out a sigh. "What are you so afraid of?"

Everything.

How could I put into words that I was afraid of rejection? If we continued screwing around like we had been doing all this time, I could still retain the upper hand and wouldn't risk being turned away when I was in too deep and at my most vulnerable. The minute I sealed *us* with commitment, it would all turn to hell, ending in a messy breakup that would leave me alone, yet again. *Like when Mom and Dad died.*

Either way, I was destined to be by myself because it was clear to me that Eli and I couldn't continue this way. It would at least be on my terms if I ended everything immediately.

Forehead creased, Eli seemed to read my thoughts loud and clear. I gritted my teeth to keep anxious tears from flowing. "I'm going to sleep."

Without a word, Eli slid out from my bunk. His mattress overhead bowed with his weight He tossed and turned before finally going still. The rhythmic sawing of his snores soon followed.

My bunk was empty and cooler than with a man in it, yet the weight of the thin flat sheet strangled me. I kicked it off and planted my feet on the vinyl floor. I threw on my overworn Smokey the Bear forest-fire T-shirt and shorts and left the cabin.

As expected for nighttime, the deck was empty, with only one crew member on watch in the wheelhouse, no doubt.

My body swayed with the gentle waves that rocked the boat. The sea was far too calm. A storm was coming. I sensed it, although there wasn't a cloud in the sky.

I wrapped my arms over my chest, staring at the bright full moon above. Its light skittered across the surface of the water like crushed diamonds.

We were still hours away from docking, but I desperately needed to get back to work—to distract myself from the bullshit I had left behind in the cabin.

My fists clenched as I replayed our *fight*.

Fighting wasn't supposed to happen in this arrangement, for the mere fact that this was not a relationship. A relationship I hadn't wanted in the first place to avoid the rush of labels coursing through my veins. *Inadequate. Broken. Fucked up.*

Relationships terrified me because one day, they would end. It was inevitable. Death was the result of life. Everything died eventually. Even relationships.

Losing my parents had taught me that at an early age. Their accident, coupled with Aunt Sherri's cold reception of her new ward, had really messed me up. I was still that eight-year-old girl searching for a hug. Only now, I searched for it in the form of dick with the promise of being held afterward.

I was responsible for the havoc in this arrangement with Eli. I supposed I couldn't blame him for wanting to escalate our status. As a species, humans always strove for more—to achieve something better and more whole for our lives. Eli was only fulfilling his primal instinct.

I was the one who was fucked up. Would there ever be a day when I would feel like I was enough? Like I was worth it?

The wind blew in my face. Change was coming.

Chapter 2

Hide the Salted Fish; A Storm is Coming

Aleki

The full moon had proven to be generous. The two baskets I had weaved from banana leaves were already filled with fish of all sizes.

My shoulders ached from spearing for longer than I could recall ever doing, and my eyes burned, in need of rest. For some reason, I wasn't tired. My mind matched the shifting winds, restless. A storm was coming, and it would be a big one, from how still the beach air had been hours before.

I gathered my spear and baskets and trudged through the sand, making my way to the thicket ahead. I barely registered the underbrush pricking the soles of my bare feet. They bore years of scar tissue to pad my discomfort.

As easy as it would have been to use a net for fishing instead of spearing, I opted for the more cumbersome option because it exercised my mind through strategy, anticipation, exhilaration for my success, loss for my failure, and mourning for the life that perished for my survival.

The moon was bright enough that I didn't need to bother with a torch in hand to light my way.

Branches and thorns whipped my broad shoulders, but I had grown accustomed to their lashes, too. I had been much smaller when I'd first landed on this island and had been able to weave through the trees unscathed. Over time, both the jungle trees and my body had grown unapologetically large, as if fighting for dominance over each other. I was one man, alone in this wild place, among many trees. Most days, I was fighting a losing battle. Yet, somehow, I was still here, nearly twenty-four years later.

How did a ten-year-old boy retain a sense of time after being shipwrecked on a deserted island without a watch, a calendar, or the guidance of his parents? By carving tallies into trees.

I passed the grove of barks that bore witness to my solitude, each covered in grooves as if infested with termites. Eight thousand eight hundred and ninety-one ticks—one for every sunset I had seen. The gashes varied: some were deep because they had been carved in anger; some were shallow because there hadn't been hardly enough time in the day to waste recording the date. And some ticks, especially the earlier ones, held traces of the tears that had fallen from my face as I mourned my parents. These marks were the only evidence of my history.

I slowed my stride as a deep grunt sounded from beyond the trees. Leaves rustled violently, warning me that I had company. Frenzied wheezes grew louder as the source neared. I braced myself for an attack.

Swift like a lightning bolt, a giant ball of fur barreled into my shins, nearly knocking me over. I crouched to the ground to welcome my visitor.

"Nice to see you, too, Poaka," I said, rubbing behind his floppy ear, which elicited a delighted wriggle out of him. For a hefty adult pig, he sure did act like a baby.

It had been many lifetimes ago when Poaka had first approached me one night when I had been trying to assemble a tent, and he had never left my side since. He was my only friend and confidant who never abandoned me—except to forage for mushrooms.

I ran my hand under his belly, measuring how full it was. "Looks like I wasn't the only one who was successful in my catch. Hope you left some mushrooms for me."

Poaka rocked on his hooved toes impatiently before shoving his hairy face into one of the baskets. His eager nose huffed at the pile of fresh fish.

I patted his head, then stood up and gathered my catch. "Not yet. Got to clean them first."

Together, we made our way back to the hut. The four-walled cube covered with a triangular roof made of mud, wood, and palm fronds seemed humble at first glance, but it was ample in terms of shelter. I had built it from the ground up with my own two hands. It had taken years of trial and error and many unsuccessful attempts before I created a dwelling strong enough to shield Poaka and me from the rainstorms and heat.

Over the years, I had collected various materials that had washed ashore, like teak wood and plastic ship sidings, and added them to the structure. And what I had eventually ended up with was a solid hut with stairs below the modest front deck. It was completely furnished inside with a bed, one sitting chair, and a dining table, all made by me. They weren't beautiful to the eye, but they were sturdy enough for my needs.

There was also plenty of room to store my father's collection of books that had washed up, completely safe and dry in the trunk it had originally been packed into. I had studied every word within the collection, particularly the hefty dictionary, learning each one's meaning and practicing its *pronunciation*. Ironically, that had been a difficult word for me to learn to say correctly. I still wasn't sure I had it right, but there was no one around to correct me.

As good of a friend as Poaka was, English certainly wasn't his strong point—granted, he understood much of what I said to him.

I started a fire in the pit and got to work on the already gutted and descaled fish. Poaka danced around me, kicking his hooves excitedly as I extracted a few bony spines that I had saved for him. He chomped on them, grunting his appreciation between bites.

Working like a one-man assembly line, I set to curing. Using salt I had boiled out of seawater, I smeared a generous amount inside of each fish, as well as on the body, before resting the prepared ones in a basket filled with more salt.

Fresh seafood was more delicious, but it spoiled too quickly in the humidity and attracted pesky flies. Curing was the only way to prevent a large catch like this from going bad. My supply had run out, and this batch would last me another month, provided hunting went smoothly, too.

I covered the basket with more banana leaves, then wrapped a scrap of a plastic tarp over the top—another thing from my collection of items washed ashore—and lowered the bundle into a hole in the ground. The basket had small gaps that would help to drain the water drawn out by the salt. The tarp over the top and sides would help keep the fish clean from any ground matter. I covered everything with dirt and packed it tightly to protect it from the expected rainfall. I'd check on it again after the rain passed.

Poaka rolled onto his side and let out a sharp grunt. He was tired, and I couldn't blame him. On most evenings, I fell asleep soon after the sun set, but tonight, my body had been too restless to stay still. However, I could feel myself slowing down. "Alright. Let's go to sleep."

I washed my hands with the rainwater I had collected in the barrel next to the hut. I had engineered a system to rig an outside shower made of old tubing that I had found, but I was too exhausted to use it now.

The cool water was the perfect relief as I splashed it onto my face, sighing at the tiny rivulets that dripped down my beard. I kept my facial hair short to avoid bugs and other particles from getting caught in it. It was uncomfortable to have little things crawling around your face especially when body hair grew like weeds in the humid weather.

I slurped some water into my mouth and swished it around, then spit it out and grabbed a twig from the collection I had left on the side of the water barrel. I chewed on it, making sure to touch each tooth. The ritual reminded me of brushing my teeth with Ma every night before bed. *Round and round and up and down.* My chest still ached for her as if she had died yesterday.

I tossed the stick into the pit and put the fire out. Poaka trotted by my feet as we made our way to the hammock strung up between two trees. I usually slept inside the hut, but the air was different, and something about it beckoned me. I would stay out until the rain started before moving inside.

I helped my buddy up into the heavily reinforced sling, and he curled into my underarm, nuzzling my side.

I chuckled. "Okay, I'll sing your song." He loved when I sang him the lullaby Ma had always sung to me. Every time I recited the words, I felt closer to her, if just for a moment.

"Close your eyes, child.

Let the winds be and the stars shine.

In your dream, your hand will find mine.

The splendor we'll see.

Sleep, my boy, and fly free with me."

Poaka's breathing slowed to a steady snoring, and I exhaled deeply, allowing my aching limbs a chance to relax.

The moon was certainly brighter than I'd ever seen it, despite the storm clouds hovering nearby, ready to stifle its brilliance. I rarely found time to enjoy nature. My day was filled with chores to keep the pig and myself alive to see another sunrise.

However, I couldn't help but savor the fleeting peace of the rustling leaves and the fragrant jungle air.

My eyelids drooped, yet I was aware that I should move us to shelter. Perhaps I could wait a little longer.

Chapter 3

Crashing into Destiny

Maris

Age 8

"I have to pee!" The seatbelt squished my belly every time I crossed my legs to try to stop an accident from happening. Bit, my stuffed bat, wobbled on my lap from my *pee-pee* dance.

"What?" Mom snapped back at me from the front seat. She immediately noticed the silver pouch in my hand. "I told you no more liquids until we reached Nana and Pop-Pop's."

She grabbed the juice pouch from my hands—and must have squeezed too hard because clear yellow liquid shot out of the straw like lava from a volcano and dripped down her wrist and onto the sleeve of her pink jacket.

"Damn it!" she shouted, holding her hand out in the air like she had touched dog poop. Her cheeks glowed red when she turned back to me with eyes big like plates. I had ruined her Chanel suit and she was mad.

"Maris Marie Schuler!" she screamed. "Look at this mess. Do you know how much this cost?"

That question wasn't supposed to be answered. Everything she owned had cost a lot. Mom liked expensive things so much that Dad had stopped asking about the prices whenever she went shopping. Nana was the same way with Pop-Pop. Everything in their house at the lake was white...like a hospital...and cost Mom's favorite price, *expensive.*

Fat raindrops punched the car, turning everything through the windows into smudgy splotches. Rain the day before Thanksgiving in Seattle was normal. It would be nice to live somewhere warm. Maybe near a beach. I would eat mangoes all day and then swim until bedtime. That was where I wanted to live when I grew up—free to play and be happy for the rest of my life.

Without removing his focus from the slippery road, Dad reached into the little cubby between the seats and pulled out a stack of white napkins leftover from our secret fast-food trips for French fries on weekends when

Mom was at Pilates class. It was his way of "seeing about dinner" for the only kid in the house.

Mom snatched a rectangle of white paper from him like she had the juice from mine. She had a problem with using *gentle hands* to take things from other people.

"It's ruined, Frank." She rubbed at the speckled fabric, but the stain stayed. "Is it too much to ask to look nice for once when we visit my parents?"

"You always look nice, dear." Dad lifted her sticky hand and kissed the back of it.

"And you *always* say that." Mom rolled her eyes. I was surprised hers never got stuck like she said mine would whenever I did the same thing.

Turning his head toward her, he smiled. "I always mean it."

As a heart surgeon, he was a serious person, but when it came to my mom, he was as soft as mashed potatoes. She could get whatever she wanted out of him. Most of my punishments came from Mom bugging Dad to *do something about his daughter.* If it were up to him, he'd ignore anything I did wrong. And it wasn't because he adored me. It was the opposite—he never paid much attention to me. I was either annoying Mom too much or boring Dad. So, I kept to myself as much as an only child could, pretending my stuffed animals were real animals and caring for them like their doctor. Bit the bat was my favorite patient, but I never let the other stuffies know that.

"I don't know why you bother to get so dressed up for Thanksgiving anyway. It's just going to be us at your parents' house," Dad said.

"And *Sherri!*" Whenever Mom mentioned Aunt Sherri, the *r*'s in her name sounded too hard. Like she was grinding her teeth to get the rest of the name out.

"Pamela, your sister doesn't care about what we wear."

Mom glared at the side of Dad's face like he was the one drinking a juice pouch. "I don't care what Sherri cares or doesn't care about."

It was a lie. Mom was always worried about Aunt Sherri's opinion, which confused me because my aunt was usually quiet.

The two sisters were like night and day. Mom's nose was usually between the pages of society magazines and blogs, while Aunt Sherri's was behind a microscope. She was a scientist…*biochemistry-ist* or whatever it's called. I didn't have much of a relationship with her because she scared me. She didn't like to be touched, so she never hugged me like I thought an aunt would hug her niece. I didn't think she liked kids at all. She seemed like she would rather be anywhere else than with her family.

I was never comfortable around her, so I kind of understood Mom's feelings.

The car jerked slightly on the road, and the seat belt cut into my belly, which was as puffy as a balloon, as we swung to the right. Dad quickly turned the wheel, and the car moved straight again.

"I really need to pee. Now!"

Mom twisted around. "No. You should have used the restroom before we left home."

"I did!" I squeezed my legs together and hoped that it would be enough to stop from bursting. Now probably wasn't a good time to let her know about the other two empty pouches that I'd hidden between my seat and the door.

"Oh God, Maris. Please tell me you didn't bring that hideous rat." Her eye scrunched at the corner as she stared at my chest.

"It's a *bat*!" She had finally noticed Bit snuggled under my arm. I never went anywhere without him. He made me feel less lonely, even when my parents were around. It was kind of funny that Aunt Sherri was the one who had given him to me as a Christmas gift last year. Mom's face had frozen when I'd opened the gift, and that had made Bit my new favorite toy. After that, he never left my side.

Of all the animals in the world, I loved bats and how much they loved each other. They were smart enough to hunt alone at night, but the coolest thing about them was how they slept. Hundreds of bats cuddled together, so warm and safe. Each *belonged* to the colony.

It was very different from how things were in my family. I didn't belong and it made me sad. When I was younger, I cried to get the attention I needed. As I grew up, I quickly learned that it was better for me to create my own world where I belonged, with my stuffies. With them, I could pretend that they needed me and that I could give them the love that I wished Mom and Dad, and even Aunt Sherri, would give me.

"Frank, help me out here. She's eight years old and still walking around with a stuffed animal like a baby."

My lips turned down. Mom could be so mean sometimes. And the brown bag in her lap was way uglier than Bit.

"So what? You walk around with your purse all day. Can we pull over, please?" Mom was concerned with everything but the most important issue: my pee. If they didn't pull over soon, I was really going to act like a baby and wet myself.

Dad laughed while Mom's face twisted like she'd smelled something bad. "No, we have twenty-five minutes left before we reach the lake house, and you can hold your bladder until then. And this," she lifted the bag, displaying the gold LV on the front, "is a designer bag. One day, you'll be thanking me for leaving it to you when I die."

I let out a huge breath. It was always the same thing: her purses were *investments*, and I was going to be so rich from the collection she was leaving behind for me.

I didn't care about *things*. I cared about being loved. I was jealous of the girls in my class. They had dates at the nail salon with their moms and got to go to the school daddy-daughter dances on the arms of their dads. Mom went to the salon to get away from me, and Dad worked all the time.

I closed my eyes and wished for something I knew would never come true. I wished I could move far away and live with the bats on a tropical island and never see my parents again.

The car swung again, but this time, it was faster, like that ride with the teacups at Disneyland, except this wasn't fun. My tummy dropped, and I squeezed the sides of my seat. Something wet and warm spread under me, a puddle of liquid soaking into my seat.

"Uh-oh! I had an accident," I cried out.

"Damn it!" Mom shouted. "Frank!"

"*Shit!*" Dad spun the steering wheel, but we rolled in the opposite direction.

Lights whirled around me, my head spinning like the car. My screams mixed with Mom's, sounding so far away from my ears, like from another planet. My body slammed forward, and Bit flew off my lap. Cold air pricked my skin. Glass met Bit, raining onto him like the water outside of the car. It was the last thing I saw before my head hit the back of my seat.

***

Cold and wet. That was how my body had felt as everything had turned black.

Now, it was the opposite. I was warm and dry. *Too warm. Too dry.*

I lay in a bed with rough sheets tucked under my chin. I should have pushed them away, but I stayed still because I was too scared to move.

Everything was wrong.

The cloth wrapped around my head was tight, scratching the tops of my ears. The beeps from the machines were loud. The TV on the wall was showing the news instead of cartoons.

And suddenly, I really wanted Mom and Dad.

Where are they? They have to be okay. I need them to be okay.

Where is Bit? I need to hug him. To talk to him.

I heard voices outside the door.

"She was very lucky her bladder wasn't punctured. The paramedics said they smelled urine when they found her. We suspect she emptied her bladder sometime before impact."

I didn't know who the man was. His voice reminded me of the way Dad spoke when he was on the phone with work.

Another voice. "What about her head?" It was serious and belonged to my Aunt Sherri. *Why is she here? Why am I in a hospital?*

"She suffered a mild concussion, so we recommend keeping her here for observation."

"When will she be able to go home?" Aunt Sherri asked.

"If her vitals check out and nothing new arises, I anticipate her to be discharged tomorrow. Will she be staying with you?"

"Yes."

Why am I going home with Aunt Sherri?

I didn't know how far from Nana and Pop-Pop's we were, but it couldn't have been too far for my parents to drive.

I watched the TV. A small boat flashed, then I saw helicopters flying in the air over the ocean, the words "Search Continues" at the bottom of the screen.

"She's been asleep, so she doesn't know about her parents yet," the man outside the door said. *Know what?*

"I'll take care of it," Aunt Sherri replied.

My head hurt trying to figure out what they were talking about, and the weird tube in my arm wouldn't let me leave the bed to go and ask them all my questions. My stomach hurt, and not from the accident. It hurt like when you knew something bad was about to happen…something you couldn't change.

Why won't they come in and tell me whatever it is?

The man spoke again. "Please make arrangements with your funeral home of choice to transport the bodies. Again, I'm sorry for your loss."

I didn't understand what he meant. Why were they talking about bodies? And where were Mom and Dad?

"Thank you," Aunt Sherri said.

The door clicked, and she entered. Where Mom had blonde hair and eyes that reminded me of my friend Jessica's tabby cat, Aunt Sherri had brown hair and small eyes that were glued to me through her eyeglasses.

"You're awake." That was how she spoke…never asking questions.

"Aunt Sherri, what's going on? Where's Mom and Dad? Are they okay?" I held my breath, hoping her answer wouldn't hurt my feelings, like my belly knew it would.

Her attention moved from me to the TV that showed a photograph of a boy around the same age as me. He had short dark hair, almost black, and brown skin. He had a nice smile, so wide that I could see the teeth that he'd lost. The background of the photo was the same blue color that Mom had chosen for my school photos this year. Blue was a good color for him. He looked like a nice person.

The helicopters came back on the screen and then the words, "New Zealand exploration family, including child, missing in the Pacific." Then under the school photo of the boy was a name, "Aleki Taylor."

Aunt Sherri stared at me again. If I could have erased her next words, I would have.

"Your parents are dead."

My breathing stopped. My stomach flipped upside down, and a sour taste filled my mouth.

I had wished to never see my parents again, and now I couldn't take it back.

Chapter 4

Ship Happens

Maris

"He's not here." Malcom's attention remained on his laptop screen as he shoveled a spoonful of fruity O-shaped cereal into his mouth. The Internet was spotty at sea, but it wasn't needed to review data, since everything was backed up onto an external hard drive when we couldn't access the cloud.

The boat swayed, propelling me into the crew mess. I quickly regained my composure, as if I had meant to tumble-walk to the booth. "Who?"

Malcom clicked through his spreadsheet, his cleanly shaven jaw working through chomps of fruity cereal. "Your boyfriend." For a grown man, he sure did relish in harassing me like a snotty teenager.

I slouched back into the ripped cushion of the bench seat, flashing him a prime view of everyone's favorite finger. "Fuck off."

He might've been my research lead at work, but I would always see him as my undergraduate roommate's smart-mouthed boyfriend. I had spent four years sharing a closet-sized dorm with Sibley and the love of her life, Malcom Jones—aspiring conservation resources management biologist. Having been subjected to the sight of his disgusting cum-stained boxer briefs on the bathroom floor one too many times should have granted me a pass from his heckling. Since then, Malcom and I had earned our doctorate degrees, yet he clearly still retained his immaturity. He might not have been a part of Sibley's life anymore, but he had been a fixture in mine for the past two years while on his research team at the university.

Malcom was a great scientist and fantastic leader. I honestly couldn't imagine working for anyone else, even if he knew the right buttons to push to irritate the hell out of me. He was like that annoying big brother whom I shared no DNA with yet couldn't get rid of.

His umber eyes glittered with amusement, nearly matching the color of his smooth skin. "Fucks before breakfast? What a way to start the day!"

Fran stumbled into the mess like I had, except with much more poise and a well-rested face. If she hadn't been such a sweet person, I'd have despised her for her porcelain skin and pin-straight hair, the kind I could only achieve after an hour with my hair straightener.

Fran Park was the kind of woman who didn't need makeup to look presentable. I, on the other hand, needed a shit ton of foundation and concealer to smooth out my nearly translucent skin stained with *party marks*— the dark spots that took your face hostage when you didn't get more than three hours of sleep on a regular basis. It would be fine if my sleepless nights ever involved dancing on tables and doing body shots off male models. But no, my insomnia was mainly because of my pitiful need to cuddle with any man who showed me the least bit of attention. Why was I such a hot mess?!

My colleague was so enviably perfect from the time she woke in the morning until the time she went to bed. In my defense, she was our resident ornithologist, which by default made her a morning person—early to bed, early to rise and all that deal. Bat people, on the other hand, were not morning people. Nighttime was our time to shine since most species were nocturnal.

The boat sloshed, and my stomach dropped. The water was unruly. If it kept up, one scopolamine patch to fight nausea wouldn't be sufficient.

"Water's getting kinda rough, huh? Eat something so you don't throw up." Fran served me a bowl of marshmallow cereal before sliding into the booth next to me.

"Thanks." I wasn't hungry, although it was my favorite, but I forced down a spoonful to express my gratitude.

"Everything okay? I heard you and Eli talking last night." Her low voice didn't keep Malcom from minding the conversation.

"We're calling it *talking*? The entire crew had surround-sound audio of you two howler monkeys fucking and fighting. I was ready with a bucket of cold water to break you two up."

"Malcom!" Fran scolded. He had managed to finagle two faint wrinkles between her brows that I hadn't known she was capable of.

"What? They get to keep everyone up with their drama and I can't comment on it?"

"Lay off, Malcom," I grumbled. "I'm not in the mood." My head was pounding, and I needed to get my shit together before we made landfall to set up nests to tag bats.

"Never mind him, he's just jealous he's not hooking up with anyone." Fran waved our boss away.

Ever since the breakup with Sibley years ago, Malcom had become the eternal bachelor, and it was no wonder why. His loose tongue scared off any woman who paid him attention.

"If that's what a relationship sounds like these days, then count me out of it." Malcom pushed his cereal bowl out of the way.

Fran shook her head and directed her attention to me. "I'm here if you want to share."

"Thanks." I offered her a weak smile.

Where would I even begin? How could I explain that I needed Eli in my bed so I could sleep properly, except now that he wanted to be exclusive and label *us*, I was damn near ready to jump out of my skin to get away from him? It would make no sense, no matter how hard Fran tried to understand it. It barely made any sense to me.

No. Deflection was the only sane option. "Do we think we're really going to make it out into the field today?" The floor heaved, jerking me forward so my sternum met the edge of the table.

"It had started raining before I came down here," Fran said.

"I spoke to the captain, and he said that we've moved into a system. We're close enough to shore that he should be able to drop us off and then we can find shelter on land to ride it out. Unfortunately, we may have to push our start out by a day or two, depending on how long the storm lingers."

I groaned. I was too excited to commence research, but I understood the potential change of plans. The shitty weather would certainly disrupt the ecosystem for a few days, throwing the bats off their usual routine.

"Morning." Eli's sunken voice cut through the room, raising the hairs on the back of my neck. *Time to face the music.*

Fran and Malcom swiveled their heads in his direction, each offering a jumbled "Good morning" in response.

He looked terrible, just like me. Eyes bloodshot and hair disheveled. His gaze didn't quite meet mine. The awkwardness was like static electricity—painful and inescapable. We still had two more weeks left on this trip, and it wouldn't be fair to our colleagues to drag this energy with us off the boat. The right thing to do would be to explain my lunacy and move past this as best we could. It was my fault that this had escalated the way it did.

So, I decided to be an adult and approached him first. "Hey."

"Hey," he replied nervously.

"Can we talk?"

Suddenly, my balance vanished, and I lurched into Eli. He caught me in his arms before we stumbled backward into the wall together. Fran shrieked as she flew headfirst over the table.

The floor tremored violently underneath us. My stomach roiled from the motion, threatening to heave marshmallow cereal chunks. Loud creaking, like when wood is about to snap in half, echoed through my ears.

Dishes smashed onto the floor. Malcom's laptop went flying across the room. Our bodies moved as if without gravitational center, rolling and knocking into each other haphazardly.

Shouting blared from above. Malcom charged through the mess, planting his palms on the walls for stability. Eli was hot on his heels.

"Eli!" I cried. But he never turned around.

Fuck.

I gaped at Fran, seeking any justification to follow the guys—a nod, a thumbs up, or maybe an "I'll come, too," but she just stared back with wide eyes, begging me to stay.

I couldn't sit still when it sounded like Armageddon up there. What if something happened to Malcom or Eli?

"Wait!" I called out, running after the men.

"Maris, no!" Fran shouted after me.

I took two steps at a time, the rough wooden edges scraping my bare feet. I pushed the hatch door and climbed up onto the deck.

Water pelted my face, and the wind tossed my body to the side like an empty plastic bag.

I squinted to make out the crew. Some were securing items with rope. Others were bolting the hatches shut to keep water from seeping in.

The captain was pulling on the crank to deploy the storm anchor, as Malcom ran over to help him. Chains clanked over the booming thunder.

"Maris!" Eli was busy tying a rope with another crewmate. "Get back inside," he bellowed.

He really didn't know me if he thought I'd sit idly by while our vessel was in danger. I had learned how to tie knots on previous voyages and would put my skill to work.

I ran to the edge and pulled on the ropes. Eli grabbed my arm. "Do you have a fucking death wish? Get back inside! These ropes are heavy, and it's too dangerous for you!"

I jerked my arm from his grasp. "I'm not leaving." Just because I was a woman didn't mean I was useless. Fuck him for thinking so.

The boat dipped, and I lost my footing on the slick wood.

"Maris!"

I couldn't stop sliding. I caught the railing and held on tight, trying to pull myself away from a wicked sea that had sprouted tentacles, ready to grab me.

The boat swayed harder this time, and my hands slipped off the bars.

And suddenly, I was falling. I could clearly see images from my life passing by: prom, graduation, my first car, my first apartment…the faces of my parents, happy and smiling, like they had been waiting all this time to hug me. With my arms wide open, I flew toward them—toward love.

And for the second time in my life, my limp body crashed hard into a wall of coldness before everything went black.

Chapter 5

True-Crime Stories – Episode 158: "Revenge of the Caveman"

Maris

They say when you're caught in a current, the best way to avoid drowning is to go with the flow. To lean back and give in. To imagine your limbs are weightless like air and succumb to the strength of the water. To not fight it when it tries to pull you under.

As torrential as the waves were, my body was surprisingly still and at peace. Like I was resting on grass on a warm summer day.

My skin no longer registered the ocean wetness, even though I was certain I was drowning. Instead, I was wrapped in warmth and dryness. I had experienced this once before, except all of it had felt wrong. This time was different. This time, I was comfortable. Like I was at peace. I didn't have the rock in my stomach that I'd had when I was in the hospital after the car accident. I was floating. I could also make out the muffled chirps of birds and the rustling of leaves overhead. A deep voice crooned a lullaby in the distance, the melody soothing me.

It was the freest I had been in a long time.

I scrunched my lids tighter, hoping to hold on to it all for a moment more. My physical body, ever the traitor, was already awake, and my nerves were buzzing.

The last thing I remembered was water. Lots of water. So much that it filled my nostrils and mouth.

The boat!

I blinked my eyes open, and they stung against the light.

What the fuck?

Overhead was a mosaic of dried leaves intertwined together.

Where the hell am I?

I pushed onto my forearms, but the throbbing in my neck sent me crashing back down. I patted my body, registering that it was swaddled tightly with…a blanket?

Attempt number two. I tried again to sit up, shutting my aching lids, moving slower this time as my neck protested. My hand rubbed the back of it to release some of the knots, and the blanket over me shifted. A light draft hit my chest, and my eyes flew open. My tits, bare in all their pointed glory, shone back at me like they were far too happy to be free in this new environment. *What in the—*

My heart stopped in my chest as I lifted the tattered sheet, and my stomach dropped. *Where the fuck are my panties?*

Panic rushed through my veins.

I clutched the fabric to my body, finally noticing my surroundings.

Wood…everywhere. *A cottage?*

A simply constructed table with one chair sat directly across from me, and shelves stuffed with odds and ends hung on the wall behind them. A slab of wood sat underneath, and if I squinted hard enough with one eye and covered the other, I could be fooled into thinking it was a counter. Random objects, like rubber tubing and glass trinkets—basically the equipment that could be found in a home meth lab—were strewn messily about the slab.

And the apparatus I was huddled on top of? It was a bed with posts that certainly wouldn't have passed a quality-control check at the local furniture store. The material under me wasn't as soft as a mattress, but it was still cushioned enough to pad my ass…my *bare* ass… resting on some strange bed where God knew what took place. I let out a squeak and quickly muffled it with my hand over my mouth.

This was how erotic horror books started. With some random chick waking up in the middle of nowhere, strapped to a bed, at the mercy of some reclusive freak who got his rocks off by rubbing his crotch on every part of her body while branding his initials into her skin with a hot iron. I swore I had read a book about it…and the idea had been sexy under the comfort of my own store-bought sheets, in my townhome in the suburbs at two in the morning. Here? Not so much.

I sank back against the wood headboard, lumpy pillows barely offering any lumbar support.

How the hell did I end up here?

At the foot of the bed, there was an ornate trunk fashioned from polished dark wood and metal locks and hinges, the kind that I'd imagine belonged at the bottom of the ocean with the Titanic or something.

My attention darted to the door to my left. It was the only one in this place, and judging by the intense light radiating through the window made of aged plastic next to the door, it led outside.

A tinge of green floated from behind the dirty window. Trees? Was I in the woods? The air was too heavy and thick to be temperate forest air. I was still in the South Pacific…I think.

Who had brought me here? Where were Eli and the rest of the team? I wasn't much into religion, but for the briefest moment, my little black atheist heart offered up a silent prayer to the mythical dude who wore a toga and sat on clouds while stalking our every move.

Bro, hear my prayer. Pleeease!

My team needed to be alive, and I needed to find them.

I moved without thinking, body prepared to run, then I remembered that this sad blanket was the only cover I had for my naked body.

Maybe if I ran for it, I could escape whatever kind of fucked up cabin-in-the-woods holding cell this was—and whoever was keeping my clothes hostage.

A sound halted my movements. It was distant and hard to make out. Hoarse and grating. Like a chainsaw.

Oh God, this is it. A mad slasher man is about to mince my body into worm food, and no one will hear my screams.

Suddenly, the door flew open. A hairy mass of black and beige barreled toward me.

I screamed, and the creature screeched in response, its shrill tone puncturing my eardrums. I shuffled back as far as I could, until I hit the headboard.

The *thing* stomped on the ground, its hooves tapping violently as it skittered to the side of the bed. I screamed again and clutched at the items scattered on the crude nightstand, grabbing the closest object I could find. I had no idea what it was. It was made of something smooth like rock and had a sharp tip, like an arrowhead.

The creature lurched at me, propping its fat head on the edge of the bed, its flat nose vibrating a snort at me.

A pig is my kidnapper? What in the Animal Farm bullshit is this?

Before I could process how I had become a character on fucking Animal Crossing, heavy footsteps clonked on the floor. The bright light that had been streaming in from outside was eclipsed by the mammoth creature blocking the doorway.

I gulped down the lump in my throat.

Cryptids really do exist...

All I could see was muscle on muscle. The ridges had no beginning or end.

Yup. This is how I'm going to die. At the whim of that green giant from the frozen vegetable packages.

Except this giant was neither green nor jolly. This beast was brown-skinned and...furious.

I let out a blood-curdling shriek that triggered the pig to join in.

The man stayed still. Wild dark hair and an overgrown beard obscured most of his face, except for his hard eyes that were focused on me. I dropped my gaze, and they landed on a flap of material between his legs. Based on the way it tented, the package underneath must have been considerably sized.

On a random one-night stand, what lay behind that loin cloth would have been more intriguing, but on a kidnapper, not so much.

"Who are you?" I pressed the blanket to my chest and pointed the stone blade in his direction. I had no idea how to fight with a weapon, but I was confident I could learn on the fly.

His expression remained stern. Perhaps he was one of those untouchable tribesmen...the ones who hadn't had contact with the outside world for their entire existence. The type that *killed* intruders.

I swallowed another pool of saliva that had settled in the back of my mouth.

I flinched when he leaned forward, his dense body crowding the space between us. "Don't come closer or I'll cut your dick off." My eyes flashed from his glare to the loincloth and then, much slower than intended, back to his face. *Enough with his dick, Maris.*

Angular jaw and stone expression remained frozen, as if I hadn't just threatened his manhood. *Shit.* Maybe he didn't understand English.

"Why. Did. You. Bring. Me. Here?" I slowed my speech, enunciating each word in hopes that he'd understand at least one of them. His prominent brows only drew closer. I huffed out a breath, sending my bangs flying up. *He's not hard of hearing, Maris!* I couldn't have been less politically correct if I'd tried.

Maybe if I used a normal cadence, I'd somehow get through to him. "Where are my clothes? And why am I here?"

Without warning, the giant marched forward, the distance between us shortening quicker than I could measure. *Jesus. This is how I die.*

I listened to way too many true crime podcasts not to know how this shit ended. Possible episode titles would include but weren't limited to: "The

Curious Case of the Missing Reclusive Scientist," "When No One Could Save Bat Girl," and the potential fan favorite, "Revenge of the Caveman."

The shadow of his heavy torso descended over me. My brain blipped, and I swung the shard in my hand.

Please let the judgy cloud dude in the sky take pity on my soul and protect me from the hot-but-scary naked lumberjack about to eat me. Amen.

I couldn't imagine that God had ever heard a prayer where a woman didn't want a ripped lumberjack to touch her, but hey, there was a first time for everything.

A sharp hiss seared my ears, yet my skin never registered his touch. I blinked one eye open and found Cryptid clutching his shoulder. When he moved his hand, I could see a light tinge of red through a thin slit of flesh. It was quite a ways from needing stitches, but it was still a wound.

Hot damn! I wounded him! My insides fluttered with pride. This was probably how boxers felt when they landed their first punch in a match.

Unfortunately, before I could dart to freedom, his hand caught my neck, pinning me to the headboard. The pig squealed from the commotion.

The stranger's grasp wasn't painful, yet it was tight enough to partially compress my vessels, depriving me of sufficient blood flow to my brain. I clawed at him, trying to pry him off, as my limbs tingled woozily like my head.

My vision clouded. The stranger bent over, picking something up from the nook between the bed and the nightstand while his other hand still held me in place. Wavy locks of onyx hair covered part of his face as he righted himself. Phantom helium filled my head. The lack of blood had a hypnotizing effect, and all I could see was him in my trance. Thick lips, the rosy color of redwood bark, parted and a huge *whoosh* of air blew hair out of his line of vision. I was transfixed by his mouth now, the way the flesh joined together at the corners, forming the most perfectly wet and supple—

With a jolt, he released my neck, sending blood rushing up my neck to be greedily absorbed by my brain. I coughed as too much air rushed to my lungs at once.

A heap of neatly folded cloth was now in front of my face. *My clothes.*

I examined the pile of expertly folded items and wondered how the fuck this guy knew how to fold like he was the manager at a clothing store. Furthermore, this was proof he had understood my words because he had retrieved my clothes after I asked for them.

My train of thought crashed when I realized what was staring at me from the top of the stack. My cotton panties were perfectly folded, like they were on display in the lingerie section, with my bra draped over them. Heat flamed my face.

I clutched the garments to me, hiding my underwear. Cryptid continued to stare at me, not moving a muscle.

"Um…thanks," I muttered, desperate for the burn to leave my cheeks.

Perhaps he wasn't a kidnapper. He would've tried to assault me by now, right? He'd had ample opportunity to, especially while I'd been unconscious, but although I was naked, nothing felt different and there were no new marks marring my skin.

My hoarse voice scraped my throat. "Can you go so I can put my clothes on?"

He let out an exasperated sigh and turned on his feet, trudging toward the door. At least he was respectful enough to listen this time, despite crossing a line by stripping me while I was out cold.

Assuming it was him who did it?

Or fuck…maybe he had help from another one of his scary friends.

The pig batted the side of the bed with his hooves, preparing to jump up onto the mattress.

"And take him, too," I called out. As a biologist, I loved animals, but not when they seemed eager to eat me alive.

Cryptid stared back at me, irritation wrinkling his golden forehead, like I had demanded one too many things.

Perhaps a little sugar would make the creeper and his sidekick go away faster. I swallowed my pride and offered a fake smile. "Please?"

The man whistled, and the pig trotted merrily to him on command. He turned around, and I was greeted by a perfectly sculpted ass. *Lord, have mercy on me.* The man was ripped.

The door creaked closed, and I finally let out the breath I had been holding, before collapsing onto my back.

Where the fuck am I?

Chapter 6

The Screech Owl Has Risen

Aleki

I didn't remember humans being that noisy. My head pounded from all the shouting. For such a scrawny person, she was loud. Her voice grated my ears like the cries of a screech owl in heat. To top it off, she had wide, round eyes and brown hair exactly like an owl.

I couldn't stand her chaos. That was why I had grabbed her throat. To stop her so my mind could have a moment to think. Strangely enough, her pulse vibrating against my fingers had soothed me, like butterfly wings flapping on my skin.

I would have expected that a person with a voice that large would be bigger in size, but she barely had any meat on her. Her arms and legs were long and thin…delicate when compared to my solid limbs. I bet they'd snap off if a harsh gust of wind ever hit her. Actually, she was the windstorm, violent and unpredictable.

Her ability to fight had surprised me. It was nothing I'd have expected from the frail and lifeless figure I had found lying face down on the beach yesterday after the storm had passed. Her skin had been so pale, yet after having seen her awake, I realized it was naturally that nearly translucent shade of the inside of a lychee. It was interesting to see how quickly it turned red when she was at a loss for words. Like when I had handed her clothes back.

I had seen women's underwear before, but never had I been tasked with removing them from an actual woman.

I blinked, remembering the moment I had found her.

I had been nervous to touch her—to touch another human. No one ever came to this island. The surrounding seas were so fierce that no one would intentionally wish to make the voyage.

I had assumed she was already dead when I'd found her. No injuries had been visible at first glance, but to my surprise, she had roused and managed to cough up water, her eyes remaining shut, too tired to wake.

With her thin body cradled in my arms, I'd carried her back to the hut. I'd had no choice but to remove her wet and sandy clothes. The fabric had clung to her body like glue held it in place as I'd pried pieces of clothing from her cool skin. Her bra and panties, as I had learned they were called from the boys in grade school, matched. They were black, like the color of midnight, and a deep contrast to her light complexion. My throat had tightened at the image that lay on my dinner table like a feast for my vision, and my insides had rumbled with something I could only describe as hunger. Not for food. For something else I couldn't begin to explain.

My fingers had instinctively brushed the tops of her bra where fabric met flesh. Little bumps had broken out, following the path my finger traced. Curiosity had nagged at me, so I pushed the garment down.

Until then, I had only seen breasts in the nude magazines conveniently hidden away in my trunk of books. Those images couldn't compare to the real thing. Two perfectly symmetrical globes, swollen bigger than my own chest, like ripe fruit with how plump they were. My mouth had instantly filled with saliva. Dark-pink peaks had stood at attention in the center of each fruit, so hard that my fingers had itched to touch them. *How would they feel if I pinched them...rolled them between my fingers? Soft? Hard? Would they change shape? Could I make them soften in my hands? What would they taste like?*

As badly as I'd wanted to find out, it hadn't felt right to touch them while she was unconscious, so I let them be.

Plus, the next distraction had beckoned me. Her panties. I'd slid them down her legs, an inviting V greeting me. A sprinkling of dark hair—the same color of Christmas gingerbread cookies as on her head—covered the part that had intrigued me the most. Or perhaps I had only wanted to see it because it had been hidden away from me like a present, begging me to unwrap it.

My blood had thrummed in my ears as I'd leaned in, examining the glimpse of peach flesh peeking out through her hair, and suddenly, my tongue had been too large for my mouth. I hadn't been able to look away. She had smelled sweet and musky. Like juice that could never satisfy your thirst, no matter how much you drank.

It had all been too much for me to handle. Confusingly beautiful. I had to shake away the cravings so I could proceed with my task without faltering. With the last of her clothing removed, I'd dried her and wiped the sand from her skin, then I untangled the seaweed that had woven into her hair.

When I had cleaned her enough, I carried her to my bed and covered her with a blanket I had stitched together using fabric I'd found on shore with a needle made from a splinter of wood. I didn't know who this woman was, but she was clearly not a threat. So, I'd let her rest.

Any interest I had in her had vanished when she had opened her mouth, screaming like some hellish creature without so much as a thank you for taking her in so the vultures wouldn't attack her sack of bones. Who was this demon, and more importantly, when would she leave? My days of wishing for visitors were long gone—except right now, I was hoping another human would show up to take her home and leave me in peace.

I took out my frustration in the dirt I shoveled away, clutching the giant clamshell I used as a hand trowel so tightly that the rim dug into the flesh of my palm.

Behind me, the hut door creaked open slowly. *The Screech Owl has risen.* Her uneven footsteps, conveying her uncertainty and fear, gave her away.

One step. Then two. She shuffled, as if rethinking having come outside, then as if she had turned to go back in.

Pause.

Another step.

Then a series of hurried ones until they stopped.

She was fully dressed and in a silent standoff with Poaka whose head had dipped like he was prepared to charge at her. From the way his tail wagged, he just wanted to play. She was oblivious to his true intent, and I enjoyed watching her on edge.

Poaka was a piglet at heart, but his size would injure her if she wasn't careful around him.

I snapped my fingers at him, signaling to back away. He grunted his protest, then trotted over to the hammock, plopping down underneath for shade.

Screech Owl's shoulders sagged in relief, and I returned to my chore.

"Where am I?" Her voice was soft and shaky now.

So, it is possible for my ears not to ring from the sound of her voice. In-
teresting.

I didn't offer a response, despite being capable of speaking. Although most of my day was spent in silence, I did talk to Poaka, and sometimes sang him his nightly lullaby. My vocabulary was vast, except my speech never matched the speed of my thoughts. Words were sticky on my tongue, like they couldn't leave as smoothly as I wished. I hadn't spoken to another human since my mother had died in this forsaken place twenty-four years ago, and I wasn't interested in doing it again with a stranger. I had nothing that I cared to say to her.

Instead, I focused on the basket of fish I'd set to cure before the storm. I poured out the accumulated liquid that hadn't properly drained because of the rain soaking the surrounding dirt.

Screech Owl approached me slowly. I could see her feet moving gingerly from my periphery, like she was stepping on hot coals. The brush underneath her soles must've been uncomfortable. She'd better get used to it fast. *No shoes around here, princess.*

She hesitated before bending to meet me at eye level. Her scent, an intoxicating mixture of some sort of spice mixed with juicy fruit, enveloped me. She had been tossed about the ocean for who knew how long and had somehow emerged still smelling like a dessert that I couldn't quite place from my former life. A life that didn't involve curing fish in a ditch.

I glared at her—a warning for her to keep her distance. Her aroma was fogging up my head and I didn't like it.

She stayed in place, her green gaze carrying a soft desperation. "You understand me, don't you?"

I did.

"My name is Maris."

Maris. It was a beautiful name that suited her well. The *s* at the end sounded endless, kind of like the waves of the sea. I wondered what it would sound like off my own tongue.

"What's your name?" she asked.

Aleki.

"Why won't you reply?"

Because you don't belong here.

My silence elicited a heavy groan from her throat, followed by a forceful exhale of air out of her mouth that sent the hair framing her face flying. Inwardly, I smirked while still tending to the basket of fish.

A hand touched my forearm. Her fingers were delicate like the rest of her body, and her touch was careful, but somehow, it sent a shock wave through my body. "Please. I need to get home, and I can't do that if I don't know where I am."

It was easy to feel sorry for her. She reminded me of a lost kid. Like I had once been. Like I still was. Perhaps it was better for her that I didn't reply. Then she wouldn't have to hear that there was no way out of this place. I knew firsthand that this island was *forever*, and she'd figure it out, too, soon enough. On her own.

She let go of my arm and took a seat on the ground. "I'm a scientist who was traveling by boat," she continued, her fingers furiously pointing at her chest, then into the distance before rocking through the air.

The strange signs she was acting out, like I was a foreigner who couldn't understand her, irritated me all over again. Any pity I had for her disappeared. She was the foreigner, not me. This woman was not only annoying, she was condescending, too.

"Fucking hell!" she shouted. She threw her hands up in frustration, and they landed in her lap with a loud smack.

A good chunk of my slang word catalog consisted of swear words I had learned in school—words that couldn't be found in my dictionary. My knowledge of curse words wasn't plentiful, but it was sufficient when I needed to let out some steam if I was carrying something heavy or a *fucking* coconut fell on my head. Fallen coconuts should always be preceded by the word *fucking*.

A loud gurgle reverberated between us. Maris clutched her stomach, and her skin instantly turned my new favorite shade of rosy red again. It had been nearly a day since she had last eaten or drunk anything, and as much as I hoped that she'd go back to wherever she came from, she didn't deserve to starve.

I took her small hand in mine, aware of how her eyes widened in response to the gesture. She tried to pull away, but I held it firmly in place and then placed a piece of fish in her palm.

She lowered her head, smelling the offering. "Fish?"

I rolled my eyes. For a scientist, she wasn't too good at figuring things out on her own.

Her focus roamed over the salt-crusted meat like it had been poisoned. Maybe if it had been, then she'd leave me alone for good.

Maris sniffed at it again.

The Screech Owl was so particular, it was grating my nerves.

I grabbed a piece for myself and scraped off some of the salt coating before putting it in my mouth. The chewiness was stiff. It still needed a few hours more to cure until it was perfect, but it was tasty enough.

She watched me the whole time, probably wondering if she was hungry enough to eat food from the man she assumed was holding her captive rather than die of starvation. Starvation would work fine, more fish for me.

Eventually, she caved. Her jaw worked as if she were chewing the bubblegum I used to love from my old life. She let out a greedy sigh, satisfied with the fish. "Thanks," she murmured.

I handed her another piece, and we ate together in much appreciated silence.

Chapter 7

Knife to the Head; Hand to the Throat

Maris

My belly was full of salted fish, which I never would have guessed I'd like, but then my stomach had threatened to open up and eat my own hand. By the time I'd realized my burps tasted like cod liver oil, I had inhaled nearly half of Cryptid's stash. That had been my sign to step away from the fish…hands in the air…nobody gets hurt. Or throws up from putrid breath.

With one basic need checked off Maslow's hierarchy, it was time to move on to the next. My successfully distended stomach was pressing on my other organs, namely my bladder, and I needed to pee. Badly.

He had stalked off with his devil-pig before I could ask him about an ideal spot to relieve myself. It probably didn't matter anyway. It wasn't like I'd find a clean bathroom or a porta-potty around here. This was a *pop-a-squat-by-a-tree* kind of a place.

I was no stranger to peeing in the forest while on assignment. Typically, I had a guide to advise me on a safe location. Urinating in wild cat hunting territory was neither advisable nor enjoyable.

I set out for the thicket of trees a few feet away from the hut. After emptying my bladder under one of the tall trees, I decided to explore. If I ever wanted to get back home, I needed to figure out where the hell I was.

As I walked, I hoped that I would find some landmarks to map out a path, but every tree resembled the other. I heard the faint sound of water rushing in the distance. A watering hole must've been nearby, which made sense—he had chosen this area for his hut for a reason.

My feet stung from the thorns and weeds that protruded from the brush. I loved nature, but shit, I never thought I'd be barefoot and stranded in the middle of it. I wished I had worn my hiking boots before falling overboard.

My neck was covered in sweat from the suffocating humidity. Thank God, I had opted for a breathable white short-sleeve shirt with a slight scoop neck and stretch pants before the storm. It was my most comfortable outfit for warm weather.

Although, traipsing around nearly naked with a strategically placed loincloth like Cryptid would have felt a whole lot better—not that I was still thinking about his lack of clothes or anything.

It was hard not to notice the sheen on his muscles when they flexed. It was like he was covered in oil or whatever muscle-magazine models used to highlight their *gym gains*. However, muscle-mag models were scrawny compared to him. He was a mammoth of a man, with more ridges on his body than the Grand Canyon. His bronzed skin only emphasized his physique—hard, like that of a gladiator. Specifically, the ones from the movies. I had a hunch that the historical ones wouldn't have been as pretty as those portrayed by Hollywood.

A rush of heat rippled through me. The air grew ten degrees hotter. I lifted my hair and flapped my hand over my sticky hairline, anxious to cool off.

Even more distracting was his face. *His eyes.* Dark-brown orbs that seemed almost limitless. They hinted at secrets, and I was curious to find out exactly what. Who was he, and how had he ended up living in isolation?

Maybe he really was from an untouchable tribe. He was certainly skillful at surviving in this environment. But where were his other tribesmen? And did that mean there were other people nearby? A lump formed in my throat as images swirled in my head of an encounter with Cryptid's family and friends. I wondered how they would react to my presence. *Not well, Maris. Not well at all.*

It's possible he had defected and chosen to live on his own as an outcast. A rebel. He certainly had the attitude to fit the theory. He never uttered a word, but I was certain he understood me when I spoke. Also, his cabin was completely furnished with modern luxuries like a four-poster bed and makeshift sheets, as if there were one of those bohemian home decor shops nearby.

He wasn't holding me hostage. In fact, he hated me, and the feeling was mutual. If the jerk had been keeping me captive, he wouldn't have left without tying me up or locking the hut door...or whatever else jungle Mafia daddies did to their captives. His absence was proof that I still retained my freedom, at least.

I had walked for too long and nothing appeared familiar. There was no sign of a beach anywhere, despite the forceful sound of rushing water. If only I could get to shore, I could build a fire—send a smoke signal so that the team could find me. What if they had already been here and left? Dread lumped in the pit of my belly.

The sky was dimming. Spots of sunlight still broke through the thick canopy of leaves overhead, though less forcefully than when I had started my excursion. The brush had also grown more unruly, scraping my arms and face as I traveled.

I was lost.

Leaves rustled harshly ahead, sending a shiver down the back of my sweaty neck. I glanced around, searched for the source of the disturbance.

It was probably nothing. Perhaps just a bunch of birds. All landing within the same vicinity. Flapping their wings against the foliage. At the same time. *Right?!*

My heart hammered against my rib cage.

A shadow eclipsed my periphery. I gasped, whipping my head in its direction, only to find more brush.

I *knew* I had seen it.

Someone was here.

Cautiously, I eased backward, praying my footfalls would go unnoticed by whatever jungle spirit was waiting to lure me into a cave and sacrifice me to the gods.

The rustling resumed, more violent and organized this time, heading in one direction—straight for me.

I sprinted away, harsh flora striking my skin as I ran as fast as I could. The fabric of my pants crackled loudly with my strides.

Tears streaked down my face. *It* was closing in on me. Its crashing footfalls were loud, like it was right on my heels.

Then, suddenly, it stopped. All of the sounds behind me, they were no more. I looked back, finding nothing, and came to a stumbling halt, panting to pull oxygen into my starving lungs. My legs burned, unable to support me properly. Using a tree against my back for support, I gripped the sides of my waist to ease the cramping.

My nervous system wound down and heavy tears streamed down my cheeks. I was eight years old again. It was the day my parents died. And like back then, I wanted my parents to wake up and take me home from the scary place. Years later, and still, no one was coming to take me home.

My shoulders shook with sobs.

Through the pools in my eyes, silver glinted in the distance. In a split second, the apparition flew toward me, and the sound of splintering wood rang in my ear as loud as my scream.

Yet, I never registered the impact of the object.

I tilted my head to the side. A knife was embedded in the bark, centimeters from my ear.

In a flash, my neck was restrained, and my gaze snapped forward again.

Him.

Cryptid's searing gaze glimmered wildly with feral need. *Hunger.* If looks could kill, his would have granted me a rapid death, leaving my carcass behind for him to devour.

His face hovered so dangerously close that my skin burned from his hot, heaving breaths. Short and quick, like a tiger when the adrenaline hits right before they were about to strike. He was the predator, and I was his prey.

My lungs ceased to draw in air. I feared that the slightest noise would trigger him.

His foreign touch moved roughly down my shoulders, holding me still.

His nostrils flared before he leaned in, grazing the side of my neck with his nose, right above my throbbing artery. The hair on his jaw pricked my skin, and the slight suction of his inhales tickled me as he memorized my scent like a skilled hunter.

It wouldn't have been smart to break free, to fight him. That was a sure way to die. Fight or flight? My sympathetic nervous system triggered neither. I stayed rooted in place with no plan other than to dig my fingernails into the trunk behind me to alleviate the constriction in my belly.

Freeze.

I shut my lids, willing consciousness to float away from my body. A defense mechanism. Separate the metaphysical from the physical to survive. Neither my mind nor my body could escape his domination. Instead, it perfused every part of me, from the blazing heat radiating from his flesh onto mine to his consuming scent of fresh rain and leaves. My eyelids felt heavy, and my chin drooped, head lolling to the side as intoxication overpowered me.

I was jolted back to life when he slammed my back hard. My eyes flew open, redirecting my awareness to the savageness that imprisoned me. Thick fingers gripped my rib cage. He held my focus, erasing all sounds around us except the ragged cadence of our breaths.

Every sweat-covered muscle of his was flexed, prepared to attack, when his hands lowered to my hips, making room for my breasts to graze his torso. The shallowest inhale scraped my nipples against his bare body. All of him was solid, from the arms that caged me in, to the firm thighs that pinned my legs, to the ridge that prodded my belly.

The beast lowered his head, his lips hovering over mine.

Would he kiss me? Or consume me?

Did it matter?

We were close enough to exchange air, his exhale my inhale.

My heart was about to burst in my chest, a whimper escaping my lips.

And then my body was cold. He had retreated, cruelly ripping away the life he had injected into my veins. His nostrils flared, as if to blow off the steam he'd generated.

Cryptid backed away, almost stumbling on his steps, his molten glare never leaving me. Where there had been pure carnal desire before, there was something new.

Doubt.

Before I could gather the right words to speak, he had run off into the jungle faster than he had just attacked.

Chapter 8

Sins Never Wash Away

Aleki

There were two ways to survive being stranded on a deserted island. The first: hunt.

Hunting was more about instinct and less about logic. Intuition over brain. All five senses worked together, triggering a primal desire to attack.

When I had first landed here, I'd had to learn quickly how to hunt. Dad had drowned during the boat wreck, which meant Ma and I had been left to fend for ourselves when we washed up on shore. Barely one week on land, and Ma had fallen ill and passed away soon after. Finding food had become my responsibility. I had started small, setting traps to catch mice and birds. It had taken many tries and a lot of failures to be able to hunt larger mammals like deer.

With time, I had proven to be an excellent hunter. I had learned to submit to my yearnings. The inner need I couldn't control. I allowed them to run free during a hunt, the urges coursing through my veins. None of my actions during a kill were filtered. I wouldn't have thought I could ever stop myself once the rush kicked in.

But I had. I'd *had* to.

It was like stopping suddenly mid-sprint. You shouldn't do it. I had stopped cold, and I was paying for it now.

The adrenaline hadn't crested naturally, and I needed my body to come down from it…from her. I could feel her all over me, through my skin, in my blood…stifling all logic. My senses were only registering *her*.

What had I been expecting to do to her back there? Snap her neck? Bite her flesh? Or something more? I couldn't pinpoint the emotion, but it was much bigger than the desire to kill. It was consuming my whole being, and there were not enough words in my collection of books to describe what it was.

The second way to survive being stranded was to find clean water.

I headed straight for the closest source. Water cascaded down the giant rock formation, spilling into a clear, turquoise pool. Large boulders surrounded the bank, encasing the private retreat.

My oasis.

My flesh burned so hot that it would melt at any second. I was a sweaty, sticky mess and needed to cleanse not just the outside, but my insides. I needed to wash away whatever it was that still pulsed through me.

I dropped the basket containing my blades and the three iguanas I had caught earlier and stripped the cloth from my waist. I dived headfirst from the rocks and broke the surface with a splash. Bubbles floated around me as I submerged myself in the cool, crisp lake. I was weightless, gliding through the water. When I surfaced, rivulets of liquid spilled from my hair and beard down my tired body.

I swam up to the platform of rocks below the stream and climbed on top of it. The shower pelted my aching muscles. I deserved the abuse for the things I had wanted to do to another human. I bowed forward into the torrent, allowing it to flow down my head.

Fuck, it felt good.

And since I was flinging *fucks* around like a naughty schoolboy, what the fuck had Screech Owl been doing so far from the hut, anyway? I had nearly mistaken her for a target from all the noise she'd been making hobbling around the jungle. She had sounded like a three-legged deer—clumsy and begging for someone to put it out of its misery. If I had aimed my blade a hair to the right, her slender neck would've been sliced cleanly in half. She was lucky I had missed this time. I rarely ever did.

I rubbed my hands over my face and then down my torso, scrubbing away the layer of dirt-crusted perspiration.

Deep down, I must have known it had been her. That was why my aim had been off. I hadn't realized it at the time, but her scent must have given her away. Spicy-sweet fear. That was the best way to describe her essence.

My touch glided down my abdomen to the painful erection that hadn't settled since I had pinned her against the tree. I was always hard after a hunt until the rush had run its course, yet my cock wouldn't give up.

Memories of my hand around her neck only made my blood rush stronger. Screech Owl...the one whose voice irritated the hell out of me, and the same one whose whimper made me invincible.

I turned with my back under the water and pumped myself in my fist, squeezing harder than usual to offset the ache. Wetness was already leaking from the tip, greedy to escape, slicking my hand as I worked myself.

Damn her wide eyes, full of terror that I'd hurt her.

Damn her rapid pulse, fragile as butterfly wings under my fingers.

Damn her soft body rubbing against mine with every frenzied breath.

And damn me for wanting to pin her down and sink my tongue into the mysterious V between her legs like in one of the many romance books from my trunk.

Intensity flooded my shaft as I thrust with a ferocity I had never experienced before. I clutched at the rock wall, bracing myself as I stood there, hunched over, grunting like the barbaric beast I was. My hips moved as my fist worked with urgency. White light flashed, and a tremor ripped through me.

"Fuck," I groaned as liquid warmth jetted out and onto my abused hand.

I gripped the wall, catching my breath. Instead of relief, I was hungry for more.

"Son of a bitch." I turned back, standing under the stream of water with my still-erect cock, and washed away the evidence of my greed.

Chapter 9

Swallow the Mystery Meat

Maris

The last bits of sunlight in the sky were hanging on by a thread by the time I had found my way back to the hut. Unfortunately, my search for the beach would have to wait another day.

Since we had been close to shore on the boat, I assumed I was still near Fiji, which meant this island was somewhere in the South Pacific. I was certain because the nearest continent to our last vessel location had been a two-week boat ride away. Judging from the newly raised stubble on my legs, which I'd shaved the last night on the boat, I hadn't been missing for more than two days, at best.

A deep heaviness filled my stomach. Perhaps it was too optimistic to assume that everyone had survived, but I couldn't let my theories turn down that dark alley of dread. I had to keep faith alive that they were all safe and searching for each other—searching for me.

I filled my lungs with breath, recharging my hope. *They are fine.* I needed to make it to a beach. I could send a signal from shore for any boats or airplanes passing by. Smoke signal would be the best way since it could be spotted from far distances. Once rescued, I could contact the university to find out the whereabouts of Eli, Malcom, Fran, and the rest of the crew.

For all I knew, they were wandering this godforsaken place just as I was, hoping to make it to the coast, too.

Glowing embers flicked to life in front of me, igniting flames that climbed the air like vines, reaching for the sky. I watched the fire dance as Cryptid pushed wood about with a long metal rod. The pig was off to the side, happily chowing down on his dinner, scraps of unidentifiable fruit and vegetables flying in every direction around him.

A crawling sensation tickled the hairs on my arm. *Slap.* The local mosquitoes must have sent out a newsletter to inform each other that fresh meat was now available on the menu. My skin was covered in red welts, some from the bites themselves and others from my incessant lashes meant to murder the damn heathens.

Slap. Slap.

Cryptid turned his head in my direction, studying my fingernails scraping my forearm. Until now, he had refused to acknowledge my existence. He knew I had returned to the hut, but failed to spare me a side glance when I'd tripped over an uplifted root or offer me a disgruntled groan when I had accidentally spilled some of the rainwater from the barrel trying to pour myself a drink.

It amazed me how he could act like he hadn't almost killed me in the jungle. Okay...*killed* sounded dramatic, but for a moment back there, I had been convinced he was going to skin me alive and feed me to the black-and-beige furball wheezing next to me that sounded like it had food lodged inside its nostrils.

I certainly couldn't forget it. My skin heated when I remembered how he had looked at me like I was his for the taking. I had never experienced that type of fear. Not even when our car had skidded on the highway, killing my parents, had I been so scared. Perhaps the most confusing part was how that fear had morphed into excitement. Like a thrill I had wanted to continue. It must have been what cliff divers and rollercoaster junkies experienced when dopamine took over their brains.

He was angry, like he couldn't stand me more than before. Earlier, I had caught him stealing glances at me when he assumed I wasn't paying attention, but not anymore. One thing I knew for sure, he was like every other man in the world, sending mixed signals and confusing the hell out of women. However, if Eli had been here, he would have argued that I was the one who was an expert at sending out mixed signals.

Cryptid's thick fingers, the same ones that had gripped me, picked up a lush frond of leaves and tossed it into the fire.

I broke the silence between us. "What was that?"

More cold shoulder.

A citrusy aroma filled the air. The leaves must've been something to ward off mosquitoes, because the little fuckers no longer helped themselves to my blood.

I bit back a victorious smile. He could play a badass all he wanted, but I was still visible to him.

A wet nose nudged my side, knocking me onto my haunches. The pig snorted playfully before rubbing his head on my lap, begging me to pet him.

Cryptid marched up to us and snapped his finger sharply. A sign for his companion to retreat.

"No, it's okay. I don't mind." The mammoth pig had scared me at first, with his size and his screeching, but now, I realized he wasn't a threat. In fact, he was kind of cute, like an oversized marshmallow with fur.

The brute stared at us, unsure if he should trust us together. I massaged one of the pig's ears, and he burrowed his nose into my belly, clearly enjoying the affection. *At least someone enjoys my company.*

The big jerk exhaled a haughty breath and turned back to the fire. He extracted a knife and busied himself with whatever task was at hand. Over his shoulder, I saw a streak of blood on his knife. I quickly glanced away. My guess was, he was preparing dinner, but I didn't have the stomach to see the carcass.

Fluttering sounds overhead drew my attention to the purple sky. A flurry of black skittered across the haze.

"Bats!" I squealed, jumping to my feet. The pig screeched, protesting the loss of my lap.

With everything that had happened, I had completely forgotten about my research. Ordinarily, there wasn't a day when I wasn't thinking about the little critters. My insides vibrated with giddiness as I watched what must've been a hundred bats flapping through the sky. I must have witnessed this sight thousands of times, and the majesty of it had never waned.

He was peering at them with interest, his hands idle for probably the first time in the short while I had known him.

The pig grunted at us and stalked away, not happy that our attention had diverted from him.

I craned my neck, tracing their flight pattern. Their roost was most likely to my left, as they flew in hoards toward the opposite direction.

"The entire colony is awake," I murmured, mostly to myself, and a little for Cryptid, too.

Like shadows, they moved with urgency, their lives depending on this one flight. "They're searching for fresh water," I continued. "After sleeping all day, they're thirsty and will glide to the nearest source and swallow a mouth-ful before heading off to hunt for the night."

If a body of water was to my right, then that would mean the jungle most likely thinned out on my left, and led to the shore. It made sense, the trees were lusher in the direction the bats were heading. I would know...I had been pinned up against one not long ago.

The warm shudder that happened so often now that it seemed to have become a habit traveled through my body, clenching my core. *Really, Maris? Now is when you decide to reminisce about the wild man's dick threatening to impale you?*

I shook my head, clearing my brain of the caveman smut that it was addicted to. Maybe he hadn't noticed anything.

His severe gaze was already on me, penetrating my skin.

Break the silence, Maris. My forced smile never reached my eyes. "I like bats."

All he offered in return was a half-hearted nod.

I was starving for conversation, and I took that as my invitation to keep talking. Planting my butt back down on the ground, I took the lead. "I study them. That's what I was doing before I ended up here. I was on my way to Fiji. Do you know where Fiji is?"

His bushy brows knitted together, as if I weren't making any sense.

I persisted. I was so desperate to get home that I would figure out where I was even if I had to beat it out of him. Okay, maybe not *beat* him, because he'd probably roast me as a consequence—like the unidentifiable animal whose body had been dismembered and put over the fire.

"Do you know which way Fiji is?" If I had an approximate location, I could figure out where the hell I was.

Nothing. No semblance of recognition of what I was asking. No gesture of caring to help.

"Are you alone here? Do you have any family?" I assumed he was solo because there was no evidence of a partner or children in the hut. Aside from the minimal furniture and random junk that littered the shelves, it was bare, like he didn't spend much time there himself.

I'd placed him around the same age as me, thirty-two, or maybe a few years older. To be in your thirties and have to spend it doing manual labor on a deserted island without a friend to call at the end of the day to vent to or family to embrace had to have been a far lonelier life than the one I lived back in Washington. At least I had friends, a rotating carousel of men, and Aunt Sherri, though none offered the kind of closeness I craved.

Cryptid's expression deepened with something I couldn't pinpoint. Whatever it was, it caused his focus to dart away from me and to the fire and then back to the pig, who had returned to his side for some petting. His large hands stroked the furry coat of the content animal, almost like he was comforting himself. They were an ironic sight to witness together—both exaggerated versions of their species.

The thick aroma of meat wafted into my nose, interrupting my train of thought, and my stomach growled. I was starving and had a hankering for barbecue. My gaze flashed to the pig, then guiltily away, catching the wild man's knowing stare. I smiled awkwardly.

"So, what did you find while you were hunting earlier?" I forced my voice to remain casual, as if we hadn't had that *thing* in the jungle.

He strode over to the fire. When he returned, he carried a stick with a chunk of meat speared on it. It was pale, almost like chicken or fish.

"What's that?"

He shook it at me again. There was something off-putting about mystery meat. I wouldn't let just anything in this mouth.

Okay, this wouldn't have been the wildest thing to have passed my lips.

Before I could take it, a hand gripped my chin. His hold didn't hurt, but it was firm. I tried to pull away and pushed against the stone wall that was his bare chest. "Let me go!"

I had succeeded only partially because my jaw was free, yet his thumb rubbed at my lower lip, coaxing it to relax. The pad was rough, like sandpaper. My lips tingled, nerves firing wildly, almost as if I liked it.

His pupils trained on my mouth, as if it was his toy to play with, and I sucked in a shaky breath, unintentionally allowing my lips to part. He moved quickly, slipping a shred of meat inside, grazing my teeth with his fingers as he pushed it into my mouth. My tongue briefly swiped his index finger, tasting the charred essence of his offering and the salt of his skin.

Our eyes locked as I chewed the tender meat, its juices exploding in my mouth. The taste was mild, much like chicken. Then again, everything tasted like chicken at first bite.

Far too familiarly, his hand closed around my throat and stroked my sensitive flesh, urging me to swallow.

I obeyed, my throat working against his grip. In the silence between us, I realized I wasn't the only one breathing heavily, loud enough to over-shadow the crackling sounds of the fire.

His intense stare cast a shiver down my spine, despite the suffocatingly hot and humid air enveloping us.

"Thanks," I murmured.

He moved to feed me another piece of meat, but I intercepted it before it met my lips. "I got it from here." It was insane how the most mundane interactions between us became charged, and I was a freak for enjoying it. I might've been craving closeness more than ever on this desolate island, but I needed space. These emotions he brought out in me were far too strange for my liking.

The urge to pull away must've been contagious because the stranger went back to the fire, as far away from me as possible. We ate in silence, ex-changing fleeting side glances yet pretending the other wasn't peeking.

I wondered how long he had been here. From the state of his hut, it must have been a while. He knew how to survive out here like he had been doing it his whole life. Certain things about him were peculiar, like the length of his facial hair. I would've imagined if someone had been here for years, their beard would be overgrown and scraggly, except his wasn't very long. Like it had been trimmed regularly. I could see his full lips through the fuzz, and the hair was neat and free of any dirt. Did he take a sharpened rock to his jaw every now and again, giving himself a good barber-style shave? One slip of the wrist, especially without a mirror, and the man would have been a goner if he had sliced his jugular.

I chuckled at the morbid thought, which earned me a tight glare from Mr. Almost-Naked Sweeney Todd.

Without warning, a deep yawn overtook my mouth. I set the empty meat skewer aside and stretched my arms overhead. It was late, and I could barely keep my eyes open any longer. I needed sleep.

He must've shared my feeling, because he rose to his feet and moved to the wood barrel next to the hut, reaching in and extracting a brown plastic container. The words *butter spread* were printed on the side. *One man's ocean litter is another man's water cup.*

I sat dumbfounded as he splashed the water onto his face. Tiny droplets dripped down his facial hair and neck. He swished some fresh water in his mouth and spit it out before reaching for a thin twig, one of many resting in another *butter spread* container on top of an old stump that he used as a table. He rubbed the stick against his teeth as if he were brushing them and then gave it a quick chew. He groomed himself like he had been doing it every night…as if it was part of a routine.

Who was this man? And why did he sometimes act like he was from another world—from my world?

I was suddenly aware of my own hygienic needs, but fuck if I was going to ask to borrow one of those stick thingies. I missed my toothbrush and face wash.

Finished with his bedtime routine, Mr. Dental Hygienist put the fire out, blanketing us in darkness. My vision took a minute to adjust to the lack of light. I could barely make out his massive frame trudging up the steps of the hut, his heavy footfalls creaking the wood underneath. The front door opened, and the pig went trotting merrily in, ready for slumber. His human didn't move. He turned to me, as if waiting for me to come inside with them.

The pit of loneliness in my stomach begged me to get up and follow him, my desire for companionship battling with my logical brain.

This was weird. I didn't know this man, yet too much questionable shit had already happened between us that shouldn't happen between two strangers. His hands had already been all over me and inside my mouth. He had seen me naked when I was unconscious, as I was certain he was the one who had undressed me.

No.

Sharing a sleeping space with him wasn't appropriate at all. But God, what I wouldn't have given to share a bed with someone to quell my anxiety.

It took all my willpower to shake my head and decline his offer.

Oblivious to the deranged battle going on inside me, he shrugged and closed the door behind himself, leaving me to spend the night with my old friends: abandonment and loneliness.

Chapter 10

Man-Just-Go

Maris

It's official. I'm never getting any sleep in this place.

My head swam and my lids drooped heavily as I lay in the hammock. I had spent all last night wide awake, tracking every suspicious noise from the bushes, expecting a bear to jump out at any moment and maul me to death.

I loved the outdoors. It was one of the reasons I had become a wildlife biologist. However, camping in a known environment with a team was completely different from roughing it solo in a location that possibly didn't exist on any map. Needless to say, my anxiety was working overtime without pay and benefits, and she was not thrilled.

Sleeping by myself was the other issue. While I didn't prefer it, I was capable of slumbering without sharing my bed, especially on work nights when the sex-then-snuggle dance impeded my schedule. However, right now, my mind was so dysregulated from too much unfamiliarity that it craved closeness. But I was not about to hop into bed with him just to quell my nerves. Forty-eight hours was too short a time to bed a Sasquatch. I still had standards. No cuddles without at least a coffee date first.

Fuck, I miss coffee. My head pounded harder at the memory of warm happiness in a cup.

If the night was noisy, the day was Grand Central Station. Birds cawed. Insects chirped. And the random sounds of branches snapping off trees ruined any chance for a nap.

I was losing my fucking mind. I was certain of it, too, because last night, I could have sworn I heard singing coming from inside the hut. It'd barely been audible over the breeze, but I had heard it. With no electricity to run a TV here and a silent stranger, where had it come from?

Maybe it was some weird paranormal energy or something inhabiting the island...like spirits. Spirits of people who had never escaped. *Fuck.*

They always said that the outfit you had on when you died became your *ghost outfit.*

I looked down at my once-white-now-light-brown Henley and dingy trekking pants against my sunburned skin. I was destined to be the ugliest ghost that had ever existed. *Double fuck.*

My latest crisis was interrupted by the hobbling pig and his owner carrying a large basket made of woven leaves and a long rod with a sharp end— kind of like the ones used for spearfishing.

My heart lurched in my chest. If my suspicions were correct, he would be going to the beach.

Jumping to my feet, I chased after him to catch up before he headed into the thicket. "Can I come with you?"

As per usual, he didn't stop to answer, and I didn't wait for an invitation. The beach would give me access to the coastline, and there had to be at least one boat passing by.

His brisk pace quickened, most likely as a means to lose me on the journey, but my determination energized me as well as one of the room-temperature energy drinks from the case on my office floor ever had.

"Do you fish often?" I happened to know firsthand that he still had plenty back at the hut. I may or may not have been double-dipping into the stash in the middle of the night. Chewy salted fish was my new fast-food restaurant *fourth meal.*

My brain worked overtime, mapping the terrain. My job was studying animals in their natural and unmanicured habitat, but this environment was too difficult to navigate even by professionals. Every turn appeared to be like the previous and every rock was indistinguishable. Only an inhabitant like Cryptid could recognize the way.

However, I was able to make out something rather curious on our left. A group of trees—three, to be exact—standing close together. It wasn't the trees themselves that sparked my interest, but the markings on them. Tiny gashes covered the trunks, too deep to be organic.

These had been made using tools. Sharp tools. The kind that only a human was capable of employing.

"These marks are interesting. Do you know what they are?" I asked, stopping to run my fingers over the uneven lacerations.

Suddenly, my hand was yanked away by a big, rough one. His icy stare froze my lips shut. How was it this man who had never uttered one word could silence me with a look?

His calluses scraped my skin as he tugged me along, leaving the tick marks and their hidden meaning behind. So many secrets. Nothing about him was obvious; he was an impenetrable fortress of mystery.

Despite confusing the hell out of me, he brought my twisted mind comfort. I stared at our hands joined together, his large one swallowing up my small one, then closed my eyes for a moment, enjoying the security of his touch. Every nerve came alive, sending trills of heat up my arm. The most intimidating beast of a human somehow made me feel safe and, in some sick way, excited me. The lunacy of it was beyond my understanding, and a part of me blamed it on the deficit of touch I was currently experiencing. My obsessive desire to be connected to another human hadn't been met since I had washed ashore. The deprivation only heightened my senses whenever he did touch me. And my body responded like that of a boy-crazy teenager, excited by a mere brush of skin.

My lunacy must've been showing because I realized we had stopped walking, and when I opened my eyes, I found him gazing at me with interest.

I retracted my hand. *Oh, for fuck's sake.* My neediness had reached a whole new level of *weird.*

I didn't need him. I didn't need anyone. *I, Maris Schuler, can be alone!*

One of his bushy brows lifted before he continued walking toward where the pig was grunting merrily ahead of us.

I marched along, this time crossing my arms over my chest, banning myself from his touch in the event I tripped or something and involuntarily reached out for the oaf.

We traveled in silence with nothing but the crunch of brush under our feet and the buzz of flies in our ears.

The air thickened and I was dripping sweat.

I preferred to work in clothes that covered my limbs to avoid falling prey to poisonous spiders. And since most of my work was usually done at night with the exception of setting up nets to catch bats, I could get away with being fully clothed and not suffocating like I was now. My vulva was officially chafing from wearing the same dirty pair of underwear. I wished I had enough courage to ditch them completely.

"Where's the beach?" I stared, puzzled, at the dense trees around us. We had been walking for some time, and instead of the foliage thinning as it did near the shore, it grew thicker. We were in the heart of the jungle.

"I think you went the wrong way," I called out. He stood in front of a luscious green tree drooping with red and orange jewel-colored fruit.

He dropped his basket, and with a brisk shake of the tree with the rod, the gem-colored fruit rained down on us, landing on the ground with blunt thuds. I covered my head, unwilling to withstand another unconscious incident while I was still recovering from the first.

"Mangoes!"

There must've been almost twenty of them lying around my feet like green, red, and orange globes.

Cryptid stooped low, tossing the ripest fruit into the basket. He moved to the adjacent tree and repeated his process of shaking so hard that the branches threatened to break off.

The avalanche sent bubbles of excitement bursting inside me, like a kid witnessing birthday balloons raining around them. I giggled with glee until the last one hit the ground.

This time, I beat him to the chase and picked up a mango before he had a chance to collect it. The pig let out a coarse snort and went to town, gorging on the feast around us.

The seemingly permanent wrinkle etched between Cryptid's brows softened at our enjoyment. His usually intense eyes lightened briefly with an emotion I couldn't place.

I squeezed the fruit in my hand, testing the slight give. Eagerly, I dug my nail into the skin and juice spilled out over my fingertips as I pierced into flesh. Saliva was already pooling in my mouth.

Unexpectedly, he reached out, taking it from my hand.

"Hey! That's mine, you big bully." His grouchy self was like a wet blanket on my emotions. God forbid I ever found any joy around here. He would make sure I was as miserable as him. It was a wonder he ever let the pig squeal in excitement.

Mr. Miserable let out a rough grunt before biting into the skin. Threads loosened steadily as he ripped it away from the orange flesh with his teeth. Strip by strip, he skillfully peeled the mango by mouth as we huddled over the ground. My gaze was glued to the confident way his mouth treated the fruit, and a warm heat rushed through my core. He could make any task erotic.

He passed the exposed, juicy globe back to me.

I cleared my throat, swallowing down excess drool in addition to gratuitous guilt. "Umm, thanks."

I sank my teeth into the treat. "Mmm," I groaned. It was the most delicious thing I'd ever tasted. So sweet and hydrating…and untidy. Nectar dripped down my chin in tiny rivulets. I laughed at the complete mess I was making as I slurped the entire thing down in record speed. Not ignorant to his attention dragging along my liquid-stained skin to the bottom of my V-neckline, I tried to wipe away the juice—and also his gaze.

He peeled another with his teeth and offered it to me.

"Don't you want any?"

He nudged it in the air until I finally accepted. I took another bite, closing my eyes this time to savor the luscious taste.

"It's so good. You have to have at least one bite." I pushed it toward him. Instead of taking it into his own hands, he grasped my wrist and lowered his head, wholly focused on me, and sank his teeth into the flesh. Juice dribbled down his lips and onto his beard, and I followed a cloudy drop as it escaped onto his bare chest. His skin was always glistening with sweat—not in a pretentious *gym-bro* kind of way, but in a sexy-lumberjack kind of way. The result of hard manual labor. The sheen highlighted the definition in his muscles, making them appear as juicy as the mango in his mouth. Maybe even more.

My tongue was suddenly too heavy, and the temperature must've risen about ten degrees because my neck was burning up.

There we sat, in the middle of the jungle, hungrily staring at each other's lips. Was he hoping for more than just sharing produce, like I was?

My belly tightened, as he held my wrist. His breath was warm on my face. Fragrant like fruit. I parted my mouth, hoping to catch a taste.

There was no one around to interrupt this moment. No one.

No one.

Realization slammed into me like a freight train, and the lustful murkiness in my head vanished.

No one was here to save me. I was stuck on this island with a strange man who couldn't answer any of my questions in a way that I could comprehend. *Shit.* I didn't even know his damn name.

What was I doing? I didn't have time for this. I needed to save myself, unless I wanted my worst nightmare to come true—to live what few days I possibly had left in isolation.

My paralyzing fear of loneliness clawed up my spine and wound around my neck, strangling me.

Clearing my throat abruptly, I shot to my feet, effectively breaking our connection. Forever the expert at pushing people away when things became too real…too intense. "Um…thanks. These were yummy." I dropped the seed on the ground and backed away. The flies must have been watching us because they swarmed around me, sticking to the mess on my neck.

Swatting at them was futile. These assholes were persistent. "Too much to wish for a shower out here, huh?" I teased, smacking one of the buzzing nuisances that had landed in the middle of my forehead. Red and brown guts smeared my palm, and I rubbed it away on my pants. *Gross.*

He nodded and gathered the basket of fruit. The pig stayed behind, chomping on the mangoes that we'd left on the ground, while I followed the man with the rod in hand.

We continued on past the hut, several yards farther, to an alcove in the bushes. Another barrel rested there, similar to the one he used to catch rainwater outside the hut. Tall stalks of something resembling bamboo had been arranged like walls to form a nook. Large, smooth rocks lay flat on the ground inside the area with barely enough space between them to see a sliver of earth underneath.

Cryptid passed me the rod and twisted a makeshift valve on the ground constructed of plastic. I assumed it was another invention made from salvaged ocean trash. Suddenly, water trickled from an overhead spout fashioned from an old water bottle with small holes poked in the bottom, attached to another bamboo-like stalk. *A shower.*

I placed my free hand under the stream, cool liquid hitting my palm. "Oh my God! You built a shower?"

He nodded curtly before turning off the valve.

It was a shame no one else was here to witness his accomplishments. If he had been in a less isolated area, he'd have no doubt been a successful engineer. He deserved accolades for building something out of virtually nothing.

"This is amazing. Can I use it?"

He nodded again and collected the rod from me and the basket off the ground, leaving me in privacy.

Wow. A real shower. Despite being made from limited resources, it was far fancier than some of the showers I'd used in motels and hostels during my travels.

I waited for his footsteps to disappear before undressing. My clothes were so disgusting that I had to peel them off my body. I stripped down completely, ditching my sweaty underwear. A shower was a rare occurrence, and I intended to take full advantage of it.

Water flowed steadily when I switched on the valve as he had demonstrated. The pressure was low, and judging from the size of the barrel, I didn't have much time to waste before the supply vanished.

I stepped under the stream and shivered when the cold water hit my skin. I tilted my head back, dousing my greasy hair. Liquid cascaded down my body, stinging my burnt skin. Gradually the ache dissipated, and I was able to enjoy the chilling sensation.

I gently cleaned my neck, and then my breasts. *Underboob* sweat was the bane of my existence, and I had been a walking factory for it over the past few days.

My eyes closed as I washed between my legs, cleansing away the memory of dirty panties. I had to admit that touching my most private parts in the middle of the jungle, with the birds chirping overhead and the breeze blowing, was liberating. I opened my eyes to take in the tranquil surroundings.

"Fuck!" I screamed and grasped at my body, unsuccessfully hiding myself from the inquisitive man gaping at me.

To my horror, Cryptid stood before me, taking in my hand that failed to contain my tits and the other that barely covered between my legs. A deep growl vibrated in his throat.

A large cloth tumbled from his clutches onto the ground. I snatched it up, instantly snapping him out of his stupor. Wrapping myself in the makeshift towel, I shut the water off.

"Dude! What the hell?! You can't sneak up on people like that when they're bathing!" He might've built the shower, but he certainly didn't have any bathroom etiquette.

He still stood there, as if waiting to see more.

I frantically waved him off. "Do you mind?!"

Finally, he stalked away.

I wouldn't have dreamed privacy would be an issue on an island with only two people, but damn it...

Chapter 11

Uncontrollable Storms

Aleki

Screech Owl was too much to deal with. One minute, she was soft and quiet…kind of amusing…but then, as soon as I blinked, she would turn into a babbling mess of words.

And I didn't want to start on the mood swings.

I was always the same: a loner, kept to myself, a person of few words—or *no words*, when it involved her. I regretted tricking her into thinking that I was incapable of speech because now I couldn't tell her to shut up when she made my head hurt.

Like when she'd been showering. Any appreciation she'd shown me for my handy construction had disappeared when I'd just been bringing her a towel. The favor backfired, and she had exploded.

Dramatically trying to cover her body from me had been pointless. Her body parts were too obvious to hide behind her slender hands. Plus, I had already seen it all before. To be honest, I liked watching her. Her skin was smooth—*pretty*. And the way it curved down her neck and over her chest, creating a secretive valley between her two perfect breasts, made something vibrate deep inside me much like when I hunted. My heart rate sped up. My senses sharpened. And whenever she looked at me with those big green eyes, I had to hold myself back from attacking her.

Like when she'd eaten the mangoes I'd picked for her. The mess escaping her lips had excited me. For some strange reason, I had only been able to think of licking the juice off her. I was sure it would've tasted better than the actual fruit itself.

Damn it.

I had let myself go there again—down the spiral of thinking of her in ways that didn't involve sewing her mouth shut. In fact, her lips were very loose in my dark fantasies.

I was losing my mind.

I wished I could go back to the way life was before, when I hadn't had to deal with her. Except, did I really want that? Could I go back to being alone?

The pile of firewood was victim to my irritation when my foot smashed into it.

Screech Owl and Poaka peered up from their dinner. She certainly wouldn't be too thrilled when she realized the light-colored meat I'd been feeding her was iguana. Another reason I should speak so I could ruin her peace, as she did mine, with the ingredient list that was her dinner.

I set about my nightly routine, brushing my teeth and washing up quicker than usual. My head needed a break from the wild thoughts that raced through it.

The faint sound of thunder rolled through the air. A storm was coming again. The clouds were thicker this evening and the air more heavy than usual.

Screech Owl had finished her meal and threw the bones into the fire pit before taking her spot in the hammock. Her frame somehow grew more delicate after another round of thunder cracked overhead. She glanced up at the sky, her body shaking like she was cold.

She caught me staring and quickly turned a rosy shade of pink, deeper than the sunburn that had settled into her pale skin. Her cheeks reminded me of two flowers in bloom.

"Storms make me nervous," she said quietly as she played with her fingers in her lap. "I don't exactly have a good track record with them."

She had washed up on the shore soon after the last storm, so that must've been what she was referring to.

I motioned to the opened door of the hut. As annoying as I found her, I would always offer for her to sleep inside. Tonight was especially one of those nights where shelter would be needed if rain was on the way. Plus, I knew she hadn't been sleeping well. This morning, she'd already been awake, with heavy dark circles above her cheeks, when I had stepped outside.

"No, thank you. I'll sleep out here," she said, offering me a weak smile. She was upset, but quiet about it. Very unlike her.

I exhaled roughly. If only she would allow me to help her.

Suit yourself.

I extinguished the fire, bathing us in darkness, and Poaka's hooves trotted on the wood as he took shelter inside.

Thunder rolled again, this time harder and louder. The storm was heading our way. A soft shudder echoed from Maris. I shook my head and stepped through the doorway before I did something rash, like throw her over my shoulder and carry her inside.

I groaned nearly as loud as the bed did when I lay down. Every muscle that worked like a machine all day finally relaxed. I was like a man in his sixties instead of one in the prime of his thirties. I often worried about how I would handle living here when I grew older. Could I continue without help?

Poaka was already fast asleep next to the bed, snoring louder than the thunder outside. He was a deep sleeper, and when he was out like this, nothing could wake him up. Thankfully, I could defend myself if needed because Poaka would've made a terrible watch pig.

Rain pelted hard outside, knocking against the wood frame.

The mattress beneath me was old and full of lumps, but it was the only one I had ever come across. My guess was it was a scrap from an old boat, much like most of my finds.

Other than the texture, everything was right about my bed. It was large enough—I'd made sure to build the frame to fit my body. It was cozy with fabrics I had collected over time, connecting them together to make full-length sheets. I had also fashioned a pillow, using discarded clothing as stuffing.

It felt *too right*, too comfortable, that it made me uncomfortable.

Clearly, I was still overstimulated from the day. I wasn't used to having someone around. And though I was separated from her by four walls, I could still feel her nearness. Like she was right by my side—a shadow. It was difficult to ignore her presence.

There was no way she was getting any sleep in the rain. She would be soaked to the bone by now and cold as the water drenched her. Her clothes would be dripping, clinging to her body. Goose bumps would dot her skin.

My dick twitched to life between my legs. It liked the visions my mind had created of her see-through wet shirt.

Touching myself had been more out of necessity than entertainment…until *she* showed up. According to one of the romance books in my trunk, men often desired to pleasure themselves based on visuals of something erotic, namely a woman. "The breeze gently blew her hair against her chest..." "The woman's lips were as bright as a ripe cherry..." "Her milky white skin pebbled under his touch..."

The imagery described on those pages—coupled with the explicit pictures from my nude magazines—had been the only material available since I had never had a real woman for inspiration. Until now.

Pushing the sheets down, I fisted myself, indulging in a few harsh pumps. I preferred to sleep naked, allowing my private areas to *breathe*.

My cock always came to life when Maris was around, which was all the damn time. Her loud voice. Her spicy-sweet scent. Her annoying mannerisms. It had all invaded my space, clouding my head from thinking straight.

She needed to go. To leave forever. Her presence was too distracting.

I tightened my grip, choking my length. Visions of her nipples peeking through her clumsy concealment when I had stumbled on her in the shower flashed through my mind. I had seen the full view when I found her on the beach, and that dusk shade of pink would forever be my favorite color.

I pictured her thin hands touching me—squeezing me as hard as I was doing now. Running her fingers over the tip, catching some of my liquid on them.

My chest vibrated with a growl as I worked myself faster...harder.

Thunder cracked again against the violent soundtrack of the rain.

The door opened. Instantly, I released myself and pulled the covers up to my chest, already aware of the identity of the visitor.

Her figure was far better than the mental pictures I had conjured. The door shut with a soft creak, locking the bad weather out. Step by step, she drew closer, bringing a different kind of storm with her.

She stopped beside my bed. Our breaths created a simple rhythm, one beat after the other, but somehow louder than any pet snores or any downpour beyond these four walls.

Water droplets skittered from her hair, some landing on the edge of the mattress while others pattered onto the wood floor.

"I don't want to be alone," she whispered softly, as if it were a secret...one she never wished to expose to the universe.

One I'd hoped she'd admit because I didn't want to be alone either.

Not tonight.

Chapter 12

Safe and Sound

Maris

"I don't want to be alone."

There, I had admitted it. Not just in my head, but aloud. For another person to hear.

The words were out there, and I couldn't take them back. I had carried them inside for so long that they had fused with my consciousness—my soul. Where they had once rested now lay a jagged wound. The admission had been painful, yet this secret had weighed me down for too long.

However, more painful than saying it aloud was waiting for his response. His stare burned my vulnerable skin, exposing more of me.

Steadily, he peeled back the thin sheet, revealing the vacant spot next to him. Enough space to alleviate my aching loneliness. It was dark, but I could make out the fabric of the covers bunched low on his waist, revealing his naked side. I visibly traced the outline of his hip, down to the side of his solid bare glute.

The gentle rise and fall of his chest matched my own, steady and incessant.

He reached out and caught my hand in his, his thumb stroking my knuckles. So warm, so inviting.

How easy it would be to slide in next to him. To curl into his side and seek the comfort I longed for. The kind I was addicted to. I could use him to meet my needs. His face was better looking than that of any man I had ever been with, and his body was that of a god.

Yes, I certainly could spend the night with him—trade sex for comfort. Except, what would happen tomorrow morning?

The same thing that always happened...I'd wake up and glimpse last night's living *security blanket* from the corner of my eye while I awkwardly tried to avoid conversation as I hurried out of bed. Then, the minute he left, my old pals Guilt and Self-loathing would suffocate me, and I would be reminded of why I needed an occupied bed in the first place. The cycle would continue like a pitiful hamster wheel, never really addressing any of the underlying anxiety and sadness I had been carrying for decades.

God, what is wrong with me? I'm so desperate for affection that I'm considering hopping into bed with a stranger.

This island was getting to me, and this man clouded my judgment. I needed to get home and focus on myself, once and for all. I needed to find the beach.

I jerked my hand back, clumsily retracting and waking a shrieking pig in my escape.

I ran.

I ran as fast as I could out the door and away without granting him another glance.

I ran like I always did. This time, it was to protect my sanity.

Rain pelted my face, and my feet splashed and sloshed in trenches of mud. My heart pounded in my throat. My vision was marred by the storm. Branches lashed my skin, stinging on contact.

Still, I didn't slow down. I wasn't stopping until I found the beach…until someone came to rescue me. This wasn't my home, and somehow, I had begun to think this life was normal.

My foot stalled on something hard, and I lurched forward, slamming to the wet earth. My eyes were heavy from tears, so tired that they drooped.

I heard my name in the distance. Thick and deep, echoing through the jungle. The voice soothed me, promising me protection.

My body shifted, and suddenly, I was cocooned in a blanket of warmth. It was as if I was floating midair, completely weightless yet still moving. *Flying.* My head rested against something firm, the perfect amount of support I needed, physically and emotionally.

My lids squeezed tightly, shutting out everything around me, because I was protected. The voice murmuring my name against the top of my head would make sure I was safe.

Chapter 13

Chasing the Runaway

Aleki

One minute, I was hypnotized by the repetitive rise and fall of her wet breasts, and the next, I was gaping at the open door, no trace of her left behind.

Maris had bolted out of the hut, away from me, as fast as the lightning cracked outside. If I had blinked, I would've missed her sprint.

I had been left sitting up in bed, completely dumbfounded by what had happened. My erection immediately deflated when the reality of her stupidity hit me.

She couldn't survive out there, especially with the high winds and slick weather conditions. Every creature around with good sense found shelter during rain like this.

I shot to my feet, uncaring of the fact that I was naked, and went after her. Poaka scampered behind me, doing his best to keep up in spite of his top-heavy build.

Thick bullets of water splattered my skin, and the wind torpedoed whole branches from trees. Visibility was low, but I didn't require eyesight to guide me. The impressions from her footsteps could easily be felt by my own feet as I jogged into the thicket, and her fruity scent was thick, despite the rain diluting everything around me. Years of relying on instinct wouldn't fail me now.

A painful yelp sounded, like an animal had been wounded.

"Maris!" My voice roared louder than the thunder overhead. It was the first time her name had fallen from my lips, and I hadn't expected it to carry so much desperation.

She didn't know this area, and the unruly landscape would make sure she wouldn't survive it.

Once I had spoken her name, I couldn't stop. My voice grew louder, more urgent, with each call.

Poaka jetted in front, his body compact and moving with purpose. His nose had picked up her trail, too. He hobbled through the wet earth as best he could until he stopped before some fallen brush.

I ran over as fast as I could, leaping over the tangle of branches and twigs. There she lay on the ground, a messy mass of hair and limbs strewn every which way—the same as I'd found her that fateful day on the beach. For a split second, my stomach hollowed out and dread filled the space. She wasn't moving, and I feared the worst.

I sprang into action, gently rolling her onto her back. I couldn't see her face clearly in the dark, but I could sense her chest expand and deflate shallowly under my hand. Relief flooded my chest, and my shoulders relaxed enough for me to draw her limp body into my arms.

Carrying her unconscious self happened far too often for my liking. She wasn't just a person who had been beached and stranded, she was fighting things within. Things that made her behave erratically and feel like she needed to run away from them.

I cradled her gently against my chest and headed back to the hut.

What had broken her?

I didn't think I'd ever know, but I'd do my best to protect her from it. To keep her from turning into a person without light—like me.

Chapter 14

Two Lost Souls; One Shared Memory

Maris

Spoiler alert: I didn't find the beach.

As a matter of fact, I'd wound up in the same empty bed, completely naked.

Déjà vu all over again.

Except I knew exactly where I was. And I knew who had carried me there and cleaned the mud off my skin. And who had left me a tattered T-shirt that was about three sizes too large to wear instead of my wet, soiled clothes.

It had been the man who was sitting next to me, teaching me, the least crafty person ever, how to weave baskets.

I was never getting out of here. I was destined to stay and watch Mr. Silence complete an entire inspiration board of crafts without ever looking me in the eye again.

Last night had made him uncomfortable.

That made two of us.

Tension wasn't new between us—we irritated the hell out of each other—but last night in the hut, with him naked in his bed and my heart bleeding out before him, that tension had gone to my head. I had almost done something that I would have regretted.

This had to stop. I couldn't go around sleeping my way through beds to be whole. I was weak, and if I stayed here any longer, I would just cover up my issue with another Band-Aid instead of exposing it and allowing it to heal once and for all.

I needed to get home and fix my head. The first person I was calling when I set foot in Washington was a therapist because I was certifiably fucked up.

I tucked my legs under me, and the hem of my worn-out tan T-shirt flared out like a dress. My guess was that it had been white a long time ago. The screen print had nearly faded away, but I could still make out the block lettering that spelled out "Bob Marley and the Wailers." At least it was a legendary artist, although I didn't think Cryptid even knew who Bob Marley was.

Underwear was no longer necessary under such a billowy shirt. It only got in the way and chafed more than anything. Soggy, tight clothing wasn't practical in this tropical environment. Plus, he was always staring at my boobs anyway, so modesty was pointless.

My craft tutor deposited the basket he had started onto my lap. Long, waxy leaf tails poked out of the circumference of the frame, made of dried straw-like twigs. He already had another one started for himself and lifted it for me to watch his method. His fingers worked more quickly than expected, catching leaf tails and weaving them over and under through the straw frame he had fashioned. He must have weaved hundreds of baskets to work as expertly as he did. His movements were far too skilled for me to follow. Or, rather, my mind was far too cluttered to pay attention.

I lifted a tail and stabbed it between the grates of straw, but the leaf bent, creating a kink I could no longer thread through. I tugged the tail, undoing the weave, and the leaf remained disfigured.

I can't even thread a fucking leaf over and under. How could I survive here? I'm fucking helpless.

"Fuck!" I screamed, throwing the basket skeleton over the unlit fire pit, nearly hitting the pig, who was flopping on his back in a puddle of mud. He scrambled to his feet and let out a haughty snort at me, rivaling my scream.

"I can't do this!" I clutched my head in my hands, bringing my knees to my chest as I huddled into a ball on my ass. Hot tears pricked at my vision. I rocked back and forth, anxiety bubbling to the surface and overflowing out of me as sobs.

Cryptid remained seated and placed his basket on the ground, watching me fall apart.

"I want to go home." My voice shook and the tears poured out. I wanted my old life back… It had been far from perfect, but it had been mine. And the normalcy of it was the only thing that had kept me from flying off the deep end from my longing for affection.

Here, nothing was normal. Every smell, sight, and sound was new, constantly triggering my nervous system and overstimulating me. This place was driving me mad.

Cryptid rubbed circles on my back, his palm taking up a large surface area to radiate warmth through my shirt. His strokes were gentle and soothing, far from his tough exterior. I closed my eyes, falling into his surprising touch.

My sobs slowed after seemingly a lifetime, and still, he patiently waited them out with me. He didn't have to console me. He could've just given me his infamous side-eye and grunt and trudged off in search of another jungle craft, but he had stayed and given me the space to pour out my frustration.

His hand left my back, and my spine rolled, as if searching for his tenderness again. Cryptid retrieved a basket that he'd already completed and

VICTORIA WOODS | WILD LIFE

filled it with random items like he was shopping at the grocery and checking off a mental list.

Slabs of firewood. Small rocks. Black rubber tubing.

Oh God, he's going to make me build something else. I swear I will lose my shit if he makes me build a water fountain.

"Listen," I said, my voice hoarse from crying, "as fascinating as I think it is that you're a closet engineer, I'm not very crafty. I don't think I'm the right person to be your intern."

Unimpressed with my argument, he took my hand in his and pulled me to my feet, the basket tucked into his other arm. The pig scuffled on his hooves, excited to find out our next moves. And I was curious, too.

Gently, Cryptid guided me, his big hand swallowing mine. Our difference in size was complementary. I shifted, and he stilled my fidgeting, interlocking his fingers with mine.

I had never held hands like this with another person before. As a devout member of the anti-relationship religion, I had made it a point to never do so with anyone. It wasn't because I hated it or was repulsed by it. On the contrary, I had always yearned for that type of touch. To have that connection with someone while doing something completely menial like walking. I had never wanted to encourage something more permanent from the men that I'd hooked up with, and the gesture would clearly have sent the wrong message.

121

It was only the third time he had held mine, but it felt different. When he'd done it the first time, he had been dragging me through the jungle like I was a child. The second time had been last night, and that was in the heat of lust.

As we walked together, we moved as equals. As two people traveling to the same destination willingly, though I didn't know where it was. I was too tired from the tears I had shed and allowed him to lead me.

We walked in silence until my legs hurt. The pig struggled to hobble along for the journey. I stopped, the fire in my calves unbearable and my feet stinging from the harsh brush.

I doubled over, holding my waist. "I can't walk anymore." The pig collapsed at my feet in agreement.

Cryptid shot us a hard glare, as if we were the most pitiful beings he'd ever seen. He continued walking through the dense trees.

I dropped to the ground, sitting next to the pig, careful to keep my thighs shut since I was *sans* underwear. While I had let Eli the Bug Guy inside my vagina, I would be damned if I let actual bugs inside.

The pig nestled his wet snout between my shin and the ground. I rubbed his ears, and he let out a contented huff. "You hated that walk, too, huh?"

His large eyes stared back at me as if wishing to agree.

"I think he forgets that not everyone is made of stone like him." I glanced to where Cryptid had disappeared.

My hand moved to the pig's exposed belly as he lay on his side. He lifted his hind leg in enjoyment. "You're a giant puppy, aren't you?" I said in a baby voice. "When I first met you, you scared the hell out of me, but now I see you're simply a ball of mush inside."

Just like your human companion. I smiled at the thought. The two of them really belonged together.

Interestingly, the pig cuddled into me as if he knew exactly what I was saying. He seemed incredibly aware of human mannerisms and emotions, like a magical animal in a fairy tale or something.

"We'll wait here 'til he gets back. What do you say?"

My nose drew in a faint smell. It was heavy and astringent, coating the back of my throat. I choked on my acrid breath, covering the cough with my hand.

The pig perked up, his nose vibrating in the air, too.

"You smell that?"

The scent strengthened, like a thick blanket around us.

Smoke.

It was coming from the direction of where Cryptid had headed.

I leaped to my feet, and the pig followed. The jungle was on fire, and I didn't know where Cryptid was. What if he was trapped? I needed to find him.

The pig ran ahead, covering his companion's tracks, and I followed. The brush thinned considerably as we moved.

The dirt under my feet changed, softening, and my feet sank with each step. More daylight shined through the trees. The landscape was morphing with each stride. My heart pounded in my chest.

Then, suddenly, I stopped running and stood in awe.

There were no more trees. Only sunlight shining on miles of white sand for as far as I could see. Blue waves painted the horizon like a masterpiece. They roared in my ears with the promise of freedom. Water. *The ocean.*

I stumbled through the sand, dumbfounded that I'd finally made it to the beach.

And there was Cryptid, standing in front of a fire. The pig ran to him.

My feet carried me to him, attracted as if by a magnet. "You...How?"

His eyes darted to the fire that he'd started with all the items he had packed in the basket, the flames crackling voraciously.

"You did this? For me? To help me get home?"

He nodded.

Tears pooled, but this time, they were happy ones. I was nothing to him except an inconvenience. He could have let me rot away with starvation when I had shown up here. Despite his grumpy exterior, he was always finding ways to help me. To care for me.

This fire was the nicest thing anyone had ever done for me.

I launched into his arms and he caught me under my thighs. I wrapped my legs around his waist, gluing myself to him with my arms around his neck. I buried my face into him, inhaling his distinct, rain scent. "Thank you," I whispered against him over and over again, my lips grazing his neck with those two little words.

He held me tight, his arms wrapped around my body in a bond that only our lost souls could understand. His nose buried into my hair, and his chest rose as he breathed in—breathed *me* in—almost like he was committing my scent to memory.

The time we had known each other had been short, but he would always remain a part of my life, even if I never saw him again. I could never forget my savior who had given me the most important gift—the chance to not only to be found, but to find myself.

And from his embrace, I knew this man would never forget me, too.

Chapter 15

Home is Where the Heart Is

Aleki

Screech Owl was gone, and silence had found me again. Except, I couldn't relax.

I lay in bed, but again, nothing was right. It was too quiet. My head was too busy. I was *too alone*.

If I had known that I would feel the opposite of her joy when she'd seen the beach, I would have reasoned harder before taking her there. She was so desperate to get home. I remembered what that was like when I was a child…the hope of being rescued soon. That the whole world had stopped and set out to search for me. Except each day that had passed without anyone coming had slowly strangled that hope until there was none left, I had no choice but to accept that this was my home until I died.

I had left her on the beach earlier, but since night had fallen, I wondered how she was. Had luck finally struck this hellscape and rescue had come for her? Or had my reality become hers and she was still sitting on the shore waiting for help that would never come?

Every inch of me itched to jump out of bed and watch from the shadows to see which fate she had met.

What would I do if she wasn't there? Perhaps I fought my impulses to leave the hut in the middle of the night because I didn't want proof that she was gone. My heart rested heavily in my chest. I'd never see her again. No one in their right mind would ever return here once they were free—at least not someone like her who so clearly belonged to the other world.

It was better for her to leave. Survival was difficult here. A person like her required social interaction that I wasn't able to provide. Hell, she didn't even know I could speak. Spending the rest of her life with a man who she assumed couldn't talk depressed even me. I could give up the charade and reveal the truth, but she would hate me for fooling her for this long.

I missed her mindless chatter. I was now suddenly aware of how much silence existed between me and Poaka. He couldn't regale me with random facts about bats or about how he couldn't eat pineapples because the enzyme, *broma*-something, burned his tongue. Her stories added variety to my day and provoked new fantasies—many of which involved me wondering what made her tongue work as quickly as it did.

Maris talked too much, but her words had filled a space I hadn't known needed filling…until it was empty again.

The night was still, except for the heavy snores of Poaka on the floor next to me. He was out and there would be no waking him up until morning when his bladder was full and needed to be emptied.

I covered my eyes with the crook of my arm and exhaled as many worries as I could force out of my mind.

The front door clicked open, and my heart stopped beating. I had imagined it. I was sure of it. No one was here, and I refused to move to feed my overactive imagination.

Feet padded softly on the wooden floor, bringing my heart back to life, its beats mimicking the steps. As they grew louder, approaching me, my heart thudded harder—wilder. That memorable scent of spicy-sweet hesitation grew stronger, permeating my senses.

Relief washed over me.

She had never left.

I lifted my arm from my head and my sharp vision registered her expression, despite the darkness. It was fallen and sad. *Hopeless.* Reminding me of the little boy who had given up so many years before her.

"No one came," she murmured, her voice hanging like the broken wings of a bird.

She wanted the one thing I couldn't provide for myself—to be saved.

I shifted slightly to my left and pulled the edge of the blanket back, fully aware that I was naked. I had often spent my days roaming without a cloth around my hips and had never given it much regard, but when her eyes were on me, I was suddenly concerned with the parts of me that were bare and wondered what she thought of them.

Her focus darted from my length to the empty spot on the bed, as if a war were going on inside. *Chaos.* I would give anything to climb into her head and listen to her mind.

She slid in next to me, her sea-salt-kissed wavy hair sprawling over her side of my worn-out pillow. "Can you hug me? Please?" Her voice was almost as fragile as her frame.

It had become a habit to reject her every request. Only lately, I found it harder to deprive her, especially when her hurt was so clear. It activated a part of my human side that I hadn't sensed in a long time. A memory of the Aleki who'd lived before this island.

I drew my arm under her light body and pulled her close. She fit perfectly into the nook of my arm.

I hadn't hugged anyone or showed affection to another human in years, and here I was, engaged in one for the second time in a day with the same woman. The first time had been because I'd believed she was leaving for good.

This time was different. She had asked, but control was left up to me.

Intimate body parts were touching me through her shirt, igniting new feelings within. Too much was happening, and I was far too self-conscious to unwind.

My discomfort must have been obvious because she took the lead. Her head lifted and rested on my chest, and her warm breath rushed out against my skin as she relaxed into me, her addictive scent below my chin.

The tension between us melted away.

How had I slept by myself all these years?

Maris shifted and suddenly threw her leg over my hip, the innocent gesture of closeness becoming anything but when her thigh rested on my hard length, which was also very excited to have her back.

Her body stiffened slightly.

She didn't move her leg. Didn't apologize. Didn't try to pretend it had never happened.

My dick threatened to explode from the light pressure of her touch.

What should I do? I had no experience with women, and I had no clue if this made her insides vibrate like it did to me.

I wanted so badly to take myself in my hand and chase that much needed release, but it wouldn't be enough. I craved more than what I could give myself.

Her hand moved from the center of my chest downward, coming dangerously close to my groin.

Would she touch it? What would happen if she did? My dick lurched with excitement and hope.

Her hand stopped, as if unsure what she wanted to do, until it fell to the opposite side of my waist.

I let out a sigh. Whether it was from relief or disappointment, I wasn't sure. Everything had changed between us.

I lifted my free hand and pulled her in closer. We lay fused together, like unsolved riddles until sleep silenced our minds.

Chapter 16

Flowers for Ghosts

Maris

In some cultures, bats represented transformation. It was believed that after slumbering all day in secrecy, they were reborn at sunset. Their reemergence was a sign of rebirth. Another chance at existence. A chance I hadn't been awarded on the beach.

Hope had shimmered so vibrantly in my chest that I'd been sure anyone could have seen it from miles away at sea, like a star in a clear night sky. I had stupidly believed that I would be rescued within hours, so much so that

I hurried Cryptid away after he'd brought me some fruit to keep on hand for nourishment. However, as the sun had set, so had my confidence.

No one had come. Not one airplane overhead. And a new dread had set in—the possibility that my team hadn't been as lucky as I had to have survived the storm.

Lucky. I chuckled at the irony of the word. Sure, I was lucky to be alive. But was life worth living when you were invisible to the world, doomed to spend your days living somewhere no one knew existed?

It was like when people survived some sort of disaster, like a house fire. Friends offering their condolences always said shit like, "At least you're alive," or, "How lucky you must be!" all while the person who'd experienced the disaster stood there with nothing but the clothes on their back and the very real knowledge that their life might never recover from the plunge into misfortune.

People had said that kind of crap after my parents died, and it had always irritated me. My entire sense of security had been stolen from me, yet I was supposed to thank some dude who lived in the sky for sparing my brain from hemorrhaging upon impact, like my emotionally negligent parents' had, and subsequently forcing me to be raised by my even colder and more distant aunt. If that was what luck meant, then slap my ass and call me *Lady Luck.*

I skinned another rambutan and popped it into my mouth. Juice exploded over my tongue when I punctured the flesh with my teeth, and the mild tartness made my lips pucker.

A moist nose shoved its way into my lap, nostrils vibrating and expanding at my stash.

"Hey!" The fruit had taken me all morning to harvest, and I wasn't going to give it up easily. I turned away to escape the garbage-disposal-on-legs that was trying to attack my treasure.

There was no hiding food from the pig. He could've given those bougie truffle pigs they used in France a run for their money, except he probably would've eaten everything he found before it ever had a chance to make it to market.

I gently trapped his snout with my hand, and his eyes shot to mine as if I were keeping him from the only meal he'd had in a week, although he had just stuffed his gut with a hearty portion of the bananas that Cryptid had harvested for us. Leaning in, I held his innocent stare. For a giant creature, he was so juvenile. The more I was around him, the less I noticed his intimidating size.

I softened my voice. "I will share my treats with you if you calm down."

His eyes darted between both of mine as if he understood my words, which was remarkable since he'd probably never heard another human speak in his life.

A loud grunt startled me. Cryptid stood in the doorway of the hut, watching my exchange with the pig. He had avoided me all morning, so I wasn't shy about giving him a taste of avoidance, too.

"Good boy," I praised, turning back to the pig. I removed my hand slowly and straightened up while he remained seated before me, no longer a frantic barge of huffs and snot. I quickly peeled away the spiky shell of a rambutan for him and tossed it in the air. He caught it and immediately swallowed it down, then resumed position. "See? Good things happen when you're patient."

I fluffed his ears and went back to peeling fruit for both of us.

Cryptid lumbered past as if I didn't exist. As if we hadn't spent the night in each other's arms.

When I had returned to the hut, I'd been defeated. I should have stuck it out longer on the beach, but with every degree the sun had traveled closer to Earth with no sign of rescue, the harder the rejection had gripped my suffocating hope. Spending the night out on the beach was lonelier than when I had spent it outside in the hammock pretending to sleep.

My brain had been too tired of thinking, allowing my feet to take over and bring me back to camp. I didn't know how I had remembered the way. It was like my body had been pulled on an invisible line that connected me back to the hut. Back to Cryptid.

I had given up. Then I had given in.

Like always when I was lonely, I'd found my way into a man's bed. Except this time hadn't been out of desperation. Instead, it was like coming home to a place where I could be completely honest and not worry about having to mask my childhood-trauma-turned-adult-dysfunction.

Despite his frequent attitude, Cryptid felt safe. And last night, he'd proven that he was capable of warmth. He had given me what I needed rather than me taking it like I always had from other men. And for the first time, I hadn't used my body as a bargaining chip.

I was in the habit of trading sex for intimacy. Some believed the words were interchangeable—a common misconception. Sex was physical, the act of fucking, so to speak. But intimacy went deeper. It had the power to make you feel whole when sex left you incomplete, especially if you forced yourself to go through with it without having a real connection with your partner.

For once, I hadn't offered myself up to a man like a platter of goods. I'd been truly vulnerable and received the intimacy I needed to ease my loneliness.

All of that had vanished when I woke up in an empty bed, yet again. And he had punctuated the insult by acting as if it had never happened.

It was almost as if I had imagined the entire thing—a dream. But I distinctly remembered how secure I was in his arms.

And I also recalled how his hard dick had pulsed against my thigh. He could pretend I didn't exist, but he couldn't fake an erection.

I watched him as he organized more wood against the hut. More specifically, I watched his loincloth shift as he bent over, hoping to catch a glimpse of the bulge that had pushed against my leg all night. My teeth sliced the rambutan in my mouth in half, and I used my tongue to dislodge the flesh from the seed.

The man might've been unfortunate to be stuck on a deserted island, but that misfortune didn't extend to his length. Cryptid was a monster of a man with a monster dick, and I was too curious to see what it looked like. *A quick peek.*

Last night, I had demonstrated control in not straddling him in hopes that he'd hold me afterward, and that certainly deserved a preview of what I was missing. I had been a good girl, and good girls deserved rewards, right? Just a glance would do the body good.

It had been fully erect for much of the night, and it must've been painful to have gone that long without coming. Maybe that was why he was cranky. Did he know how to *take care of his business*? He had to, right? It was something all men instinctively knew. I mean, if apes could do it on their own, certainly a man stranded should know how.

His cock sucked me so deep into the rabbit hole of dirty desires that I hadn't noticed the pig gobbling fruit from my lap. I tried to push him off and failed, falling over as rambutans rolled in all directions around me. I opened my mouth to curse the lug out, but the seed inside went rogue and slipped into my throat. It traveled down my esophagus, but not without a fight.

Coughs and gags racked my body, until I was on all fours, hacking like a cat with a furball.

When the tears finally cleared, I was face-to-dick with the loincloth that had distracted me almost to my death.

The cock's owner stared down at me with nothing but a raised eyebrow, as if I were an idiot.

Not funny, Universe.

I scowled and stuck out my hand. "A little help here?" My voice was still hoarse from escaping death.

Instead of being a decent human being, Cryptid ignored me and walked away.

"Jerk," I muttered. That man was insufferable.

I pushed myself up and dusted off my palms and knees, watching him as he headed for the line of bushes. His hair was down and the old rubber band he used to secure his bun at the crown of his head was missing. I'd only ever seen his tresses loose when he was about to go to bed, and I had never really taken the time to appreciate them. Luscious, wild waves cascaded down his neck, the tips grazing his broad shoulders. He was a darker version of Tarzan, both in appearance and in mood.

He examined the full blooms dotting the wall of dark green leaves. He plucked two ruby-red hibiscuses and turned to the side, his profile visible as he brought one of the flowers to his nose and inhaled. Fleetingly, he resembled a little boy, his innocence visible in that hard exterior.

My heart softened as I approached him. "Those are beautiful," I said. "Going on a hot date or something?"

He faltered at my voice, shuffling backward. I had intruded on a personal moment.

I held my breath as his lips parted, expecting miraculous words to escape. Only, nothing came out. Instead, he walked off.

"God, I wish he could talk to me," I said aloud to no one in particular, and the pig snorted. I turned my focus to the black-and-beige spotted bundle sitting on his hind legs, begging me for more treats. I stooped before him and patted his head. "Reading your friend's mind is exhausting. How do you do it all day?"

The pig grunted. How was it that this animal with hooves could carry on a conversation better than his human?

"Where do you think he's off to?" I asked my animal companion.

All I was met with was a blank stare.

"I don't blame you. He doesn't really tell us anything, does he? How about we find out ourselves?" I patted my thighs, and he stomped excitedly. "Let's go."

We followed behind at a safe distance. If Cryptid could hear us, he didn't let on. I was rather surprised, between the pig's hobbling and my clumsiness, we made more noise than a train.

The trees with the mysterious tick marks were on our right, and I was immediately filled with overwhelming heaviness. My fingers involuntarily skidded over the grooves as we passed by. I didn't know what it was about them, but a sense of foreboding twisted my guts into knots. The trees communicated deep grief, telling me a heartbreaking story.

The island had a way of speaking louder than its inhabitants could, like it had a life of its own.

The brush thickened, making it harder to tail my target while still maintaining ample distance between us. The pig had a tougher time wading through the vines on the ground, and every so often, I'd have to stop and untangle his legs.

Jeez, where the hell is Cryptid going?

There were too many trees to see clearly. I had lost him, but the pig still trotted along, and I trusted that at least he knew which way his companion had gone.

I was ready to give up this spy mission and head back to the hut when I spotted him through the leaves. There he was, hunched over on his knees, his shiny locks covering his face like a curtain. He held the two flowers in either hand, resting them on his lap.

Two dirt beds lay before him side by side, separated by a line of small rocks. They were too perfectly arranged to be natural. Someone had created them intentionally—like graves.

He set the flowers down by his side and pulled at the weeds that tangled over the soil, working diligently and exercising so much care in cleaning the beds—gardening with no garden. Then he carefully scooped up and covered the beds with new soil.

Gently, he laid a flower on each fresh bed and stared at them for a while. I could finally see his face as he turned it to the sky, eyes closed and hands resting on his lap. He was so still, he didn't seem real anymore—like a carved statue posed deep in prayer.

The pig was restless at my side, his legs wrapped in weeds. He let out an angry grunt, disturbing the peace.

Cryptid's focus shifted toward me, pricking me with its sharpness.

He stood up and stalked closer. His size overwhelmed me.

"Umm, I was looking for…"

My mind raced as I stared wide-eyed back at him, hoping an excuse for my nosiness would present itself, but I was never fortunate enough for things like that to happen. Being on the island was proof of just how unlucky I was.

"The trees." I pointed up to the canopy that enveloped us. "They're interesting, huh?"

He glared at me, clearly seeing through my bullshit. Then he stormed off, leaving me with the ghost of whatever emotion had gripped him moments earlier.

Chapter 17

Kiss of Breath

Aleki

Screech Owl had inserted herself into every part of my life, and it was overwhelming. I couldn't visit my parents' graves without her following me. She was messing with my head. And my body wasn't spared either, much to my dismay. They kept teaming up to coerce me into acting on the urges that rushed through me. All she had to do was cough and my blood would pump furiously, as if I were hunting.

I had messed up the night I held her. All the distance that I'd carefully imposed between us had disappeared. My resolve was weakening, and if her supple lips fell into one more pout, I'd cave to the pressure and do something stupid like surrender my hut and all my belongings and follow her around on all fours, much like Poaka did.

My pig had betrayed me, preferring to stick by her side instead of remaining by mine.

First, she couldn't stand the animal, and now, she couldn't go without calling for him anytime my inattention was too much. He'd even started answering to "pig," completely ignoring my use of his name when we were alone. I would catch him gazing off into the sky as if waiting to hear, "Come, pig!"

And don't get me started on the new sleeping arrangements. After the one night we slept together, the lusty haze that had robbed me of logic had worn off and I had decided to never allow it again. Of course, she was oblivious to my inner dialogue because I'd stupidly pretended I couldn't speak, so she'd slid into my bed again…and again…and again…until it became our new bedtime routine.

Every night, her warm body would nestle into mine as if I were her mate. Instantly, my skin would light on fire from the attraction. And my dick? It throbbed to find a home inside anything it could fit into.

The temptation was far too great; it was a miracle I'd yet to take myself in hand and release the tension she'd infected me with right next to her in bed. It was like an illness, one that started in my groin and spread to my whole body, overtaking every part of me. Maris wasn't a screech owl, she was a disease. A deadly one that wouldn't stop until it conquered me.

She had full control of not only my bed and my pig, but my body, too.

Pretty soon it would be the whole damn hut. *My hut.* The one I'd made with my bare hands, back before I'd had the distraction of long legs, shapely hips, and skin fair enough to bruise easily if I grabbed her too hard.

Unwillingly, I pictured dark-blue marks on her thigh left by my fingers. My erection shifted my loincloth out of place.

Damn it. I needed her gone.

She was going back to the beach, even if I had to drag her there.

No more missing her. No more pesky feelings. No more thinking.

I wished for quiet again—for peace—and for my body to stop pressuring me to discover more of her.

I could see her from the treetop on the other side of the pool, the waterfall cascading between us. She had found some string from my shelves, and in her high-pitched voice as bouncy as her breasts, asked to use it to make some sort of contraption.

Her attention was stuck on whatever it was she was creating. Something about using it to study bats. Poaka chased the end of the string while she worked, making her project his own.

I broke branches off and dropped them below to prepare more tinder for fire, but my gaze was glued to a patch of skin on her leg revealed when she had sat down and her shirt had ridden up. Her thighs were still new to the blazing tropical sun, unlike the rest of her, which had turned cherry red before settling into a light-rosy color.

Splinters embedded into my fingers as I grasped the wood hard because all I could imagine was gripping her silky skin. Her complexion reminded me of the cold glasses of strawberry milk I used to devour as a kid.

A whole body of water and a waterfall separated us, and I could still somehow smell her soft hair and yearned to bury my nose in it, filling my lungs with its spicy-sweet scent. It was so real that my mouth watered for it. I would have bet her skin tasted just as good, too, like cinnamon candies.

She abandoned her string project and slapped her leg with her hand. The smack was loud, but my ears registered it at a near-deafening volume that somehow masked the rushing downpour from the rocks. It rang through my ears, the sound carving itself into my brain. The sound of her flesh made my insides scorch hotter.

Another slap.

Fuck.

I yanked hard at the branches. I needed to get a hold of myself. She was only a woman, and although I was now old enough to qualify as a man, I couldn't spend my day gaping at her like a hormonal teenager. I had real problems to worry about—like survival—and Screech Owl was too much of a disruption.

I was done thinking of Maris. *Done.*

Until she let out a scream that pierced my ears with the sharpness of a blade. I snapped my attention in her direction to find her on her feet, her body twisting into strange positions like she was trying to crawl out of her skin. The screaming didn't stop. She clawed at the back of her shirt, desperate to put more space between herself and the fabric as she leaped away from the spot where she'd been sitting.

Poaka started to his hooves and screeched wildly, matching her screams.

My entire being sprang into action, and I scaled down the tree. The second my feet thudded onto the soil, I bolted around the pool so fast that I thought my legs would fall off.

When I finally reached her, her contortions were too violent for her to speak coherently. She kept slapping at her body, tears pouring down her face.

I couldn't figure out what was wrong because she wouldn't stay still. I needed her to stop moving before I could figure out how to help her.

Without caring about handling her tenderly, I pinned her to the ground, my knees on either side of her body. She wouldn't stop crying out, repeating "Ow" over and over.

And then I saw them on her neck. *Fire ants.*

Too many to count, scurrying all over her perfect skin, and leaving trails of angry red bites.

My eyes went to where she'd been sitting. A mound of dirt lay next to her string project. A nest.

Fuck. There were so many ants swarming, swiping them off with my hands wasn't enough to get them all.

My head spun, glancing at the pool. I needed to get the ants off her. Too many bites could do serious harm.

I stripped off her shirt and lifted her, hoisting her thighs around my waist. My skin tickled as ants crawled onto me, but I held her twisting body tightly against mine. After inhaling a deep breath, I jumped.

Cool water consumed us as we sank to the bottom, our bodies separating. Maris's arms and legs flailed. The water wasn't deep, just hitting my waist if I were to stand up. The ants only needed a few more seconds to dislodge, and then they'd wash off her skin. Longer contact with the crisp liquid would help the swelling from the bites, too.

I grabbed her shoulders and held her under with me, and her eyes widened. Even under water, I could hear the sounds of her protests amid the bubbles she created with her frantic movements. She hadn't been prepared for the plunge and must've been starving for air.

Thinking fast, I grabbed her head tightly and sealed my lips around hers, creating an unbreakable connection. She went still against me. I loosened my lips, and when she did the same, I forced breath into her mouth. Then I bit her lips to force them closed to keep the air in.

She watched me, eyes sparkling under the crystal liquid. I nodded, assuring her it was okay to exhale. I could hold my breath much longer than her due to years of training while deep-sea fishing.

She pursed her lips, and tiny bubbles escaped as she breathed out. I cradled her face to guide her.

I nodded again, signaling it was time to ascend. We rose together. As fresh air hit her lungs, she sputtered, coughing up what had been trapped inside. I wiped the water from my face and pulled the rubber band out of my hair, looping it over my wrist for later. Rivulets from my wet locks ran down my back.

Red welts had already started to form on Maris's skin, but luckily, her face had been spared. I caressed her shoulders, gently examining the bites. They would swell more by tomorrow. I cupped my hand in the water and splashed some onto the bumps.

She braced a hand on my chest for balance. "They sting so much, but that feels good." Her voice was hoarse from hacking.

She closed her lids and angled her head away, allowing me to bathe her. Droplets trickled down her smooth skin, guiding me to discover a new set of bites on her chest. I splashed her there, too, my hand skimming over her body, careful not to press too hard.

Those drops of water drove my gaze lower. Her breasts skimmed the surface of the pool, pink nipples peaked from the cold. My hungry vision ate them up. While my fingers ached to touch them, to roll the buds to see if I could make them pointier, I didn't.

Her focus was on me, like she was fully aware that I was memorizing her. Her breathing quickened, causing them to heave. She braced her other hand on my hip, sealing our connection.

I wanted to play with her breasts. To test their weight in my hold. To massage them. I dripped liquid over them and watched how it rolled down to her nipples and hung off the tips before falling back into the pool that kissed my skin.

I could have gone on forever, if she'd let me. My mouth craved to taste them, and before I could stop myself, I let out a deep groan that rippled the aquatic surface. It startled her, and she immediately covered her naked chest from me with her arms. Our sights lowered, where we could both see the distorted image of the magical V between her legs.

My length twitched its appreciation.

I turned away. It was too much, and the way I was yearning, I wanted to ram her against the rocks and bury myself inside that V.

I climbed out onto the soil, water sloshing from my thick frame. I needed to get away from her before I hurt her already injured body.

"Thank you," I heard. I turned slightly to see her peeking from behind the rocks at the side of the pool, only her face fully exposed. "Thank you for helping me. I don't know what I would've done without you."

I let out a grunt of acknowledgment before walking away.

I didn't know what I would have done to her just then, but I knew I *shouldn't* do it.

Chapter 18

The Honey Scene

Maris

It was a rainy evening again, and the already little tropical bubble that contained Cryptid, the pig, and me had become microscopic inside the dry hut.

The dwelling had no natural lighting, but tonight, he had fished some candles made from beeswax, I guessed, from the shelves behind the dining table. We had dined on more of the chewy mystery meat that I had yet to identify and some papaya harvested earlier. I ate better here than I did at home, every meal consisting of protein and a shitload of fiber, pun intended. And I missed toilet paper.

Cryptid was busy cleaning up, and the pig was already asleep on the floor next to me as I sat on the bed. I was a bit worried about how easily and deeply he fell asleep, like he'd gotten into a stash of nighttime cold medicine or something. I actually wished he'd share his drugs with me so I wouldn't be awake to deal with this stupid itching. My skin was on fire, but scratching the fire-truck-siren-red welts only made it itch more.

I let out a frustrated groan and dropped myself flat on the bed. "These fucking bites! I wish I could rip my skin off!" My nails dug in harder, dangerously close to drawing blood. Surely, the viscous liquid would cool the discomfort.

The mattress against my back was uncomfortable. I jumped off the bed and paced back and forth, irritated like a squirrel searching for its tenth consecutive lost nut. Cryptid stared at me like I was losing my mind.

I was.

I shot him a deadly stare back. "What are you looking at? Take a picture. It'll last longer." I stuck out my tongue and screwed up my face, hoping to scare his attention away. Instead, he furrowed his thick brows harder.

I was still on edge because of what had happened at the waterfall. He had saved me from turning into ant food, yet that damn tension between us had wormed its way through yet again. It was always there. After every damn encounter, even a bodily danger event, it was a reminder that I hadn't had sex in forever. I had turned a new leaf and was trying hard to keep my vagina quiet. Unfortunately, the universe was conspiring against me by constantly sending the definition of masculinity to undress me. It was exhausting being this strong, and I scorned him for always being there for me.

I might've sounded immature, but I wanted someone to blame other than myself this time. It was either Cryptid or the pig, and the furball wasn't awake half the time to fault.

The scratching was only magnified the more worked up I got. I slapped my thighs, the sound echoing loudly. The pain canceled out the itch temporarily, and it felt so good. I slapped myself again, this time on the backs of my legs.

A husky grunt from across the room responded to my smack. Over my shoulder, his intense focus was on me, brimming with something much darker than anger. My knees wobbled in response.

I swallowed that lump in my throat that he was so good at inducing. "It's the only way to get the itching to stop."

He cast one more lingering view at my backside before turning away to the shelves. I watched his broad shoulders flex, the candlelight casting a soft glow on his already golden skin. His back was so muscular that it reminded me of ridges in rock. And his ass was firm like two boulders.

I mindlessly scratched my thigh while my mouth watered.

VICTORIA WOODS | WILD LIFE

When he turned around, I was greeted with the view of his chiseled abs. It was such a shame that a man this beautiful was hidden away on an island with no one to witness him. No one but me.

Perhaps it wasn't so much of a shame, then. Even if I was swearing off sex, I could certainly indulge my eyes, right?

My gaze traveled down the valley of where his abs met, stopping at the small jar in his hands. "What's that?"

He tapped the surface of the dining table.

"I don't understand…"

The jar slammed onto the table. I stumbled backward as Cryptid started for me until my back hit the wall. I was cornered, and his body was so massive that it blocked every direction I could run. "Wait, what are you doing?"

With too little effort, he threw me over his shoulder, my top half dangling over his back and my butt under his chin. I banged my fists on his back. "Put me down, you big oaf."

My ass hit the table first, followed by my back, and then my head, which thudded hard. "Ouch! What the fuck was that for?" I rubbed my skull. "You're such an asshole, you know. For someone who can't talk, you sure have no problem ordering me around."

I shoved my way off the table, but he pushed my chest with such force that I fell back down. I let out a frustrated groan. "If you weren't the size of an elephant, I'd punch you in the face for that."

My nails dug into the skin on my neck, scratching the bumps with fury, frustration only heightening the urge for relief. He swatted my hand away, then opened the jar, his stare warning me not to dare itch again.

I eyed the amber-color liquid. "What's that?"

To my surprise, he pushed his coated finger past my lips. Our eyes locked as it made contact with my tongue.

Sweet. Sticky. Thick.

I lapped at the syrupiness with my focus on him. A rush of air escaped from his lips. My insides squeezed at his reaction—the fleeting moment I overpowered him. I might not have been as physically strong, but there were other ways to exert control, and whenever I succeeded, I wanted to giggle with glee.

That was *us*—what fed the tension that always existed. The struggle for power. I was addicted to it. As much as I enjoyed pulling his strings, I loved that he didn't give in easily. It was as if he was resisting his urges like I was.

Two players. One game. The question was, who would lose?

The candle flames flickered and crackled while rain battered the exterior of the hut, entrancing me.

I sucked harder, taking in more of his finger, tasting the trail of sweetness. Cryptid's focus never left my lips.

"Honey?" My voice was husky and deep.

He nodded.

"That's smart. For the swelling," I said, lying with my knees bent and my feet flat on the tabletop. Honey had wonderful anti-inflammatory and antibacterial properties that made it a viable alternative for wound care when traditional medication wasn't available.

He extracted more of the substance from the jar. The cool honey coated one of the bumps in the dip of my neck, soothing me like ice. He massaged it in, and I let out a moan of relief.

One by one, he treated the bites, moving lower, toward my shirt. And with each treatment, my anxious muscles relaxed. The reason should've been the sweetener itself, but I knew it was his touch—the gentle pressure he applied as he rubbed each node.

He hooked his fingers on the loose neckline of my clothing, and I lifted my upper back slightly to allow the fabric to move at his whim, yearning for more alleviation. The shirt was so big that with very little effort, I could slide it down my body and pull my arms free.

It stopped short of revealing my nipples, yet the rest of my chest was free for his viewing, and he took complete advantage of it, pressing honey all around my breasts. His interest lingered longer than before, massaging larger circles that extended beyond the perimeter of each wound, on skin that didn't need care, but still craved it.

I watched the rise and fall of his upper body as his breath sharpened while he ate up as much of me as he could see.

The stinging had subsided, and a new heat built internally. One that radiated through my body and made everything pulse to life. The baseline tension between us had been disturbed, and there was no way to bring it back down. *I wasn't going to try.*

I slid my shirt down farther, allowing my breasts to break free with an excited bounce.

He sucked in a harsh breath as his heated stare roamed over my nipples. Despite the warm climate, they were still perky, and he was the reason.

His finger plunged once more into the honey before he deposited the jar onto the table next to me. He rubbed the messy glob onto the tip of my peak, stickiness dribbling down my tender flesh.

I arched into his touch, encouraging his exploration. For once, he understood my meaning and began to draw circles along my longing skin. He played with me like I was his greatest wonder. His forehead wrinkled, and I wanted to smooth away those lines of curiosity.

This was new to him. I sensed it from the way he touched me, like he had never experienced another woman before. He was fixated on the things that his predecessors took for granted when they saw my body. The men I'd been with had seen countless breasts before, but this man touched me like mine were the only ones in the world. I was a sculpture he sought to comprehend, studying how it all fit together. How it had been made.

This went beyond worshipping—it was an awakening.

His tented loincloth could barely contain him any longer. He was big, that much I could tell from how the tiny fabric tremored with each jerk of his cock. And I wanted so badly to do some examining of my own, but I feared it would scare him. If this was all new, I didn't want to frighten him away with my assertiveness.

Fingers pinched, rolled, and teased me until my toes curled and my core was shaking. I watched as he put those same fingers in his mouth and sucked off the remnants of the honey that had touched me.

And then he lowered his head and tasted me directly from the source, swiping his tongue over my nipple. I nearly convulsed.

Weeks without sex. Without the sensual touch of a man, and now that it was happening, I was hopelessly desperate for more. It wasn't my need for security. No, I just wanted him. For the first time in my life, I wanted to prolong sexual intimacy and not race through it to get to the part I craved.

And I craved *everything* he was doing.

His tongue swiped over my peak again, and I moaned so loud that his eyes flashed to mine. The muscles in his jaw flexed with worry. He was concerned that he hurt me.

I cradled his head in my hands, his thick hair tangling between my fingers, loose as it always was before bed. "It hurts so good," I whispered.

His mind worked to process my meaning.

"Don't stop," I urged.

He nodded.

His mouth descended on my nipple again. This time, he took all of it between his lips and sucked. His beard tickled my skin, shooting off nerve endings through my breast.

Fingers still twined in his wild tresses, I clutched his head in place, trapping him against me. My hips rocked, but I found no relief in the nothingness against them. "I need more," I moaned.

He feasted on me, nipping and sucking my skin with the extra pressure that I enjoyed. I liked it rough, and Cryptid was giving me what neither Eli nor any of the men I had been with ever had before.

His big hands palmed my breasts, playing with them possessively. They were his as long as he kept touching them like that.

He buried his nose beneath my cleavage, where he inhaled me deeply. The act was primal. Animalistic. Like he was satisfying some basic need to memorize my scent.

Lower and lower, he tasted me until he reached the neckline of the shirt around my abdomen. His touch glided gently over the bites on my midsection, but I was too full of adrenaline to note their irritation anymore. He tugged the shirt lower, stopping at my hip bones.

Gently, he applied more honey on my bumps, between administering kisses onto my unblemished skin. Except they weren't regular pecks. He was devouring me.

My belly trembled with anticipation. His solid hand pressed my midsection to calm the movement while he met my gaze.

"I'm okay. You make me feel like there are butterflies in my stomach."

He took my hand and placed it on his sculpted abdomen.

"You feel them, too?" I asked, hopeful.

He offered a crooked smirk, and I melted inside. His frown was stand-ard on his face, and on the rare occasion a hint of a smile broke through, it turned me into putty.

God, he had a beautiful face. All of him was magnificent, but his face, which generally carried a lot of seriousness, was achingly gorgeous. And when he grinned, he was years younger and almost carefree. A man like him deserved to smile more. A man like him deserved so much more than being trapped in isolation.

Suddenly, my clothing was pulled all the way off, and I was completely bare to him.

On propped forearms, I awaited his next move.

The imaginary butterflies flapped straight into my heart. Even in our heated state, he prioritized my well-being, caring for my bites with the honey on my ankles. That area and my ass had taken the worst beating since I had been sitting cross-legged on the anthill. They'd been the first points of contact for the pests.

He worked diligently, healing each bump before moving up to my calves, sensations intensifying.

My knees parted wider, presenting myself to him as he massaged my inner thighs. He paused, completely entranced by my folds. It was the same admiration he'd had when he peered at my bare breasts—like he wanted to discover all of my mysteries. I was high off that rush, that I was a man's first. That I would be the reference for all his sexual encounters after me. The one he could never forget. And the best part was this had happened organically and was not something I had forced, like I had many times before.

"Have you ever seen one before?" I asked.

He nodded. Maybe he wasn't as new to this as I had thought.

"Have you ever touched one?" I asked.

He shook his head, the innocence in his eyes glimmering in the candlelight.

"You can touch it, if you like. I won't mind."

I won't mind one bit.

His throat worked, and then his finger carefully traced a line around my entrance. I tipped my head back, enjoying his treatment. Round and round he went, his fingertip slipping deeper inside with each pass. My pelvis took on a life of its own, drawing micro-circles to mimic his motions. My body bowed when he found my clit with his thumb.

"Fuck."

He gently pinched my tender flesh, the bite reverberating through my core. I reached down and showed him with my own hand over his how I enjoyed getting myself off, and together, we drew tight circles on my bud.

"You're doing such a good job," I murmured in encouragement.

He discovered his own rhythm, rubbing me off to it like I was an instrument. My insides turned molten with heat.

Suddenly, a thick finger plunged into me, and I dropped my head back with a moan. He slipped his finger back out, then plunged it in again, and my body was on fire as I watched him, my gaze colliding with his.

He labored slowly, too slowly to induce orgasm, but it made me greedy for more.

I sank onto him, rocking back and forth, fucking his hand like a needy slut. *His slut.*

He worked me well as he discovered this new skill. I lifted my feet off the table and rested my ankles on his sturdy shoulders.

The rush within built to a frenzy, the promise of release beyond my grasp. "That's it. Keep going. Do you feel how wet I am for you?" I moaned. "Don't you dare stop."

He fucked me faster, and my hips bucked at a violent pace. "Oh God—"

And then reality hit me like a freight train.

I couldn't call out his name.

I didn't know his name.

I didn't know *him.*

He was a stranger, and I was splayed out on a table, desperately chasing an orgasm from a man who couldn't even say the word. He was yet another notch on my bedpost, and I couldn't ever make the relationship anything more than a good fuck because I didn't know him.

This wasn't right. I wasn't right.

I kicked him away and bolted off the table, any potential orgasm shattered by the cold splash of realization that had rained down on me.

His hands moved for mine, but I shook him off, too freaked out to endure his touch. "No. I'm sorry, I can't."

What could I say to offer a coherent reason for my mental spiral? That I was addicted to touch? That I had stooped so low as to let a man I didn't know anything about fondle me? That I was taking advantage of a man who seemed to have very little experience with women, if any?

No...this was wrong. Cryptid, or whatever his real name was, didn't deserve to be treated like this. He was too good. Too good for me.

"I'm sorry," I muttered again, before grabbing my shirt and tripping over my feet as I ran out the front door and into the rain, like I always did.

Chapter 19

The Come Back

Aleki

The door slammed, and it was as if Maris had never existed. Except she was still everywhere. The phantom pressure from where her ankles had been wrapped around my head remained. My finger was still slick and warm from her vagina. And my ears still buzzed with her breathy moans. I could still smell her musky scent. I lifted my finger t o m y n ose, i nhaling t he memory of her that was only moments old.

Had I done something wrong?

Her responses to my actions had convinced me that she had been enjoying it. She had encouraged me to continue. Begged me not to stop. And I hadn't wanted to stop.

I'd had no idea that my touch could make another person react that way—that it held such power to make a woman's body melt like that.

Had I mistaken my ability? Was I terrible at what I had been doing to her? My experience was limited to my hand on my own dick. Handling *tits* and *pussies*, as they were sometimes called in the books in my trunk, was a foreign adventure.

It seemed so much easier on paper. The man would hold the woman and kiss her body until he shoved his cock inside her, and then they would *come* together. They made it sound so simple. And none of the books mentioned standing with a painfully stiff shaft. I was more confused about a woman's body than I had been before I had offered to treat her ant bites.

I should have stuck to the original task of covering her bumps with honey and then turning in to sleep. But as was the case whenever she was near, I had lost track of my goal and chaos had followed.

I hated chaos. My days had been routine, and I preferred them that way. Then Screech Owl had shown up and terrorized my life with her loud voice and unpredictable behavior. And long legs. And perfect breasts.

My cock jerked painfully, threatening to explode as I pictured her lying on the table like a meal ready for me to eat.

"Fuck!" I cursed out loud, slamming my palm onto the table still warm from her ass.

Without untying the cloth, I squeezed myself hard. It twitched eagerly for attention. I pumped hard, more violently than usual, imagining what it would have been like if it had been my length inside her rather than my finger. My hips thrashed back and forth as I hunched over, tending to my needs.

My release was halted by the sound of the door opening, and I spun around with my back facing the door, cock still in hand.

The door closed again and soft footsteps paired with what must have been drips of water sounded on the floor.

"I'm sorry." Her voice was small, coming from the opposite end of the table.

I stayed rooted in my spot, waiting for her to elaborate.

"I'm really fucked up. I don't know how to explain it properly, so bear with me." She drew in a heavy breath before continuing, "My parents died when I was eight."

I blinked my eyes shut, remembering my own parents and how they had died when I was only a few years older.

"We were on our way to my grandparents' house for Thanksgiving, and it was raining. The car swerved and rolled. My parents didn't survive, but I did. Everyone said I was lucky to be alive, but I didn't feel that way. My parents were never the warm-and-fuzzy type that kids were supposed to have. I ended up moving in with my even more emotionally distant aunt. She was a difficult woman to make mistakes in front of, and I was full of them. Hell, I guess I was the biggest mistake for her because she'd wound up raising a child that she never wanted in the first place." Maris let out a sad chuckle that tugged at my heart. Her voice sounded so hollow, like she was moving through life playing the role of herself. The role that she believed everyone expected of her.

She continued, her shaky breath filled an endless pause to her explanation. "I use men to find the safety and comfort I never had in my childhood."

I had been aware of her need for security, but I hadn't realized she used men to fulfill it. The problem was too big for me to understand how deeply it ran, but I would try.

"And when I came here, I really tried not to slip into my old ways. I didn't realize it at the time, but I'd been given a fresh start to learn to be alone, to create my own security. And I tried so hard to be strong. I mean…you're…well, *you*…and it hasn't been easy to resist."

I grinned as her voice wavered. *I wasn't easy to resist.*

"But I did it. And then just now, I sensed I was slipping back again, regressing into the me that I've never liked. I realized that this was different…like I wasn't rushing through it to get to the part where I could push myself into your arms so you'd hold me. What we were doing made me whole."

I had felt the same way when I was exploring her body. Like it was a part of me, a path that was okay to cross.

"Then, like a lightning bolt striking me, I realized that we are strangers. I don't know anything about you. I was taking advantage of you…just like all the other guys in my past. They were all jerks who had been all too eager to sleep with me, but not you. You're too good for that. I don't want to do that to you. I never want to look back and lump you in together with them in my memories. You're a good person who is always trying to help me, especially when you hate me, yet we barely know each other. I don't even know your name, for Christ's sake."

She let out another laugh, livelier this time. "I've been calling you Cryptid in my head since we met."

Cryptid? Like a mythical monster?

She approached, coming to stand a few steps behind me. "What's your name?" Her voice was soft and gentle, as if we were meeting for the first time.

I wanted so badly to answer, to give up this farce, but she would hate me. With her history, I risked pushing her back into the protective shell that she had built from childhood. It was clear that she was having some sort of breakthrough in her own life, and I didn't want to mess it all up. She couldn't continue feeling guilty for corrupting me, when I was as fucked up as she claimed to be.

I turned around, showing her the man that she thought was full of good, with my hand still around my cock, my loincloth completely soaked with pre-ejaculate.

Maris was wearing her shirt again, now damp from the rain. Her attention bounced from the intensity in my eyes to my poorly concealed length within my grasp.

I should have hidden it from her, but I didn't care to. This was all of me.

She stood there, as if unsure how to proceed. I had scared her frozen. Disgusted her with my barbaric ways.

If she had any sense, she would run far away, leaving this cryptid and this island behind.

"Do you touch yourself often?" she asked, her eyelids unexpectedly heavier than before.

My cock pulsed, acknowledging her question.

"Are you touching yourself because of me?"

Her curiosity disarmed me. It was direct, yet intrigued.

I nervously nodded my head.

She didn't run.

"Does it feel good?"

I nodded. *So good.*

Her steps were slow as she crossed the distance between us, closing in on me like I was her prey, until she was right in front of me. I could smell the heady aroma between her legs. My blood rushed furiously. I administered a pump to alleviate the throbbing she caused.

She licked her lips as she followed my movement, and I imagined those wet lips where my hand was.

"Can I touch you?"

I didn't hesitate to nod.

Her fingers went to my leg, skating up my firm thighs. Her touch was feather soft. It moved up under my cloth and grazed my testicles. She gave them a gentle squeeze. My breath was uneven, and heat flushed my stomach.

"Your cloth is wet," she hummed, playing with my sac.

I was far too aware of the moisture from how the fabric clung to my engorged flesh.

Her thin fingers undid the knots at my waist with strong determination.

The drenched fabric fell to the ground with a soft *thud*.

I wondered what she thought of me. Did she hate how I looked? I'd bet that to her, I was an animal since she was used to seeing humans dressed in clothes.

Her sight roamed over my length, aimed straight for her like an arrow at its target. It was telling me: "That's the one I want."

Did she want it the same way? Did she want me? I was too innocent for a woman of her experience. Surely, I'd just disappoint her.

She traced a line from my base to the tip with her finger, as if measuring me.

A sigh, almost like a whimper, escaped her. "Fuck," she whispered. "You're huge."

Her appreciation nourished me, boosting my confidence.

I did look *huge* in her small grasp. She stroked me with the perfect amount of pressure only once, before I reached for her waist for balance.

She did it again, and I let out a harsh groan.

"Am I hurting you?" she asked. Now she was the one worried about me, when before, I had been afraid that her moaning had meant I was causing her harm.

My tongue thickened in my mouth, and even if I could have responded to her, I wouldn't have been able to speak.

I shook my head.

She smiled and swiped her finger over the tip, disturbing the bead of fluid that had accumulated there and robbing me of breath.

"Has anyone ever done this to you?"

Never. I hadn't known what I'd been missing—how good it could be when someone else touched me. I would die if she didn't do it again.

Over and over again, she pumped me hard. I let out a husky grunt.

"I know you can't speak, but I love to hear your sounds. They're so sexy."

Sexy? This must have been a dream. There was no way this attractive woman was calling me sexy. She must have had her pick of any man where she was from, yet she was enthralled with me. No, this couldn't have been real, but I didn't want the fantasy to end.

She worked faster, eliciting more noises from me. It was hard to stay upright with how voraciously she rubbed. My lids fell and I threw my head back, relishing her touch.

Then, suddenly, I was encased by something warm and wet. I snapped my head down to find her on her knees before me. Her mouth was around my cock, her cheeks hollowed in, constricting me. Her hand was at the base, guiding me onto her tongue.

Fuck. My body was electrified, as if I had been dead all these years and she had zapped me to life. How could I ever come back from this?

Her head bobbed back and forth, taking in more of me with each pass.

How big was her damn mouth? How far could I reach inside of there? I felt the back of her throat with my tip, and I gripped her head, holding her in place. She choked around me, squeezing me tighter, her cough vibrating through my erection.

Stars danced in my eyes, blinding me from how heightened my other senses were.

Her hand went to my sac, playing with it like she was testing ripe fruit, and I lost my mind. My whole body shuddered violently, and I dug my fingers into her scalp while hers gripped my hips as she gagged on me. Hot liquid rushed through me and filled her mouth. She sputtered while attempting to swallow it down.

I tried to catch my breath and pulled out of her, checking to see if she was alright. She was more beautiful to me than ever before, her eyes glossy and tears staining her cheeks. Her swollen lips were wet with my release and fixed into a mischievous smile.

She had enjoyed it.

My heart was ready to burst at the sight of her.

What had she done to me? And how could I make it happen again?

Only she mattered right now, though. She had confessed that she used sexual acts to seek comfort.

My legs threatened to give out when I quickly blew out the candles. She waited for me on her knees in the darkness.

I lifted her up from the ground, and she wrapped her legs around my waist.

"What are you doing?"

I was carrying her to bed, where I would hold her for as long as she needed me to.

I understood what it was like to be alone, and together, we didn't have to be anymore.

Chapter 20

Liar, Liar, Loincloth on Fire

Maris

I had finished my mist net.

And I had given Cryptid a blow job.

I wondered which of the two I was more proud of. Definitely the blow job, with the net coming in a hair behind.

I grinned like a fool as I carried my accomplishment. Last night had been a night of firsts. It had been the first time a man had licked honey off my body, which had surprisingly really helped my bumps improve—or maybe that should've been attributed to the stampede of endorphins shout-ing at my body's immune system to calm the fuck down.

It had been the first time I shared the truth about my baggage with anyone. And he appeared not to have judged me for it. In fact, he had held me all night like I needed. I'd had the chance to wake up wrapped in his arms without having had to exchange mediocre sex for cuddling. He had given me my pride back.

According to my assumptions, it had also been the first time he'd ever received a blow job, and his response made me want to give him ten more. How could a guy as hot as him be deprived of fellatio? If he'd lived in Wash-ington, women would've been throwing themselves all over him. His size alone would've attracted news attention. People would've written articles about it. "Giant Jungle Man Has Even Bigger Cock." And for a guy who was living without the standard hygiene necessities found at drugstores, he kept himself pretty tidy down there.

And the way he had choked me with his length...I'd been afraid he might impale my voice box, leaving me unable to talk like him.

It was so fucking hot.

And I wasn't mad at myself. I had been initially, when he'd finger-fucked me, like I was taking advantage of him. Like I was too messed up for this innocent guy to get involved with. Like I needed to save him from my-self.

So much so that I'd poured my heart out to him with brutal honesty. Yet when I had seen him touching himself, *because of me*, I couldn't resist. He had desired me as much as I wanted him. And I had wanted him badly, without needing to receive anything in return.

To my surprise, he acknowledged my confession and had gathered me up in his arms, refusing to let me go all night. Nothing else sexual had happened again, but honestly, it had been refreshing not to have to worry about putting out to receive intimacy.

It was perfect and I was on a high. If I smiled any harder, I swore my teeth would fall out.

The sun bathed my skin. The birds chirped merrily. My bumps barely itched, although I resembled a short giraffe. I was happy.

And I was productive, too. My net was complete, and I was ready to hang it.

If I wasn't returning home anytime soon, then I would resume my research.

The lack of technology would be a challenge, but I could certainly observe bats in their natural habitat and file details away in my head for later when I returned home.

If I ever returned home.

Luckily, I stumbled upon a spool of string in Cryptid's cupboards. Typically, mist nets were made of very fine material, making them difficult to be detected by the ultrasonic radar that bats were capable of. The string wasn't quite that fine, slightly thicker than sewing thread, but it was better than nothing. The most important thing was that it wouldn't hurt them in any way.

I'd had a hell of a time weaving the strands together, nearly going cross-eyed. The pig had almost ruined all my hard work when he'd trampled through it to chase a bird.

Thankfully, the net was alright and safely tucked under my arm as I trekked to the nearest still-water source, a pond not too far from the hut. The waterfall would've been a larger reservoir for the bats to drink from, but they weren't fans of getting sprayed with liquid. Nocturnal bats typically liked to dip down quickly during flight for a sip on their way to search for food. The pond was less threatening for the little winged creatures.

I set my net down, searching around for the best trees to use to hang my net. There was still ample time left before they'd wake up, so I could set everything up and then come back right before sunset to check for visitors.

I had found some twist ties to tag their feet. Cryptid's shelves had proved to be a hoarder's dream because I'd also found rubber gloves which I had sterilized in hot water to keep from introducing any bacteria when I touched the critters.

Two large trees looked ideal. Each had lots of low-lying branches that I could easily reach without help. When the bats flew from wherever their roosts were, they'd close in for a drink first before hitting the net. I would be hiding in the bushes nearby, keeping careful watch. Tagging would be quick, and then I'd free them right after. The tags would help me keep track of them, if by chance I saw them again. I could note their locations in hopes of finding their roosts.

I was about to hang the contraption when a sound in the distance froze me in my tracks.

A melody.

From a song.

With *a voice.*

It was distant, but I could hear it. How could that be?

Unless…someone was here. Another person! To rescue me!

Abandoning my project, I hurried in the direction of the singing.

"Close your eyes, child."

The song grew louder. The voice that sang it was deep and carried a husky rasp, yet it was beautiful. Like a beacon, I was drawn to it. It was like the North Star and I was a lost ship coming home.

"Let the winds be and the stars shine."

My feet pelted the ground as I ran toward freedom.

"In your dream, your hand will find mine."

As quickly as I'd let my hopes soar, it all came crashing down.

I stood in shock, peering at the source from behind a branch.

Cryptid was kneeling in front of the pig, de-seeding a papaya while singing him a lullaby. *A lullaby!*

The words flowed out of his mouth with as much familiarity as a routine—like it was something he'd been doing for years. And judging from the pig's reaction, this was nothing new for him, either.

That little traitor. I should have barbecued his ass when I first saw him.

Betrayal stung in my chest. I was going to roast Tweedledee and Tweedledum for this.

"Hey, can I have some?" I asked, my voice high-pitched and shaky, effectively halting their little campfire song.

Cryptid's eyes bulged like they would fall out of their sockets as he shot to his feet. The pig fidgeted in his spot.

I stalked up to them. "You can fucking speak?!" I shouted at him. The pig jumped at the crack of my voice.

Cryptid didn't utter a word.

"What now? Lost your tongue again? How long were you going to fucking keep this up? Until I got eaten by a shark or something, when you wouldn't have warned me first that you saw it coming for me?" I was reeling. I couldn't believe that I'd assumed he was such a good guy, thinking that he was too good for me. I would never sell myself short in front of a man ever again. They were all scum.

"Listen, I can explain," he said, his hands in the air. His words came out clunky and cloaked by an accent.

I smacked his chest, which did nothing to his sturdy frame, further stoking my anger. "Explain what? How you lied to me?! For fuck's sake, we've been intimate, and you—What? Thought you'd keep this secret from me the whole time?"

"I'm s-sorry," he stuttered.

"I had your dick in my mouth, you asshole! You were willing to keep this lie going for so long that you couldn't spare telling me before jizzing down my throat?"

"What's 'jizz'?" he asked, repeating the word carefully.

I stared at him, dumbfounded one second, and the next, I launched at him, punching his wall of abs. The impact hurt my knuckles more than it hurt him, but I didn't care. "That's the first question you ask me, mother-fucker?!"

He grasped my arms, and I yanked them away. "You better watch your-self tonight. Sleep with one eye open."

The pig grunted from the ground. "You too." I pointed my finger at him, blazing with heat. "Wouldn't want you to sleep too close to the fire pit, would we? You might accidentally fall in, you little—"

Cryptid interrupted, his voice low. "His n-name is Poaka."

I scowled at him. "Now you want to speak so much that you'll cut me off? You got some balls, dickwad!"

"Sc-ree-ch Owl, listen to me—"

I snapped my head around to face him, stunned. His words might've been rough, but I heard them clearly. "What the fuck did you call me?"

"Uh, sorry. It was m-my n-nick-name for you in m-my head."

I hadn't expected I could have been more offended, but finding out he had been referring to me as one of the most annoying animals in the entire animal kingdom tipped me over the edge.

"You had a n-nick-name for me too, remem-ber?" he said, referring to my admission of calling him Cryptid last night.

"That was the only name I had for you, asshole, because you refused to talk to me! Why did you lie to me?"

He opened his mouth to speak, but I put my hand up to stop him. I couldn't bear to listen to his excuse. All this time, I had been praying he could speak so I could get some answers, so I could have companionship, and now his voice made my stomach turn. "You know what, never mind. You'll just lie to me again."

"I p-promise—"

"What's your name?"

His gaze lowered to the ground, like a puppy who had been caught peeing on the floor. "Aleki." The pronunciation of his name was smooth.

I tested it out on my tongue. "Aleki."

He peered at me, hopeful that I was giving him another chance to explain.

But he didn't know who he was dealing with. "Fuck you, Aleki," I spat, before storming off.

Chapter 21

Apologies, Who is Ariel?

Aleki

I couldn't remember the last time I had been afraid of another person. Maybe that time at age seven when I'd lied to my mother about brushing my teeth for a whole week. When she had realized my toothbrush was never wet, she yanked me into the bathroom by my ear and interrogated me about it. I had denied everything, of course, and tried to convince her that it always dried quickly after use. She'd made me do it in front of her so she could test the bristles herself. I had nearly peed my pants because I had been so anxious and frightened that she'd pull my ear again. I always made sure to brush my teeth after that, even if it involved using a twig.

Again, I felt like a scared seven-year-old, but this time, I was afraid the explosive woman sitting near the fire was going to yank my ear. If she did, I deserved it. Something told me she wouldn't hesitate to chop the whole thing off if I spoke out of place.

The fire cracked, sending sparks into the evening air. I approached her, but she didn't look up. She was freezing me out, or at least trying to. The little wrinkles on the bridge of her nose deepened, as they often did when she was disgusted by something, like when Poaka pooped in front of her while she was eating. I now ranked with pig feces on her list of repulsive things.

I stayed put. It was only the two of us on this island, and she couldn't ignore me for much longer. She was a social being. And though I was proof that she didn't need someone to converse with, she needed someone to listen. Another human. Her admission had helped me understand how her lonely childhood had caused her to crave human companionship. In my case, the pendulum had swung in the opposite direction, and the loneliness had forced me to keep to myself. Maris sought what she had missed out on, whereas I was so bitter that I sank deeper into the very thing that had wounded me. Which one of us was the healthier of the two?

This time, I wouldn't choose reclusiveness again. I moved to the right to obstruct her focus on the roaring fire, only to be met by the smooth surface of her cheek as she turned her head away to evade me.

I knelt, unsuccessfully tucking my oversized body in to fit in front of her. "M-Maris."

Her gaze snapped to mine, the ice in her eyes melting away for the briefest moment.

Years had passed since I had spoken to another person, and I was rusty at it. I had never suffered from a stutter, but the lack of practice with another human combined with my nerves created one. It frustrated me that I couldn't spit out words, but Maris didn't show any sign of misunderstanding.

Despite my impediment, it was the first time I had called her by her name, and I was surprised it had affected me as much as it seemed to have affected her when it rolled off my tongue. I liked the feel of it.

"Say it again," she ordered, her thawing vision holding mine.

I inhaled much needed courage and exhaled her name as if it were my own to breathe out. "Maris," I said softly, my tongue rolling through each letter smoother than before. My shoulders relaxed slightly.

Then her eyes hardened again, colder than before. "I just wanted it to be the last thing you said before you went up in flames. Goodbye, asshole."

She shoved my shoulder, catching me off guard, and I tumbled backward, missing the fire by only a hair.

I composed myself, taking a seat on the ground like her. "L-listen, I know you're an-gry. If I were you, I'd hate m-me, too."

"Good, then push yourself into the fire and spare me the effort."

"Will you l-listen to m-me?" I touched her knees tucked to her chest.

"To what? More lies? I poured my heart out to you, and you stood there holding your chub in silence, playing the part of a man void of voice! Do you understand how mean that is? You deceived me. Instead of responding or answering any of my questions, you simply stayed quiet. Who does that? You're more of a stranger to me than I imagined."

My head raced to keep up. Maris always spoke quickly, and now that she was angry, the words were rushing out like hornets on the attack. Despite my respectable vocabulary thanks to my book collection, she used a lot of colloquial terms I hadn't learned yet. "What's a ch-chub?"

She snapped her fingers in my face. "Wrong thing to focus on right now, nature boy!"

I sighed. I was failing miserably at this. "I'm s-sorry. I wish I could m-make it up to you, but it all happened s-so fast. After all this t-time of being the only p-person here, you w-washed up on shore and I p-panicked." Speaking became slightly easier as I continued, "I wanted you to wake up and leave. You were loud, and I wasn't hap-py about it. I wanted my p-peace again."

"Gee, thanks." She rolled her eyes. "That's the worst apology I've ever heard. I think I want my peace again, too, so please go back to being silent."

"I p-pretended not to speak so I didn't have to d-deal with you. Then, as time p-passed—it never seemed like the right t-time to admit the t-truth."

"Do you know how much stress and anxiety I could've avoided if you had spoken to me? Answered my questions? I could have figured out where

I was or who you were with one sentence instead of worrying that you were some creepy forest-dwelling creature who was going to kill me."

I laughed and the tension rolled off my back. I loved her dramatic sense of humor, even if I didn't understand it sometimes. "You thought I was a c-creature."

"Kinda why I referred to you as Cryptid in my head."

"Which c-cryptid?" To my knowledge, there were a few of them, but I didn't know the specifics.

"A Sasquatch," she said plainly, as if it were common knowledge.

"What's a Sas-quatch?" I took care to pronounce the word just as she had done, even if it came out much slower.

"A forest-dwelling creature…Stay focused, Aleki."

Although she was angry, I still loved hearing my name on her lips.

I took her hands in mine and cheered inwardly when she didn't pull away. If I kept her talking, her anger would crumble eventually.

"Th-things changed. Having you around b-brings me peace. I realized this after I left you on the b-beach. It sur-prised me that I was sad of the p-possibility of you being rescued and return-ning to your world for good."

Her fingers wiggled in my hold.

"You told me how you crave hu-man bonds because of how lonely you were as a ch-child after your parents died. I under-stand that because when I was sh-shipwrecked here, my parents died."

"How old were you when you came here?"

"Ten."

"Damn," she said under her breath. "And you've been living here all this time? Alone?"

"Well, Poaka has been with me for many lifetimes." I smiled. Poaka and I had been through it all.

The corners of her eyes softened. "Your parents. You said they passed away. Are you sure?"

I nodded, images from the worst day of my life flashing in my head. "My dad died during the acci-dent and his body washed up with us. Ma and I were so scared. Dad was an ad-ventur-er, and loved trips like this."

"Trips like this?" she repeated.

"Dad loved traveling to remote locations. He was ob-sessed with chas-ing danger. Sky-d-diving, c-canyon climbing—anything that resulted in a thrill. Ma and I relied on him for his survival know-ledge on our trips. He read maps, or-ganized all the g-gear, and knew how to operate the radio and navigate the c-catamaran."

She brightened. "You traveled in a catamaran? That sounds so bad ass."

"It was, until it got him k-killed."

"Good point. And still, I can't imagine bringing a kid on those wild journeys. It must've been wild."

"I hated it. We lived in New Zealand, but we left every other m-month for some trip. I missed school often and wanted to stay p-put so I could be with my friends. I wanted life to be b-boring for a bit."

"You needed a routine," she offered.

I shrugged. "Doesn't every kid?"

"I suppose so. I had one with my parents, and then again when I had to go live with my Aunt Sherri, but I still turned out messed up." Her mind flew far away from the present for a moment before she regained her senses. "So, how did you end up here?"

"We lost signal and were s-stranded at sea. Dad couldn't p-place where we were because the ra-dar had been down for too long, and we had drifted really far from our last known l-location. Then a storm hit."

"Of course. Fucking storms! Always Poseidon fucking with humans and laughing."

"Po-sei-don, the Greek god?"

She pointed a finger at me. "That's the dude. Vengeful little fucker."

Half of my mouth tugged upward. A smile. Only she could make me smile.

I had read about him in my copy of *The Odyssey*. Maris could hold a grudge, warranted of course, yet she had nothing on Poseidon. He was the master of contempt.

"So, Daddy Poseidon attacked your boat and then what happened?" Her interest warmed me.

"I don't really re-mem-ber too much, except Ma screaming and a lot of water f-flooding my nose and mouth. Then I woke up. My face was c-covered in sand and my c-clothes soaked. Ma and Dad were face down on the beach. I woke Ma up f-first and helped her as she choked up w-water. Then I tried to wake Dad up, but he wouldn't m-move." The bits that I remembered were as strong as the sun's rays, burning my mind.

Maris took my hand in hers. "Oh, God, Aleki. That's horrible."

I swallowed back tears. It had been a long time since I'd replayed the whole story, and saying it out loud for the first time was difficult. I could smell the sea air, feel the grit against my skin and the hollow pit in my stomach as Ma sobbed over Dad's lifeless body.

"You don't have to continue if it's too hard to share," she said gently.

I shook my head. I wanted to share. I had kept silent for too long and starting this story had been like opening a dam, all of it ready to pour out. I needed it to pour out. "Ma ended up getting sick. Her skin got really hot, and she looked p-pale."

"Infection," Maris suggested. "Perhaps from aspirating water."

I wasn't a scientist like she was, so I took her word for it. "She died a week l-later."

Maris's eyebrows drew closer. "Is that why you put flowers on those two dirt beds?"

I nodded. I still remembered the day she had followed me out there when I was visiting Ma and Dad's graves. I went often to clean them of weeds and offer new flowers. I sometimes talked to them about things, mostly complaining about life.

Her face twisted like she wasn't well.

"Are you okay?" I asked.

She hugged herself tightly. "You were only a child when you had to bury your parents. I remember attending my parents' funeral, and that was the hardest thing I had to do. I can't imagine having had to bury them myself."

"Ma helped me with Dad's g-grave. We cre-ma-ted him on the beach and spread his ashes deep in the jun-gle since he was too heavy to carry. And then when she was too sick to w-walk, she wanted to stay with him. So, I knew she would want to be b-buried next to him."

A tear dripped down Maris's cheek, and I wiped it with my finger. I didn't need them, but for some reason, watching her cry halted my own tears. Caring for her first was my priority.

"And no one ever came to find you? Not even your family?" she asked, quietly crying.

"We didn't have much family in New Zealand. Dad wasn't cl-close to his, and Ma's were back in India. She n-never spoke to her family either. They didn't like that she broke her en-ga-ge-ment and ran away to m-marry my father." I had never met any of my family in India, but I still connected to my culture through the way Ma raised me. I may not have spoken or understood her mother language, but my heritage spoke strongly within me.

"My only family that I talk to is my Aunt Sherri. We were never really close, but I still think she's looking for me right now. Where are we, by the way?"

"I'm not sure. Somewhere in the South Pa-ci-fic. Dad n-navigated east of the Cook Islands, and I think we were cl-close when the storm hit us."

"That was how I ended up here, except we were on our way to Fiji, and then the storm hit, and I fell overboard." She let out a soft chuckle. "Guess the universe had some weird-ass plan for us with all this inclement weather."

"Terrible plan," I agreed.

"Yeah." She chewed on the inside of her cheek. "You said you were ten when you landed. How long have you been here?"

"Twenty-four years."

"Fuck. Decades?! That's a long time. So, wait, that makes you thirty-four years old?"

I nodded.

"We're close in age." She motioned in the air between us. "I'm thirty-two."

It was remarkable that we had so many things in common, like age, the loss of our parents, this island.

"How were you able to keep track of time so well? I can barely keep up with how long I've been here. It feels like years already."

"The trees."

Realization dawned on her. "The ones with the marks on the trunks? Like they'd been attacked by sloth claws or something."

"I m-mark each day that passes."

"Like a calendar?"

I nodded.

"Wow." She took a minute to digest everything. It was a lot of information, even for me, and it was my own story. "So, how do we get out of here?"

"I don't know. I never really tried to l-leave."

Her face twisted like she had eaten something sour. "What?! Why not? It sucks living here."

It wasn't so bad. "I was young when I came here, too young to think of a good es-cape plan. I didn't know how to build a boat. It took for-ever to learn how to start a fire on my own after Ma died. I was skinny and helpless and b-barely able to find food." How would I ever have braved the ocean to find civilization? Eventually, as I grew older, this place became my life, the will to leave was replaced by daily chores to keep me alive.

"No boats or planes ever randomly passed by?"

"You s-spent time on the beach. You saw how d-dead it was."

She bit her lip.

"I don't think anyone knows this pl-place exists," I said.

"Does that mean we're just going to die out here? That's so morbid."

I shrugged again. "That was my plan."

She shoved me gently, this time careful not to push me into the fire. "Ugh, you're not helping my anxiety."

"S-sorry," I said.

"If you were only ten and all alone, how come you speak like an adult? And don't tell me that Poaka is a magical pig who can speak."

Poaka's ears perked up with his name, but he continued scarfing down some fish guts I had saved for him after today's catch.

I was flattered that she thought I spoke like an adult when I felt like I was failing to keep up with our conversation. The flow was much easier, yet I still found some words difficult.

"I learned from books."

"You have books?!" she shouted, her eyes gaping wide. "And you didn't share them with me? Asshole! I was bored out of my mind this whole time, and you didn't have the decency to offer them to me?" She crossed her arms over her chest. "God, you must really hate me."

"I guess I have a lot to a-apologize for now."

"This is far worse than you lying about speaking."

She was dramatic, and I found it endearing. "Dad had p-packed some into a trunk, and it wa-washed up with us. I've added a few m-more over the years that I found on the b-beach." People loved throwing stuff away into the ocean in plastic bags, which were insanely protective.

"That's how you amassed your collection of…"

"Junk?" I completed the question for her.

"I was trying to be polite, but yeah, your shelves are like Ariel's secret lair with all the knick knacks."

"Who is A-riel?"

"Ugh, really?" Maris waved her joined hands through the air like a dolphin fin. "*The Little Mermaid*?"

I stared at her blankly, no record of anyone named Ariel coming to mind.

"Hot jailbait redhead in a shell bra and fins, with a weird obsession with legs?"

"I don't understand any of that. I c-collect whatever washes up since I never know when I m-might need it."

"I see there's a method to your madness now." She smirked, and it melted my insides.

"W-will you ever forgive me for lying to you?" I asked, hopeful we were making progress. I missed her. I wanted to fix things between us.

Her focus fell to her lap. "Probably. But right now, I still need to be mad at you."

Human emotions were complex and difficult to understand after years of not having to deal with them from another person, but I was willing to try.

"I understand," I said.

Chapter 22

Bat Kisses; No Rabies

Maris

Three nights had passed since Cryp—Aleki—had poured his story out to me and I hadn't said more than a handful of words when his apology tour was over. I was grateful he had finally shared the full truth, but I was still upset that he'd lied. And more upset with myself that I had been intimate with a man who had been lying to me.

I had slept outside on the hammock each night, even though he'd argued with me to take the bed. Poaka had also tried to get back into my good graces by slumbering outside with me. I had, of course, forgiven him because he was a pig, and had promised to never to threaten to turn him into bacon again.

Life was lonelier than before, despite this new knowledge that Aleki could speak. It wasn't so much that I was mad at him anymore. Instead, I was annoyed with myself for entertaining the cock of a guy I barely knew, like I had back home. Only time and space would allow me to forgive myself before ever forgiving Aleki. Yet again, my personal baggage was meddling in my relationship with men.

The trees rustled before Aleki and Poaka emerged from the thicket. The pig jetted for me and nuzzled his nose into my lap. I patted his spotted fur, greeting only him. "Where were you all day?" I asked.

Aleki's jaw relaxed with the conversation, even if I was just speaking to Poaka.

"We brought you m-mangoes." He rested a woven basket full of red fruit in front of me. He knew I loved them, and he was doing everything he could to get back into my good graces, too.

He had also been freer to speak around me, which improved the flow of his words. The stutter didn't bother me. I understood that decades without human conversation must have weakened his communication skills. As he practiced more, he progressed, independent of whether or not I replied back.

"Thanks," I said with no desire to eat them.

He let out a sigh and knelt in front of me, before peeling one of the mangoes with his teeth as an offering, just like he had the first time he had ever brought me to the mango tree. I didn't accept. He dropped the fruit onto the ground and Poaka, of course, jumped at the opportunity, chomping loudly on the rejected fruit.

"How long are you going to keep ignoring me?" Aleki asked, crestfallen. Emotions must have been hard for him, since he had lived most of his life without human interaction. I could only imagine how numb his mind had become after doing the same thing day in and day out for over two decades, but I was the epitome of mood swings. One minute, I could be anxious, the next excited by fun stationery supplies with cute animals on them, and then swerve a harsh left to *Hangry-ville.* And it was all normal for someone like me, who had lived most of her life in a modern, fast-paced world.

So I replied as any self-respecting woman would, in modern-world text talk. "IDK. K. Byeee."

Aleki let out a hiss. "Stop using your weird m-modern slang so I can't understand you. I want to learn, but you're not m-making this easier."

I had found it entertaining to use chat language with him, putting in little effort while still retaining my amusement.

He rose to his full height, his arms crossing over his chest and his shadow cloaking me from the late afternoon sun. "You're acting like a mean girl," he scolded.

My mouth fell open. "How do you know what a *mean girl* is? Your vocabulary is basically the regurgitation of your dad's eighties-era dictionary."

VICTORIA WOODS | WILD LIFE

"That's right." He grinned. He had been doing that a lot more lately, especially with every snide remark that left my lips. Must've been because he could finally share the load of his trauma with someone else and didn't feel as weighed down. "I'm not a c-complete idiot, Maris. I know some things, too."

God, I loved it when he said my name. I was also glad *Screech Owl* hadn't stuck.

"Are you hiding a computer here, too?" I hit back.

"No, but I did find a magazine called *C-Cosmopolitan* in a plastic bin that washed up yesterday." His New Zealand accent was very strong and *very sexy*. A lot about this man was sexy. However, I was a hard-ass who couldn't get out of my head, which made it difficult for me to move on from fights. He had underdeveloped speech, while I had underdeveloped resolution skills.

"Did it have any good makeup tips? Because I could really use some concealer to cover up these mosquito bites on my chin."

He let out a breath that made his strong shoulders sag. "Maris, I miss you."

I stared back at him, steeling my heart. "I'm right here."

"I know, but I miss how you were—how we were."

"Like when I would be talking for hours, and you'd ignore me?"

"I never ignored you. My brain wouldn't let me. I hear everything you say."

I swallowed the lump in my throat. It was hard to stay mad at the oaf when he was being so sweet.

"I just have a lot going on in my head right now," I said, suddenly tired of launching daggers at him.

"Come with me." He held his hand out.

I didn't take it. "Why?"

He pulled me to my feet, tugging me along behind him. "I'm going to get your head to *chill*."

"*Cosmo*, again?"

"Yeah, I read some article called 'Getting your Cort-isol to Chill Out.'"

I rolled my eyes as I stumbled behind him. His hand engulfed mine, a protective glove, as we traveled through the trees, passing the waterfall. It was still bright out, but darkness would arrive soon, and we were still walking.

"Where are you taking me?" I asked.

"You'll see."

We stopped when we made it to the pond, and I let go of his hand. Insects swarmed the area, sticking to my skin. I slapped them off and stared at their guts on my hand. *Gross.* I'd have killed for some hand sanitizer.

"Did you bring me here to feed me to your pet mosquitoes? How romantic."

His thick hand clasped around my neck savagely, and he jerked my chin roughly to the side with his thumb. The maneuver was very *him*: dominating.

"Oh my God! The net!" I jumped out of his grasp and ran under it. There, between two trees beyond the edge of the pond, was my net. I had forgotten about it when *voice-gate* had happened and dropped everything, including my supplies.

He'd hung my net for me. The height was perfect, high enough to only catch bats and not the other walking wildlife passing by, but still low enough for me to reach it. He had even pulled the netting taut enough to create a wide catch surface.

I approached him. "When did you do this?"

"Earlier today. I f-figured you could use some help getting that up."

"It's perfect. Thank you," I said, clasping my hands to my chest. "The sun will set soon. You should go back to the hut. I'll wait here to see if any bats show up." I took a seat on the ground, unable to look away from the net.

Instead of leaving, Aleki sat next to me and folded his long legs into a pretzel shape, like mine. "No. I'm staying here."

"I'll be okay. I promise."

"That's not why I'm staying. I want to s-see them, too."

"You do?" I asked in surprise.

He bumped my shoulder with his. "Only if you want me to."

I wanted him to stay. I loved that he was into this as much as I was. I nodded.

We waited for some time, engaging in random conversation about his old life in New Zealand and mine in Washington, as the sky darkened.

Suddenly, a mass of black covered the sky, tiny bodies gliding choppily through the air over the pond.

I leaned over to him. "They're awake!" I whispered excitedly, my lips brushing his skin.

We watched in awe as nearly fifty fluttered chaotically before half of the brood swooped lower.

Aleki covered his head.

I grabbed his arm. "They won't come for us. They want the water before they go hunting." We were sitting under cover of a canopy of trees and out of their way.

I clutched his arm to my body as we watched them take sips of refreshment without stopping before swooping back into the sky. They flew over the net.

"Oh, no," I said, pouting. The net was probably too low to catch them. "Damn, tonight was a bust. I was hoping we'd at least catch one."

"It's okay, I can raise the net." He moved to get up.

I could still make out his handsome face in the early evening darkness. "No, really, it's okay. We can adjust it next time."

Soft clicking disrupted the dreamlike haze that I was experiencing watching him.

"What's that sound?" Aleki asked.

"A bat!" I whispered. "Stay here." The incidence of rabies in bats was low, but we weren't in an ideal setting for a person to be infected. My rabies vaccinations were up-to-date, so I was in the clear. However, Aleki risked exposure if he wasn't careful.

I ran over and saw a furry little dark-brown mass wiggling against the strings of the net. It didn't hurt them, but he was anxious to be on his way to find food.

I worked quickly, slipping on my rubber gloves and grabbing a twist tie. I gingerly removed him, his little heart beating furiously under my fingers. Most people were scared of bats, but I knew the importance of this little guy, and that made him precious to me.

Wrapping the tie around his foot, I carefully tucked in the sharp edges so he couldn't hurt himself. I had trimmed the ties considerably, but some of the wire still protruded.

Keeping any prodding to a minimum, I quickly checked him over to make sure he appeared healthy and strong. Then I walked to the other side of the net, where his friends had flown off to, and released him.

"Happy hunting, little one," I whispered, watching him disappear into the distance.

I slipped off my gloves and dropped them onto the ground, careful not to touch the exterior of the rubber.

"What does the tie do?" Aleki asked.

He had vacated his spot on the ground and stood tall against a tree.

"It lets me know that I've already seen this guy. If I cross paths with him again, I can make note of the locations he frequents. Usually, the tag would be linked to a radar and carry a chip so I could follow him using research software. Out here, I'll have to use my memory to record his sightings."

"How will you d-differ-entiate bats if you're using the same c-color tie for each one?"

"I couldn't find anything with various colors." I was working at a disadvantage here without all of my tools from the university.

"I think I may have some c-colored rubber b-bands back at the hut. Remind me to find them for you," he said.

I clapped excitedly. "Oh, that'd be perfect! I can assign each bat a different color."

"And before I forget…" Aleki disappeared behind the tree and came back with something in his grasp. "You probably could use this to record your in-for-ma-tion."

He handed me a spiral notebook with a pen. I opened it and could barely make out the cursive handwriting on the yellowing paper.

"It's only on the first few p-pages. The rest of them are blank."

I marveled at the journal. "Where did you get this?"

"Dad's trunk. I figured you could use it for your r-research."

"Don't you want to keep it? I mean, it has your dad's writing. You should save it."

Aleki chuckled. "I saved it for over t-two decades. It's t-time to put it to use."

"This will certainly be helpful. Thank you. For all of this." I waved my hand at the net, my throat tight with emotion. "This was amazing." I launched myself at him, squeezing his torso. His arms wrapped tightly around my body, returning my affection. With my ear to his chest, I heard the steady drumming inside that my own heartbeats fell in sync to.

He shifted and I lifted my attention to his warm gaze. He towered over me, but the distance between us was closed easily enough by attraction. Our lips met. He was warm, and his beard tickled my skin. I turned my head to the side and slowly opened my mouth, inviting him in as I slid my fingers up to grip his hair.

Then his tongue slipped into my mouth, and I eagerly met it with mine. His kiss robbed me of my breath.

Fuck, he's a good kisser.

I broke our bond, gasping for air.

"*Cosmo?*" I asked.

He grinned, only one corner of his mouth rising. "'Ten Tips for Kissing Like a God-dess.'"

I giggled. "You're a regular Aphrodite, then."

He studied my face like he was gazing into my soul. "You're very pretty."

Heat flushed my cheeks, and nerves fired through me. "Was that one of the tips in the article? Compliment your partner?"

"Yes, but that's not why I said it." He tucked a piece of my hair behind my ear, hungrily eyeing my lips for more.

We kissed again, with the stars bearing witness to two lonely souls joining together as one.

Chapter 23

Love with the Power of the Ancestors

Maris

"I still can't believe you were keeping all these books from me." I skimmed my fingers over countless spines, all neatly stacked together inside of the richly colored wooden trunk. I was still stunned that it hadn't sunk to the bottom of the sea with how sturdy it was.

I was like a kid in a candy store, as I searched the stash. The boys were all here. Dickens. Vernes. Hemmingway. I even spotted the beat-up dictionary that Aleki must have studied every day to widen his vocabulary and fight boredom.

"It was there, in p-plain sight. You could have open-ed it."

"Yeah, but it was your private belongings."

Aleki shot me a smirk. "When has that ever s-stopped you before?"

I pointed my finger at him. "Are you calling me a snoop?"

Sure, I wasn't above prying. Hell, I had learned to hack phones to find dirt on the guys I was sleeping with while they were snoring right next to me. The FBI was no competition for my skills. I'd been raised on Matlock and Carmen Sandiego. *Investigation* was my unofficial middle name. Still, Aleki hadn't had to call me out like that.

He brought my digit to his lips and pressed a soft kiss to the pad. "I would never if I value my l-life."

His gravelly voice still disarmed me and had a way of melting my insides, even if I was still annoyed that he'd withheld it for so long.

There were a few covers with shirtless men and busty women in flowy dresses.

"You were really holding out on me. Look at all these romance novels!" Though I was a Mafia girl, I loved all romance books so much that a part of me wanted to strangle Aleki for keeping them a secret.

He avoided my gaze. "They were Ma's."

I could tell from the wear and tear of the pages that she hadn't been the only one to read them.

My attention was disrupted by the big fat letters on the cover of a magazine. *Playboy.* "Man, your dad's tastes were…diverse," I said, eyeing a copy of Chaucer's *The Canterbury Tales* right next to the image of a blonde with huge round breasts. I flipped through the pages—for the articles, of course.

"The sea is a l-lonely place." For a change, it was Aleki's tan cheeks that turned cherry red. As a serial blusher, it was amusing to witness it happen to someone else.

"Are you nervous I'll hurt your magazine?"

"Why would I c-care when I have the real thing?"

Now, it was my face that turned crimson.

"Which rem-inds me…" Aleki grabbed something from between the nightstand and the bed. A white plastic bag, which was tied at the top.

Droplets of water flew as I undid the knot that bound the handles. The thick material swished as I opened it to peer inside. "*Jane Eyre*!" I squealed, pulling out the weathered paperback. It had seen better days, but the binding was still intact, and the pages were remarkably free of water damage. "This is my favorite book!"

I had read it over ten times and never tired of the love between Jane and Mr. Rochester.

"What's it about?" he asked, cocking his head to examine the book over my shoulder.

"It's the original single-dad–nanny romance. And the age gap is chef's kiss! Where'd you find it?"

"It was f-floating in the bag where I was fishing."

I inhaled the musty scent the pages still held, as if it had just been plucked off the shelf of a library. "Damn, this island is weird. It's like someone keeps sending you gifts."

"Yeah, I guess s-something out there is m-making sure I get whatever I need." His eyes bored into mine with a heat that singed my soul.

The attraction between us was hard to fight. It was there any time we looked at each other. Although we had kissed and made up after our fight, he hadn't pressured me for more. Except, it was clear that we both lusted for much more.

I cleared my throat, unsure how to navigate the tension, before redirecting my attention back to the trunk. A glint of red beckoned me from between two books. I pulled on the fabric, and a silky pouch slightly larger than my palm came loose. A gold snap secured it shut. "What's this?"

Aleki took it from me. "It was my mother's." He rose to his feet and walked to the shelves near the dining table.

Maybe he didn't want to talk about it.

I was vocal when it came to admitting my own emotional baggage, but Aleki had been alone for years with no one to share his feelings with, so maybe it would take him longer to break the habit.

"Quiet your thoughts and f-follow me." He took my hand and led me out of the hut, *Jane Eyre* still in my other hand.

Poaka bounced up and scampered along behind us as we walked past the fire pit and toward the thicket.

"Where are we going?"

"Out for pizza."

"You and those *Cosmo* magazines." I rolled my eyes, then spied a small bottle in his grasp with the red pouch. "The last time you pulled out an un-named jar, *things* happened."

"Scared it will hap-pen again?" he teased.

"You wish," I muttered, trying to play off my chest flushing with warmth at the memory of the sticky mess of *the honey night*.

His deep rumble vibrated through my core, warning of the sins we had yet to commit. Since the night when he had covered me in honey and I had given him a blow job, we'd only kissed, and suddenly, my mind was playing out fantasies I had never dared to act on before.

"Don't overthink it." Aleki knew whenever my thoughts were racing. "We're here."

I took in the dazzling sight before me. Sparkling water skittering over polished rocks, smooth like black pearls. The canopy overhead was thick, but beams of light broke through the leaves, spotlighting the brook with a golden glow. The scene was magical.

"This is beautiful," I gasped.

Poaka ran for the brook and dipped his snout low for a drink of the crystal liquid.

Aleki and I took a seat on the bank and watched Poaka hop around to avoid the running water catching his nose.

"It's so peaceful here," I said to Aleki over my shoulder, enjoying the tranquil sounds of the birds chirping in song overhead.

He placed the red pouch in my lap. "Open it."

I unfastened the snap and withdrew three small cards. Photos.

"Oh my God, is that you?" A chubby baby with a gleeful smile looked back at me. He was no more than a year old. His cheeks were chunky, and his thick hair was sticking up in all directions like he had just woken up from a nap. His grin was wide, only a few teeth ornamenting his gums.

"That was on my f-first birthday."

"You were so cute!" I flipped to the next photo. A woman with long dark hair with the same baby, in front of a sheet cake with balloons in primary colors. Baby Aleki had his little arms wrapped around her neck, and there was a black beaded bracelet around one of his wrists. The pair were cheek to cheek, completely blissful as they stared into the camera.

"That's my m-mother," Aleki said.

"She was beautiful." Her dark eyes and silky black hair complemented her flawless brown skin.

"She was." His voice carried a heaviness just underneath the nostalgia.

"You look like her."

"You think?" he asked, tilting his head with interest.

"Totally. Your eyes wrinkle the same way at the corners when you're happy." I looked back, catching his warm gaze. We were often able to say so much more to each other without words.

His lips met mine in a gentle kiss, moving slowly, savoring me. When we pulled apart, his eyes wrinkled at the corners. *Happiness.*

I flipped to the last photo. "Your dad?"

"Yeah."

Aleki and his mother were joined by a man with his arms around them. His skin and hair were lighter—sandy blond. He was handsome and fit completely with the little boy and his mother. They were the picture of a perfect family.

"Your parents loved you a lot. I can feel it from these photos."

"I l-love them, too." *Present tense.* Love never died, even when the object of it had.

"They'd be so proud of the man their son has become."

A shiny film cast over his eyes, and he blinked it away. His heartache made my own heart hurt. He had been handed a shitty fate, and I couldn't even begin to unpack the trauma he must have endured…alone.

He lifted my hair gently, pulling out the strands that had tucked between my shirt and skin.

"What are you doing?" I packed the photos carefully back into the pouch and set it aside.

"Quieting your mind," he replied.

His fingers gripped my scalp, applying pressure as he massaged the base. Goose bumps broke out over my neck as the indulgent sensation washed over me. *Ugh, it feels so good.*

My nose picked up on a perfumy aroma, and I let out a whimper. "Is that jasmine?"

"Yes," he said from behind me. "I use it for hair oiling."

"Hair oiling?"

His fingers worked between my strands, kneading just above the hair line above my ears, and all the tension in my body vanished.

"Ma used to oil my hair as a child. Her m-mother and grand-m-mother did it to her when she was younger, and since she didn't have a d-daughter, Ma did it to my hair to carry on the tradition."

"Ahh. That's why you have such beautiful hair, then."

"That, and Ma's genes."

From the looks of the photo I'd just seen, he was telling the truth. His mother's hair had been gorgeous, like onyx. "This is such a beautiful ritual."

"Sometimes she would use a m-mix of oils. I made this one from j-jasmine flowers and coconut oil."

"What was she like?" I asked, shifting positions and tucking my knees under my chin as he coated my locks in the fragrant oil.

"A lot like you. Spirited. L-loud. Funny."

I chuckled. "She must've been a great woman. I wish my mom had been more nurturing like yours. I would have loved to have my hair oiled by her as a kid. I would have begged her to if I had known it felt this good."

"Do you miss your m-mother?"

I played with the pages of the book next to me as I considered my answer. "Yes and no. Does that make me a bad person?"

"Never."

I let out a sigh. "I obviously miss her. What kid wouldn't miss their parents after they died tragically when they were so young? However, if they were still alive, I think I would still have struggled with seeking love from outside sources."

"Maybe if my dad had survived the cata-maran accident, I would still have blamed him for it."

"Do you blame him now?"

Aleki gathered my hair into a high ponytail with one hand and raked his fingers along my scalp at the base. "If it weren't for his n-need for adventure, my f-family would have been safe at home. I had wished for it on that l-last trip—that we'd never have to go on a b-boat again. Someone or something must've been l-listening to me."

I remembered my own wish before the car accident. "Right before our car crashed, I wished to live on a tropical island far away from my parents. For years, I blamed myself for killing them. I guess the universe was listening to both of us." The laugh that left me was heavy and void of anything positive. The universe obeying children's wishes was wild work. Many times, I had wished that Bit, my toy bat, had turned into a real one. I would have taken that instead of the whole deserted-island deal. "I *wish* I'd never made that wish."

"I don't."

His confidence startled me, and I looked over my shoulder. "Why not?"

"Because I never would have met you."

Our lips met again, and the kiss grew deeper and more consuming than before. Our broken pasts were fusing together into a complete present, with the promise of a future worth wishing for.

We broke apart after some time, and Aleki refocused on my hair.

"Read me your book."

Poaka overheard the command and abandoned the patch of mush-rooms he had been busy feasting on to plant his burly body next to me.

I rubbed his head before rocking in my seat and folding my legs into a pretzel. I cracked open the paperback. "You're going to love this one."

The brook babbled softly in the background as I thumbed through the pages, finding the first chapter.

Aleki oiled my hair tenderly and carefully, as if I were his whole world. And I read for my boys in the only world I wanted to be in.

Chapter 24

Iguana, Don't You Wanna?

Aleki

"Tilt your hips back a little m-more." I pressed my hand in on her lower abdomen, dead center between her hip bones, angling her pelvis back against me.

"Bend your knees a little." I skated my hand lower, down the inside of her thigh, before tickling her kneecap.

"Ah, that's perfect. Now, look straight ahead and c-control your breathing." I moved my other hand to the base of her neck, correcting her position to open up her airway.

"Good girl. G-grip it with your hand and don't let go." I wrapped my hand around hers as she fisted my steel rod to demonstrate how to grip it properly.

Maris erupted with laughter, her body shaking and tears rolling down her cheeks.

"What?" I asked, completely confused, stepping away as she fell out of the proper form I had created.

"You sound like you're directing a porno."

"Pornography?" I clarified. I knew that it involved naked people having sex, but I'd never seen one in real life.

She nodded vigorously, unable to speak through her fit of laughter.

"Maris, be serious. This is im-por-tant for you to learn." I sighed. Her habit of distraction took some getting used to. Focus came easily for me since there had been nothing in the way of it before she had arrived. But, Maris was constantly jumping from thought to thought, like a frog landing on lily pads.

"I'm sorry," she wheezed out, gasping for air. "I keep picturing you with a mustache and a velvet jacket like some seventies porn lord."

I grabbed the spear from her. From the way she was waving it around, this *movie* would quickly turn from pornographic to horror.

"Oh, come on." She pressed a hand to my chest. "Don't be a grump. It's okay to have a little fun, you know."

"You need to learn to hunt. What if s-something happens to me?" The possibility was real with the influx of storms or the threat of disease. It wasn't a matter of *if* it ever happened, it would be *when*, for both of us. And if I was injured first, she would be left helpless—and very hungry.

She twisted her nose up at me, then flashed a brilliant smile. "What could possibly happen to you? You're my Cryptid, remember? My mythical man-beast with the muscles of ten men and the invincibility of a superhero."

We had made up from the speaking debacle and she was no longer freezing me out. To be honest, my assistance with her research was what had broken her force field of ice. She loved bats, and bringing her closer to them had brought her closer to me.

"You will need more skills than you already have to s-survive." She had learned a few things from me, like how to harvest fruit from high trees and kindle a fire. Starting the fire wasn't the issue for her, learning to keep it going was the challenge. Through a lot of practice, she had been able to start one to sterilize her research equipment, but none of that was worth it if she couldn't hunt. Protein would keep her strong against the elements and was vital to her existence. This was a serious matter, and right now, she was too distracted to listen.

Her expression sharpened and her eyes narrowed. She sauntered up to me like she was ready to eat me alive. My tongue thickened in my mouth. She grabbed the spear from my hand and tossed it aside. "I have more skills than you could ever imagine, jungle boy."

Her hands went to my solid chest, and though she was much smaller than me, I backtracked as she pushed me against the trunk of a tree, my back grazing the rough surface.

She tilted her head to the side and bit her bottom lip, and all I could focus on was how red it became under the pressure and how hard my cock was from the idea of it bleeding.

She put her hand on my neck and pulled me down, sealing her lips around mine. Since our first kiss, we hadn't been able to control ourselves. Almost everything we did together somehow ended with our lips together and our tongues all tangled up.

Kissing awakened something that had been stagnant inside me, like I had been asleep for the past twenty-four years and had suddenly woken up drifting in the clouds. This had to be what heaven was like, if there was one.

I was lost in her, never reaching my fill. I clutched the fabric of her shirt at her waist, pulling her in, and she rubbed herself against my body, igniting a flame. She really was an expert at kindling fires, in more than one way.

My cock begged for her heat against her body.

She explored me, measuring each crevice of my abdomen with her fingers. Her teeth nipped at my lip between devouring kisses. I loved the variety, the unpredictability she brought to everything she touched. It was an excitement I had never experienced before.

Her touch wandered to my loincloth, where she fisted my length in her hand. It was the first time she'd touched me there since she had wrapped her lips around me in the hut. The sound from my throat when she swiped her thumb over my sensitive tip was foreign to my ears, like a wild beast grunting amongst the trees.

I trailed my lips across her neck, kissing, sucking, and biting her soft skin. I wanted to mark her as mine, to leave my imprint forever.

"Aleki," she moaned. "I need you."

I needed her, too. I had been going at her pace ever since she had forgiven me, but my body was desperate for more. I wanted to touch every part of her, all at the same time. The feeling was urgent and suffocating—like if I didn't, I'd die.

I pushed the hem of her shirt up, exposing her breasts. I bent down and licked the valley between them. They were perfect and her nipples were always pointy, commanding attention from under her clothes. I sealed my lips around a nipple and massaged it with my tongue. Her body arched into me, and she pumped my dick swiftly. It ached painfully to be somewhere different—somewhere deeper and tighter.

"Fuck me, Aleki. Please." She wanted to help me hide it away, too.

I pulled the shirt over her head and growled as I took in her perfectly naked body. She was beautiful. My one stroke of fortune on this forsaken island. All mine.

She wrapped her legs around me when I lifted her, pressing her wetness against my waist. I lowered us to the ground, careful to lay her only on soft brush. Our kisses were frenzied, breaths rivaling the fervor of the birds chirping overhead. I swallowed each one of her tiny moans, stealing them away so they were only mine to hear.

"Do you know how to fuck?" she panted against my lips.

"No." Obviously, I hadn't. I didn't know what I was doing—I was acting only on instinct. Raw, primal instinct.

"Tell me if you don't want to. I'll understand," she said.

Her consideration was a product of her own overactive mind. At first, I had found her annoying, but I had quickly realized that it was because she had too much racing through her head. She didn't just think about herself, she worried about everything else around her, including me. I now understood her frantic behavior and was touched by how she cared for me when she was clearly desperate to satisfy her own needs.

"I need to," I murmured, ripping off my loincloth to free my cock to explore her.

"Do you want me to show you how satisfy a woman?" she asked.

I nodded.

"Lie down," she instructed.

I lay next to her, and she climbed on top of me. Her knees were on either side of my hips, but she wasn't touching me yet.

Her breathing was elevated, but her eyes were soft and gentle. "Tell me if I hurt you."

I reached up and cradled her cheek, and she melted into my touch. "There's no way you could ever hurt me."

Her hand went to the base of my cock, and I watched with bated breath as she centered me in line with her core.

Then she lowered herself onto me, sheathing my tip. I had finally come home. Not my home back in New Zealand or any place of this world. This was my universal home. The home my soul belonged to.

I groaned with satisfaction.

"Are you okay?" She paused, my dick shallowly cloaked by her apex.

"Please. Keep going." I yearned for more.

She carefully guided me into her, inch by inch, until gravity took over her efforts and carried her the rest of the way down.

We moaned in unison. I had never felt so whole in my life.

"Fuck, you're so thick," she murmured. She rolled her hips around, and her walls loosened around me. She was good at this, knowing all of these sexual secrets, and still, I hoped she knew how special this was for me. I was lucky my first time was with a woman like her.

"I'm going to do that again, okay?" she asked, her palms pressing into my chest.

All I could do was nod my consent.

She slid up and down on me, waxing my cock with her slick warmth. Each stroke built heat deep inside my abdomen that radiated through my body.

"Does it always feel like this?" I asked. I had only ever used my hand in this way, and her mouth had been far better. But *this* was indescribable.

"No, not like this," she admitted, her swollen folds tapping against the base of my length. I was proud that I had given her something she hadn't experienced before, like she had for me. "I love riding you."

I watched her as she rode me at a steady pace, her flowy hair curtaining an expression of deep concentration on her face.

"You can go f-faster if you want," I said, encouraging her. She was being careful not to break me. I could handle rougher.

She grinned and bit her lip again. I immediately hooked my finger under her chin and pulled her to me so I could nip at her juicy bottom lip.

Her movement picked up, and her breasts bounced mesmerizingly as she fucked me faster.

I didn't know where to put my hands, so I settled on her hips, enjoying her work on top of me. It was like I was moving her, and that only made me stiffer inside her channel. *Sexual control.*

I dug my heels into the dirt so my hips could rise off the ground to meet her each time she descended on my shaft, and she tightened around me. She liked it, too.

In the middle of the jungle, she fucked me with a freedom I had never seen from her before.

Our hips moved chaotically as the blaze heightened between us. Her cries were as loud as my grunts. Every thrust of my hips brought me closer to release.

Then, suddenly, she screamed. She wasn't hurt, and I didn't stop. Her cry only spurred me on to drill into her harder. Her body bowed taking all of me, and I soon exploded into an inferno as pleasure ripped through my body. I filled her with my warm liquid, gripping her roughly and slamming her onto me to take every last drop.

"Fuck," I cried out.

She collapsed onto my chest, her sweaty skin sliding against mine. I held her while the rush calmed.

After some time, she lifted onto her forearms, grinning brighter than a star. "Hey, you."

I wove my fingers into her hair, and rubbed my nose against hers. "Hey, you."

"How do you feel?" she asked.

Like a fucking god.

"Amazing," I admitted. "Let's do it again."

"Woah, you gotta give yourself more time than that."

"Why? I c-can never get my fill of you when you make me feel like I've been r-reborn."

"Your dick needs a rest. Women can go multiple times, but men need a little break."

I focused on where we were still joined. "But I'm ready."

I would no longer be denying myself the sweet bliss I had experienced. The door had been opened, and I was never closing it again as long as she was willing and able.

She lifted her hips lightly, testing my statement. Warm semen seeped from inside her, down my base and onto my pelvis.

"Damn, that's impressive," she said in awe. "How are you hard again? This doesn't happen to other guys."

I grinned smugly. "I guess I'm not like most guys."

She giggled as I flipped her over, still inside her pussy. I grabbed her leg and placed it over my shoulder, ready to fuck her into oblivion. And then I'd flip her over again and do it ten more times. My insides were awake, and there was no sedating them ever.

"Look," she whispered, pointing to a branch overhead. "Is that an iguana?"

A giant lizard sat on the branch, its attention on us.

Keeping my gaze on the lizard, I pressed my finger to my lips, quieting her. With my dick still buried deep inside of her, I reached over for the spear and aimed it at the reptile.

"What are you doing?" she whispered.

I launched the spear, narrowly missing the animal and hitting the branch, scaring him away so that he scurried down the tree and away from us.

"Why were you going to kill it?" she asked. Her leg fell from my shoulder, but I kept her hips in place, still connected to her by our intimate areas.

"For dinner. That's what I was teaching you to hunt."

Her whole face twisted. "Oh my God, you've been feeding me iguana this whole time?" Her belly heaved and she made strangled noises that only aroused me more—I kept picturing my cock in her mouth again, gagging her.

"If I didn't, you would have starved."

"A giant lizard? Ugh, that's so gross."

"Oh, be quiet. You loved when I put meat in your m-mouth."

She blinked at me. "Did you just make a dirty joke?"

I didn't understand her meaning.

"A sexual joke?" she clarified.

I grinned. "Maybe."

Then I threw her leg back over my shoulder and thrust deep. She moaned, forgetting that she had survived off of iguana meat all this time.

Chapter 25

Clubbed by a Caveman

Maris

"I have cum all over my stomach."

"Cum sounds better than ejaculate. Younger. Cooler." Aleki swirled his finger in the pool of cloudy semen on my stomach, displacing the edges and sending droplets of viscous liquid dribbling down my sides. "Are people still using the word *cool*? It was popular when I was a kid."

"They are. *Cool* is still cool," I said lazily, my body too tired to laugh yet somehow still anxious to find out what he would do to it next.

Aleki's speech had smoothened out considerably. Truth be told, he'd had endless practice, which advanced his progress. For someone who had refused to speak, he sure did love to run his mouth now, and I loved hearing every word.

Sometimes the stutter would return when he was heated, like when Poaka had inhaled the entire stash of fish that had been meant to last us until the next full moon. I had never heard Aleki so angry, yet he had never been sexier with his neck muscles bulging and his fists clenching like some sort of hot ring fighter.

He traced trails around my belly button, filled with his essence, then drew his finger down through my patch of hair.

I grimaced. "I haven't had an opportunity to groom out here." I tried to pull his hand away, but he stopped me.

"I love it. I love all of you." We lay together, naked and sexually sated for the moment, as the hammock rocked us under the afternoon sun.

I studied his pelvis, marveling at how groomed he was down there. "How do you take care of that? Chiseled rock and some duck fat as shaving cream?" Or maybe he was concealing a secret salon behind his hut.

"Scissors," he replied matter-of-factly.

I mockingly smacked my head with my hand. "Duh! Scissors. Why didn't I think of that?"

"I can't tell whether you're being serious or dramatic sometimes."

VICTORIA WOODS | WILD LIFE

I waved my hand in a flourish. "I like to call it *serious drama*, thank you very much."

"I love your serious drama." He slipped a wet finger inside me, and my eyes rolled to the back of my head as my body bowed in response.

"Aleki, I'm still sore." I had barely recovered when he had finger-fucked me to orgasm while I jerked him off, sending cum erupting over my body.

"Should I stop?" he whispered against my ear while plunging another finger inside, filling me.

"Never." I never wanted this to end. Aleki was the first man I didn't want to rush through sex with. The intimacy was unreal, and I was never guilty after. For once, my mind was quiet instead of racing through all the reasons coitus had been a bad idea.

His fingers were magical, extending deep and upward, hitting that special spot that made me moan.

My hips undulated with his thrusts, and the hammock rocked violently. Orgasm rushed through me quickly this time, flexing every muscle of my body. I cried out. He took my mouth with his, swallowing my cries as my body came down.

I broke the kiss to catch my breath.

"For a guy who just learned how to have sex, you sure do know how to please a girl."

"I have the best teacher." He lifted his fingers to his lips and sucked off our juices.

My core clenched at his delicious filthiness. "I never taught you to be this dirty."

"I added my own touch." He grinned, and my heart fluttered.

As much as I adored having him worship my body, it was time to come up for air. "I need to take a shower."

"Stay for one more round," he begged.

I pulled out of his hold and leaped out of the hammock.

"Nah-uh, you're not going to trap me again with those pitiful eyes."

He chuckled. "It worked last time."

"Which is why I'm leaving so I won't be convinced by it again. I want to go search for the bat colony." I had been tagging them every evening and observing their flight patterns. I had a general idea that their roost was past the waterfall, but I didn't know exactly where. I needed some time to explore the caves.

"You're going without me?" The expression of pleading washed away and was replaced by the grumpy forehead creases that he had worn like a uniform for the first weeks after we'd met.

"Well, you said that you needed to go fishing to replenish our stash that Poaka ate, so I figured I'd do that while you were busy. Divide and conquer?" Fishing would take him a while, and I was too excited to start my search.

"No," he said plainly, all lightness from earlier vanishing.

I must've heard wrong because it had sounded like he was ordering me. "No?"

"You're not g-going." *Fuck.* The stutter was back, which meant he was furious.

"Okay, then come with me," I said, trying to calm whatever *this* was down.

"I can't, I have to go fishing," he said, unwilling to budge.

"That's why I was going to go alone." I wasn't understanding his issue.

"I forbid it." His tone was firm, as if I were his property. Sure, he owned my pussy, but he didn't own me as a person.

I pinned my fists to my hips, our combined arousal dripping down my thighs. "Um…you're not the boss of me."

"I am when it comes to your safety. You're coming fishing with me."

I wasn't going to give in to his unreasonable behavior. I was perfectly capable of finding my own way without falling into danger. "Like I said, you're welcome to join me, but I will be searching for the roost."

"S-stubborn," he chided.

My gaze narrowed in on him. "What did you call me?"

"You heard m-me."

"You must not value your life. No one tells me what to do."

All I saw was red. How dare he call me stubborn when he was the one who wouldn't let me move about of my own free will? He had no idea who he was messing with. I wasn't some doormat who would obey his commands.

Hell no. I was a grown woman with multiple degrees to my name, author of numerous research papers, and the owner of a townhome that I had paid for with my own hard-earned money. I was an independent woman, and I didn't take orders from any man.

"You know what?" I said. "I think I will come fishing with you."

"Good, glad you came to your senses." He rose from the hammock.

"Yeah, I'll be able to drown your misogynistic ass in the ocean on my way to search for the roost."

He let out a sigh. "Maris. You're not familiar with the geography of the island. S-suppose something happens to you and you go m-missing? What will happen then?"

I crossed my arms over my chest and gave him the most severe side-eye ever recorded in history. "And you say I'm the dramatic one. I can walk without falling to my death, you know. I've been doing this kind of stuff for a living for years."

"Yes, but you're always with a team and you have t-technology to help you find your way if you're lost."

I tossed my hands in the air, completely frustrated. It was like arguing with a wall…a solid wall…a solid wall of rock covered in a sheen of sweat that smelled like dominance.

Stay focused, Maris. Fuck the wall and his dominance. Fuck the patriarchy!

"Aleki, can you relax a little bit? I'll be fine."

"I know you will be because you're not going."

"Ugh, why are you such a caveman daddy, and not in a hot way right now?!"

"I have no idea what that means, and I don't think I want to know."

Without warning, I bolted before he had time to argue with me again, making a naked run for the thicket.

He was too fast and pummeled me from behind. My cheek slammed against the ground as we went down, skidding in the dirt.

"Get off me," I yelled, trying to buck him off.

"Not unless you promise not to run." He pressed his entire weight onto me.

"No." I'd never give in.

"I can do this all day, Maris." The mockery in his voice urged me to thrash harder, but he was too strong.

"No, you can't," I said through gritted teeth. "You need to go fishing, remember?"

His hips bucked and his hard cock rubbed against my ass. "I just cleared my schedule. The only thing I have to do is you." My sensitive flesh tingled to life at his prodding.

Fucking hell.

Like a wuss, my body betrayed me and submitted, pushing back against his dick.

He used his hand to guide himself inside me, stuffing my sore pussy from behind. I dug my fingers into the dirt as he pumped.

He slowly and deliberately licked the cheek that was exposed to him. "You're mine to protect, and I will never allow you to hurt what's mine. Do you understand?" His speech was as clear as day.

He thrust into me until the burn turned into an ache for more. I moved with him like an animal in heat, moaning in response.

"Answer me, Maris," he barked.

"I understand," I cried out as he fucked me hard, splitting me in half.

"Good girl," he ground out, breathing heavily against my back. "That's my good fucking girl."

I would resume the argument later, but for now, I was going to shut the fuck up and take his dick like a good girl, as if I were the star in a romance novel.

Chapter 26

Poaka in Peril

Maris

"Have you seen Poaka?"

At the sound of my voice, Aleki turned his head toward me but stayed stooped above the shower floor, holding a white plastic wand. The shower tubing had fallen victim to birds who had pecked holes through the surface to hide their seeds, clogging the water flow. Aleki had been busy all day, replacing it with a PVC pipe he'd found in the water while fishing.

"He's not with you?"

"Oh, yes, here he is." I flourished my hand beside me. "Meet Poaka, the magic pig, wearing his very special invisibility cloak!"

Aleki stared at me, too bewildered to interrupt.

"For his next trick, the Great Poaka will transform into a golden egg." I waved my hands in the air and snapped my fingers.

Aleki abandoned his project and dusted his palms off on his thighs. "Why the attitude?"

"I've been looking for him all afternoon." I pinned my fists on my hips and tapped my foot, praying he'd catch up soon and help me find Poaka.

"Where's the last place you saw him?"

"By the thicket. I had left him to get a basket, and when I returned, he was gone." After breakfast, I had called him to pick some longans with me. He had a habit of devouring half of whatever I was eating, so I had figured if I took him with me, he'd get his fill during harvesting instead of harassing me later when I sat down to enjoy my treat.

After Aleki's tantrum when I had attempted to find the bat colony on my own, I'd decided to lay low with exploration, sticking to the area around the thicket. It wasn't because I was afraid of him. I needed my pussy to heal properly before he decided to punish me when I defied him again—which was inevitable.

In my hurry with Poaka, I had forgotten to grab a basket, so I'd run back to the hut. Instead of following me, he had scampered away. I'd assumed he had been excited for our activity and had headed off to the tree, but when I had gone to find him, he hadn't been there.

Aleki nodded his head, his expression flat as if I'd told him the sky was blue. "Okay."

I sucked air through my teeth, casting the most judgmental glare I could muster. "Some pig-dad you are! Aren't you worried he's lost?" My relationship with Poaka was barely a blip in time compared to his relationship with Aleki. If this was how Aleki treated his friends, I wanted to disqualify myself from the running.

"Poaka never gets lost. He always finds his way back to me," he said, unaffected.

"You sound like a Christmas-card commercial." I sighed. "He could be in danger!"

"Poaka? He's a danger to himself just walking." Aleki snorted, and my palm itched to smack the smirk off his face. "I'm sure he's fine. Maybe he's off roaming. He knows the jungle better than me."

I worried my bottom lip as images of Poaka being cornered by a bear played through my mind. I wasn't sure if there were bears nearby, but in my head, they were big and scary with razor-sharp teeth.

"You're worried about him, and nothing I say will quiet those thoughts, huh?" Aleki tapped my temple softly before pressing his lips to the spot.

"I wish you'd use your mind-reading abilities to find our pig," I jabbed.

His brow hiked. "Our?"

"Yes, ours. The furry blob eats nearly half of my meals, so that practically makes him my brother." Poaka was an important part of my life now. He was like the dog I'd never had. He followed me everywhere and snuggled in my lap anytime I sat on the ground. If he wasn't on my heels, his phantom footsteps were.

"Fine. I'll help you look for him," Aleki caved, and we started our search.

"Thank God. I was ready to go with plan B to convince you and pop out a tit."

Aleki halted. "Wait. I could have gotten to see a nipple if I'd held out a little longer?"

I pulled his hand and dragged him along so as not to waste another minute. "You would've gotten to see both if you had helped me at the start of this conversation."

"It's not too late to change your strategy." He pawed at my shirt from behind, pulling it up to sneak a peek, but I batted him away.

"Ease up, caveman. Pig before tits."

I led him to where I had parted ways with Poaka, and we called for him. No luck.

Aleki scanned every direction, waiting for a mass of cream-and-black to barrel into us. "That's so strange. He at least comes when I call for him."

We continued through the coarse jungle.

The trees were so densely packed together that I struggled to see in the limited sunlight that reached us. The brush underneath swallowed my feet with each step, vines winding around my ankles like tentacles. This wasn't a welcoming place at all.

"I don't ever remember seeing this part of the island," I said.

"I never come out here." Aleki was having a difficult time weeding through the terrain, too.

"Why not?" I asked. He didn't strike me as the type of person to ever be held back by anything.

"Snakes."

Something brushed my leg, and I screamed. Aleki caught me as I leaped away. The image of a slimy snake slithering up my leg flashed in my head, convincing me I had been bitten. My leg tingled, and I knew I was going to die without an antidote available. *Oh God. Why me?*

Aleki examined the ground. "Vine."

I slid from his arms, my cheeks heating. "Oh, okay." I tried to play off my dramatic response, but Aleki grinned like an idiot.

"Ass," he said, biting back a laugh.

"What'd you call me, motherfucker?" I estimated that if I slapped him, I would have a two-second lead if I ran away right after.

"I want your ass tonight as payment for putting up with your theatrics."

"You're a freaking sex maniac." Everything was about sex to him. The man couldn't get enough.

"No, I'm just a maniac for you."

I rolled my eyes.

We heard a grunt in the distance and froze.

"What's that sound?" I whispered.

Aleki sprang into action, sprinting toward it.

"Poaka!" I shouted, struggling to keep up.

Under a tree, trapped in a nest of vines, was Poaka. He thrashed against the thorns pressing into his body, embedding them further into his flesh. His high-pitched squeals pierced my eardrums.

Aleki rushed to free him, but I caught a glimpse of a shadow in his path. Black stripes on silver skin. I had seen that pattern before on research trips.

I grabbed Aleki's arm, keeping him from advancing. "Snake!" It was highly venomous and slithering straight for Poaka. One bite could take down a human and no doubt kill a pig.

I sprang into action, running as fast as I could.

"Maris!"

I stomped on its tail, effectively gifting it a new target: Me.

The creature swerved and lunged at me, missing.

With reflexes faster than lightning, Aleki darted out and caught it around the throat before it could strike at me again.

"Protect your eyes!" I cried. He turned at my voice, narrowly missing a violent spray of venom.

Aleki hurled the snake into the air, throwing it far away into the brush.

I moved hastily to Poaka. "Quick, let's get out of here before the snake's friends show up, too."

Aleki ripped the unruly plants around Poaka into pieces. "What did you do to yourself, buddy?"

I gently peeled the spiky threads away. Blots of blood on beige fur did not escape my notice.

In the field, I had sometimes had to free bats from man-made traps, so I was able to work calmly on a moving subject. Poaka writhed from pain, and Aleki helped to keep him steady as I extracted the thorns.

"Poor baby. I knew you needed me." I hated myself for having left him. My gut had told me that he was in trouble, but I hadn't acted fast enough. "I'm so sorry for leaving you. Please forgive me."

Aleki tried to console me. "It's not your fault."

"If we hadn't shown up…" My voice broke. It destroyed me to think what might've happened if we had arrived seconds later. I kissed Poaka's head between his ears, and Aleki took over the task of de-vining.

Poaka settled some when the thorns had been removed. His fur was a mess, weeds and fibers tangled all through it.

A short bush nearby caught my eye. I plucked one of the stalks, and gel oozed from the tear. It was related to aloe and was exactly what I needed.

"This will help your cuts," I said gently and smeared the viscous liquid onto a laceration.

Poaka shrieked violently from the temporary sting.

"Shhh, it's okay. You'll be better in no time." I continued to apply the substance to each wound while Aleki held him still.

"He loves you," Aleki whispered.

A fat tear ran down my cheek. "I love him, too," I admitted. Poaka was more than just an overgrown pig. He was my family.

Chapter 27

Daydreams and Nightmares

Aleki

"Stay still." Maris plucked a weed from Poaka's fur as he tried to wriggle out of her hold. I couldn't blame him. His grooming session was uncomfortable, especially since she was doing it with a plastic fork.

Maris focused intensely, the tip of her tongue sticking out of her slightly parted lips, as she extracted weeds, food, and bugs from Poaka's coat. She was careful not to disturb his cuts, which were still healing from being trapped in thorns. "You really got yourself into it, didn't you? And now you're so stinky!"

He was a pig, after all—one who wasn't a fan of water.

Poaka dived under her knee, burying his snout and attempting to slide through for a quick escape. "Just one more," she said, prying a beetle from her burly moving target.

Poaka let out a shrill squeal as he jumped.

Maris's arms went around him, guiding him back onto her lap. "I'm sorry. Shhh," she soothed, petting him softly. He cuddled into her like a baby, soaking up the attention.

Suddenly, images of Maris with a baby in her lap flashed through my mind. *My baby.* Her belly swollen with another little one.

I stood marveling at the mental picture of her eyes glowing with love as she soothed our child.

I had never had daydreams like this, but then again, I had never had this life before.

She caught me mid-reverie. "What?"

I smiled. "You two are cute together."

She peered down at Poaka, who was as still as if he were asleep. "It's mostly the furry pig. He can make anyone look cute."

"It's funny how much you love him now."

"I've always loved him." It rolled off her tongue so smoothly that she almost fooled me. *Almost.*

"Liar."

"Okay, fine. He was frightening at first. Big and always pushing me around. After the snake attack, he's grown on me."

"Just like me?" I asked smugly.

"Just like you," she purred.

She adored me, and though we couldn't keep our hands off each other, underneath the lust, there was something more—something deeper that tugged at my heart when she smiled at me. The same feeling that made my stomach drop when I was away from her for too long.

Despite all the happiness, a nagging question prodded at me. "Do you miss your old life?" I asked.

Her face fell, and that pit in my stomach returned. "Yes."

Hearing it dampened my newly found happiness.

"Don't you miss it?" she asked, turning the question on me.

I hesitated. I would've immediately answered yes if I were still a child. Initially, I had missed the luxuries of the modern world. The convenience. The people. Ice cream. Except, things had changed. I had changed. Hope disappeared. "I don't really remember my old life. This is all I know. This island is my life now, and I don't think about anything beyond it."

She worried her bottom lip. "You never wanted to go back home and meet someone? Fall in love? Start a family and have some cute little baby Cryptids?"

My mind stretched to consider those new goals. "I guess I never considered it. How about you? Do you want those things?"

She shook her head frantically, disrupting Poaka's peace. He fled her lap and ran for the trees, far away from the plastic fork. "No, no. Marriage isn't my thing."

"Why not?" A part of me was disappointed, even if she hadn't specifically answered the part about having children.

"I'm not good at relationships. I purposely keep men at a distance. Hell, I've never really committed to anyone. I used random guys for comfort and safety, and I never really moved forward into something serious."

"Why?" Hearing about her past men wasn't easy, but I was curious to know what had scared her away from them.

"I'm afraid that things will end, and that I can't control it. I guess it has something to do with losing my parents at such a young age."

"So, you had boyfriends?" She must have had a few since she had lived in the modern world longer than I had.

"I'm not sure they would qualify as *boyfriends*. There were certainly guys I saw regularly."

"Were you seeing guys *regularly* before you came here?" It turned my stomach to ask that question, yet I wanted to know.

"Kind of." She blinked rapidly. "There was this one guy who was on my research team, on the boat that I was on before I fell overboard. His name was Eli. I had hooked up with him off and on for a few years, but he wanted more. I freaked out and ended things the night before the storm."

I treaded carefully into this dangerous line of questioning, "Did he take it well?"

She shrugged and offered a half-hearted laugh that didn't reach her eyes. "I don't know. I kinda fell off the boat before finding out."

I didn't like this Eli. I was certain he was out there somewhere pining for her. I would have been too, if I had been in his place. Maris would have been difficult to forget. The memory of her would be far more painful than death.

"Would you go back if you were rescued tomorrow?" I asked, willing my voice to remain casual. If she scared away from relationships easily, then I needed to proceed with caution.

She remained quiet, her mind blaring wildly inside of her head.

"I won't be offended by your answer." I wanted her honesty, without worrying about me.

"Yes, I would go back," she said.

If I could have traveled time and retracted my question, I would have. "This...*thing* between us would end?" I didn't know how to label it now, especially since she didn't like commitment.

"I wouldn't want it to," she admitted.

Maybe she'd want to carry on this relationship with me and Eli at the same time. The idea bothered me. I refused to share her. "It would have to end because I wouldn't want to leave."

She blinked slowly, stunned by my words. "Like, not ever? Not even for me?"

I could never go back. I had spent too much time away from civilization to be reintroduced again. Wearing clothes and working in an office would be too great an adjustment for me. I would find daily life miserable. Life here was the only one I was capable of enduring.

"I won't be offended," she repeated my lie to me.

I was afraid to voice my rejection. That I wouldn't leave for anyone. My life was here, and if I left, I'd lose my purpose. I plastered on a weak smile and sat next to her, my arm brushing against hers. "Let's not talk about things we don't have to worry about anytime soon."

"Okay." Her head dropped onto my shoulder, and I rested my head on hers.

After some time, she spoke. "I would miss you, though—if it really happened and I was rescued tomorrow."

I pressed a kiss to the top of her head, inhaling her spicy-sweet scent and committing it to memory. "I would miss you more than you could ever know."

As uncertain as I was about our future, I was convinced that good things never lasted.

Could I ever go back to a life without Maris now that I knew what I would be missing? If she went back to her old life? To Eli?

Chapter 28

Acing the Oral Exam

Maris

My body was weightless, floating on soft, puffy clouds. Glittering light peeked through white, bathing me in warmth. Birds twittered a melodious song.

Feathers tickled my inner thighs. I wriggled against their delicate assault. The feathers traveled upward, leaving a trail of sensation in their wake. Higher and higher they moved, teasing my skin.

The feathers joined together as one, swiping at my entrance, electrifying my nerves. My back arched, and the stroking continued at my sensitive folds. This was heaven. I supposed I must've died and levitated here.

Suddenly, pleasure rushed through my clitoris, awakening me.

I was in the hut. And the clouds were the bed. And the feather—Aleki. He was naked, just as I was, and very comfortable between my legs.

"Good morning," I said, grinning. I played with a tendril of hair that had fallen over his eye. I loved it when his dark hair was loose, adding to his wild and savage appearance.

"Good morning." He pressed a kiss to my inner thigh, and I shivered at the sensation of his facial hair brushing my sensitive skin.

I stretched my arms over my head, and he tracked my breasts as they pulled. "This is a wonderful way to wake up," I crooned.

He reached for me, rolling my nipple between his calloused fingers, which sent shockwaves down to my core. "I'd have to agree." His attention returned to my pussy, where he continued licking me.

I held his head in place and rolled my hips while he teased me. He was good, but I could make him better.

"Flick it with your tongue using small circles."

He followed my direction, and my inner walls clenched. "Like that," I breathed out.

I clutched his hair like he was a fuckboy whose mouth I was using for pleasure.

My body was still lazy from sleep, serving as a blank canvas for tension to build faster than usual. Release would come swiftly, and I wanted to maximize the experience.

"Fuck me with your fingers," I ordered.

Aleki slipped two digits inside. I took him easily since I was still wet with his cum from last night.

Slick noises filled the air between us as he fucked me while abusing my clit with his tongue.

I gripped his hair and bore down against his mouth, nearly suffocating him with my pelvis.

A sharp scream ripped through me and I splintered into pieces that drifted off into the abyss. A farewell lick down my seam, lapping up the arousal that seeped out, made my body shudder.

Aleki pulled his huge body over mine and lay to my side, his lips fixed into a mischievous smirk.

I wiped some of my arousal from the corner of his lips with my finger. "What?"

"You taste like fruit."

"What kind?" I purred.

"Something juicy, yet tart."

He was adorable when he was mentally placing something for the first time.

I rolled to the side to face him, my body sated. "Funny, because that's my stripper name. *Juicy Yet Tart.*"

His brow furrowed. "Wait, are you serious?"

I wasn't, but I enjoyed fucking with him. "Like a jellyfish sting."

His eyes widened in disbelief. "You really take your clothes off to dance…for strangers?"

"Yeah, can't you tell by my moves?" I shimmied on the bed, though I looked more like a dying fish.

His lips set into a thin line. He was clearly perturbed. "Well, now you only strip for me," he said with finality.

I batted my lashes coyly. "So possessive. Careful or I might mistake you for one of those jealous men from back home."

A coarse growl vibrated from his throat. "I bet they don't please you like I do." He pounced, his face inches from mine, and I could smell me on his lips. It was heady and addictive.

"Aleki," I gasped as he sank into me, filling me up. He was bigger than any man I had been with before, stretching me wider with each stroke.

His hips undulated so he hit my nub with the most delicious friction. I held on to his ripped biceps while he powered into me.

"No one can please me like you," I admitted between panted breaths. He quickened his pace, feeding my greedy cunt with his cock.

I was mercilessly obsessed with this man.

Chapter 29

Going with the Flow

Aleki

The waterfall was my second favorite place on the island. The first was between Maris's legs.

She unleashed something inside me, and now that I'd had sex, I couldn't get enough of it.

Except, I hadn't been inside her in two days, and I was completely confused as to why. It wasn't for lack of trying, either. Each attempt to romance her earned me a shove away and some excuse that she was too busy or too tired.

She had even started wearing some of the clothes she used to wear when she first came here—particularly her pants and underwear. At least she still wore the oversized T-shirt I'd given her.

I preferred that shirt because it gave me easy access to her body. Now I couldn't spontaneously pull it up and bend her over a rock while we were out picking fruit. And although I could still reach up for her breasts, I stopped when she complained they were too sore.

Was she mad at me? What did I do?

I waded through the pool, warm after a day of sun, and while it felt great on my muscles, my mind was concerned with Maris.

Evening was approaching, and she had declined to set up the bat net again. She said she was exhausted and needed a break.

She sat near the edge, knees tucked into her chest and arms wrapped around them, no ants in sight this time. She was staring at the waterfall as Poaka played with a nut at her feet. She was in a daze, a far cry from the animated person I was addicted to.

I splashed in her direction, careful not to wet her, but hoping to cheer her up.

She glanced over, remaining huddled in a ball.

"What are you thinking about up there?"

"Nothing, just relaxing." Her voice was strained. Maybe I had been keeping her up too late at night.

I should have let her recover.

"Well, relax in here with me. It's nice, I promise."

She offered me a tight smile. "I'm okay here."

Maybe she was mad because I had told her she was weaving baskets incorrectly...but she hadn't seemed upset at the time.

"What's wrong?" I asked, wishing I could get into her mind. To really analyze what went on inside.

"I'm not feeling well." Her face was a bit pale and puffy, despite still looking gorgeous.

Flashbacks of Ma's illness hit me. She had lost her color and became too weak to stand.

Panic struck me, and I rushed closer to her. My words felt sticky again. "Tell me what to do. How can I m-make you better?" She was a scientist. She would know best how I should help her.

"I'll be fine if I rest."

"Maris, you're hiding s-something from me. Please, tell me what to do." She was in danger. I knew it.

She brushed me off. "It's nothing."

I slapped the rocky edge of the pool hard, causing her to flinch. "M-Maris. What's wrong?" I bellowed, sending Poaka scurrying into the brush.

"I got my period, okay?" she shouted back.

I stood there frozen not knowing what to do. I knew of periods because the older boys at school used to make fun of each other by calling everyone the different types of feminine products. I knew girls bled every month and needed those products when it happened. Only, I didn't know the details, like how long it lasted or how girls managed it each month.

Maris wrapped her arms tighter, making herself smaller. "Why are you looking at me like I have a plague?"

"I d-don't know what to do or say."

She relaxed slightly. "You don't have to do anything."

"Don't you need items for the blood?"

"I do. I sterilized one of your towels in hot water and cut it into rags. I hope that was okay."

"Of course. I can search the beach for more things you could use."

"That'd be nice. Thank you."

"Are you sure you're okay? You don't seem well."

"It doesn't feel pleasant, but I'll be alright."

"How come?" She must have been in pain judging from her tight expression.

"I usually get cramps and my lower abdomen hurts for a few days. It sucks."

"I'm sorry." It was a shame what women had to endure, and I wished I could go back in time to my school to shut the boys up when they were making fun of periods.

"Are you sure you don't want to join me?" I moved my hand through the water. "It's warm today and it might soothe your cramps."

"I'm bleeding like crazy, though."

"So? It'll be like you're soaking in a bath."

Her face perked up. "You don't mind?"

"Of course not." I extended my hand to her.

She hesitated, as if thinking of another excuse not to take it. Eventually, she gave up and undressed, peeling off her clothes and exposing her perfect body. When she pulled her underwear down and stepped out of them, I saw a splotch of red on the rag tucked inside.

She took my hand and carefully slipped into the water. Ripples swirled below her breasts. I expected to see a sea of red around her—but there was none.

I gently drew her closer to me. "I thought there would be more blood."

"It's not like a downpour or something. It's more like a heavy drip that wanes as the days pass."

"Why did you hide it from me?" I asked, caressing her arms.

She shrugged. "I was embarrassed. Shy? I don't know. It's kind of a private thing." Her hands fidgeted against my abdomen.

I tucked my finger under her chin and lifted her face to meet my gaze. "You don't have to hide from me. Anything that happens to you, happens to me."

Her lips spread into a radiant smile. "Why are you so sweet?"

"Is this why you didn't want to have sex?"

"Yeah, it's a bit crazy down there," she said, pointing downward.

VICTORIA WOODS | WILD LIFE

"I don't mind blood." There was nothing about her that would repulse me.

She grimaced. "Yeah, but it's uncomfortable."

"Let me take care of you." I planted a kiss on her neck.

"I'm not used to allowing a man to do that to me."

I pressed another kiss to her lips and then lifted her, and she immediately wrapped her legs around my hips.

"I'll get you messy," she whispered, holding on to my shoulders.

"Impossible. It'll wash away."

I braced my hand so she could lay back and float peacefully. It was about to be her favorite time of day, the time when her face lit up the most.

Suddenly, the purple sky dimmed, shaded with black specks. The bats fluttered overhead, working overtime to keep up with each other.

Maris's eyes glittered with excitement, and her mouth opened to release a dazzling giggle at the sight of her favorite animal. My heart could have burst.

"I could stay here forever," she said.

I hoped she did. I really hoped she did.

Chapter 30

Half-and-Half

Maris

Was I falling in love with Aleki?

Whatever it was between us was growing exponentially, but I didn't know quite how to place it. It had transformed from hate to tolerance to lust, and now to this *thing* that made my heart flutter anytime he was near. I suspected I already knew the answer, but I needed time to digest it. I had never fallen in love before or even opened myself to the possibility of it.

This was insane. Aleki was someone the universe had forced on me versus one I had chosen on my own. I hadn't vetted him or weighed the pros and cons of committing to him. Hell, we belonged to two different worlds. None of it made sense. Yet, when I was by his side, everything felt right. Like I belonged. I no longer had to consciously extract the safety and comfort I desired from a man. He gave it to me willingly, without expecting anything in return.

Was that what love was?

Or maybe I was just obsessed with him, or specifically obsessed with his dick? It was certainly a nice one, and Aleki had mastered the use of it in no time. He was, no contest, the best sex of my life.

Maybe I had simply fallen victim to good dick.

Then why did I still feel complete when we were together while not having sex?

I didn't have much of a reference for love. Aunt Sherri had never dated when I'd lived with her. And my parents had been the result of an arranged situation.

What was it like to fall deeply and madly in love?

Was it secretly thanking the universe when another day passed by and a rescue crew hadn't shown up for me? Or maybe it was giving up the idea of returning to my old life. It probably was looking forward to falling asleep in his arms every night.

Fuck. I am in love.

What do I do now?

I sat on guard near the net, waiting to see who would show up tonight. It was possible for multiple bat species to exist in an ecosystem, and that was certainly evident by the variety of bats I had witnessed.

I'd tagged a number of flying foxes, which didn't use echolocation for navigation. Instead, they relied on their excellent senses of smell and sight to find food, namely fruit and flowers. Although they sometimes slept in caves and other rock crevices, they mostly roosted in trees, snuggling close for protection and warmth.

I was fortunate to have also seen a few mastiffs, which foraged near treetops, and long-tailed fruit bats, which enjoyed grazing in the lower lands.

It was a thrill to see them up close, especially since each one I came across was healthy. They were thriving without other humans around to destroy their roosts and food supply. Their biggest threat was the environment. Changes in climate or proliferation of unwanted predators could threaten their population.

Another big risk to bats was disease. Specifically, a new fungus that had spread over the past few years, called white-nose syndrome. It was suspected to have originated in Europe and spread to North America, effectively diminishing population numbers. The fungus usually wreaked havoc in winter while bats hibernated. It manifested as white fuzz over their muzzles and caused intense itching. The discomfort was enough to wake them prematurely, before the climate warmed in spring. The afflicted bats would find out too late that hibernation wasn't over when they ventured out into the cold for food that wasn't available.

White-nose syndrome was highly contagious, so if one bat had it, the entire colony, including the pups, were at risk of exposure.

The disease was heartbreaking, but thankfully more prevalent in areas that experienced cooler winters.

The pitter-patter of wings filled my ears. The little ones were on their nightly adventure.

I waited with bated breath for them to descend for a drink from the pond. I'd had to change the position of the net because they'd caught on quickly to its position. Some flew overhead, while some swooped underneath.

As if it was being drawn to a beacon, one drifted into the net. I scurried over, with clean gloves on and rubber bands that I'd boiled in a metal pail over the fire outside the hut.

I carefully removed the bat from the soft webbing and studied it over.

A Pacific sheath-tail! I couldn't believe my eyes. I had studied them in Fiji and had the opportunity to visit their roost. Their population was small, only about five hundred individuals in the world, and here I was, holding one of them on a potentially undiscovered island!

He appeared to be healthy, so I quickly tagged his foot and sent him on his way.

I pulled the net down so no other bats could fly into it and raced to find Aleki. He was off curing more fish because I refused to eat iguana since I'd found out it was the mystery meat he'd been feeding me. Now, I was basically on the Pilates Princess diet of fish, fruits, and vegetables, minus sporting the luxury leggings.

Aleki had remained close by despite my constant reassurance. It was like he expected me to be swallowed up by a volcano or something.

I found him hunched on the ground with his basket of fish, and he stood up when he heard my hurried steps.

"I found it!" I ran up to him and grabbed his shoulders.

"Found what?" he replied, blindly matching my excitement.

"A Pacific sheath-tailed bat!"

"And that's amazing, right?"

"Totally! There are only a few in the wild, and I found one here, which means..."

"There are probably more?"

"Bingo!" I stabbed his hard chest with my finger. "I bet scientists haven't ever ventured here to research them. What if there's a thriving population? Like hundreds, perhaps thousands of them, just hanging out?! This is phenomenal, especially since they're endangered."

His arms wrapped around me, showering me with the warmth and security I'd spent my life searching for. "I'm so happy for you!" He had little idea of the gravity of what I was going on about, but he was as thrilled as I was.

"We have to find their roost," I said.

"Do you think you can?"

"I don't know. I need to try. God, I wish I had a GPS location."

"I'll help you," he offered. The last time I had tried to go off on my own, he'd impaled me from behind to teach me a lesson.

"You will?"

"Of course! I know this land better than you, and I can help with the landscape."

"I thought you didn't want me exploring off on my own because I'd get hurt?"

"I'll be right by your side."

I hugged him tighter, and he pressed a kiss to my forehead. We were going to work as a team to find the bats.

Partners. It was a word I assumed would always paralyze me. The idea of being so intertwined with someone else that you depended on them for happiness terrified me. Commitment was beautiful, if it was never broken.

Something had changed inside me, though, clearing the cloud of fear that had always hovered around. I longed to be one-half of *us*, so long as Aleki filled the other half.

I spoke against his chest. "Aleki?"

"Maris?"

"I think I love you." My heart stilled, bracing itself for rejection. One that never came.

"I *know* I love you," he whispered into my hair, embracing my consciousness with his love.

Life pumped through me like blood, touching every part of my body in a radiant warmth I had never experienced. Nothing in my life before this man existed. He was the only thing that mattered in my present, and the only future I yearned to have.

Chapter 31

Lovely Lullabies

Aleki

The fire crackled and sparks jumped into the evening air almost as excitedly as the stick in Maris's hand moved in the dirt. It was only the two of us by the fire pit, since Poaka had decided to turn in for the night.

Maris worked quickly, using the pointed end to draw what I assumed was the map of the island. Except the series of circles and lines resembled the bicycle I used to ride around for hours after school.

Damn, I miss that bike.

"And if we follow the trend of their flight pattern backward, their roost must be beyond the waterfall."

She sat back on her haunches, pride radiating from her. She tapped her pointing tool against her thigh for several beats. "So what's beyond the waterfall?"

"Nothing more than trees. Then farther along, the beach."

"Hmm." She touched her finger to her chin. She was a feisty mix of charm and brains.

"Oh," I said, remembering something. "There are also caves."

Her eyes widened, and before I could ask what I'd said wrong, a smack landed on my arm, stinging my skin. "You didn't say anything about caves! You were going to keep them from me? The roosts are probably in there."

I rubbed the area where she had slapped me, even if it didn't hurt. I wanted her sympathy, and maybe a kiss on my bicep—a long, slow kiss with tongue. "I wasn't trying to keep them from you. You never asked."

"Remind me to be mad at you later. Now, more about these caves. How far are they from the waterfall?" She resumed drawing in the dirt again.

I played out the path in my head. "It's a decent walk, but not impossible."

"Impossible for you or for me?" she asked, her eyebrow hitched. "Because we're not working with the same level of muscle here." She pulled her sleeve up to her shoulder and flexed her arm. Sure, it wasn't comparable to mine, but she had toned up considerably since she had first arrived. She was stronger. More capable.

"You can do it. I believe in you. And if not, I'll carry you." I'd carry her everywhere if she'd let me.

She stabbed the end of the stick into the middle of my chest. "You're just saying shit like that to get into my pants, aren't you?"

My gaze drifted down to where her shirt gaped from her parted legs. If I dipped my head lower, I would earn an eyeful of my favorite sight. "You're not wearing pants."

"So you weren't trying to get into them?" She licked her lips and batted her lashes.

"I'm always trying to get into your pants, whether they're on or not."

"Interesting…Do you want to wear my bra, too?"

I paused, reconsidering the words I had spoken. "What? No, I didn't mean...ugh."

I'd had enough of talking. I pushed my loincloth aside and hoisted her up and straight onto my throbbing dick before she had a chance to protest.

She sank swiftly, encasing me in her velvety warmth. "So ready for me, even when you're playing coy."

"I have to be when you pull stunts like this. You're distracting me from my map." She lifted herself, her feet on either side of my legs for leverage, then drove back down onto me. Her back arched and she moaned into the night.

"Then let's continue discussing it." I tipped her so her pelvis was at an angle, and she ate up my length with her undulations. Her body melted with my touch.

"We're here." I circled her left nipple with my tongue, flicking the hard tip. Her breath rushed out unevenly.

"And this is the hut." I sucked her other nipple between my teeth, giving it a gentle tug before running my tongue between her breasts. "This is the valley next to the waterfall. It's filled with dangerous curves."

"Mmm," she hummed as she ground herself against me with each stroke of my cock.

"Through the waterfall and past the pool, you'll find a thicket of trees." I traced my fingers along her belly, registering her muscles working as she took me. I stopped right above where we were joined, grazing the hair there that I enjoyed so much.

I found the bud between her legs with my finger and treated it to tight circles. Her body writhed freely, shielding none of its emotions from me.

I memorized how she moved, soaking all of her in. Every time with her was like the first time and was committed to my memory as if it was the last.

"I love you," she murmured.

"I love you, Maris. More than anything in this world. Nothing exists without you."

We chased our orgasm and shattered together, proof that we were one.

I caught her in my arms and held her to me as I filled her with my hot arousal.

Peace overtook us for some time. How long exactly, I couldn't say. Time never mattered when we were like this.

Naked in front of the fire, we basked in the lingering glow of orgasm.

She sighed dreamily. "That was…amazing," she murmured.

"You're amazing." I squeezed her shoulders. "Should we get back to planning for tomorrow?"

She hung on to me, her body too exhausted. "I don't think I could even if I tried."

Victory flickered in me. I loved the effect I had on her.

I cradled her in my arms and stood to carry her into the hut. I'd come back to put the fire out after I got her settled inside.

"No," she objected. "I want to stay in the hammock tonight."

"Are you sure?" The hammock wasn't very comfortable to sleep in. She'd wake up with a backache. Although it was old, the bed was much more supportive.

She nodded. "I want to spend the night with you under the stars."

There was a time when we would both have snarled at the idea of speaking kind words to each other, let alone *sweet nothings*. However, we were a far cry from those two strangers who were forced to live together many moons ago.

Romance was our new routine—one I could endure forever.

I carried her to the hammock and gently placed her inside, then I left to extinguish the fire. Smoke temporarily filled the air.

She made room for me when I returned, and I positioned myself under her before she curled into my body.

"Can you sing me that lullaby you always sing for Poaka?" she asked.

"Oh, you don't want that." It was one thing to sing for a pig who couldn't tell me how horrible I sounded, and another to do it for the woman whose opinion mattered the most to me.

"I did ask for it, so…yes, please!"

Heat pricked my ears. "Maris, my voice isn't that great."

"Are you kidding me? Your voice is sexy."

I had heard incorrectly. I was sure of it. "You think my voice is sexy?"

She played with my fingers, stroking each one with her own. "Ever since the first time I heard you sing."

"Funny, because I remember you were mad more than anything."

"Well, at first, I thought it was sexy, then rage registered. So, about that lullaby…"

My tactic of distraction had failed. "I was hoping you forgot."

She grinned. "Never."

"This is my curse for having a smart girlfriend," I teased.

"*Girlfriend*?" Her head drew back. "I'm your girlfriend?"

My insides wavered—had I scared her off with the title? We had already professed our love for each other, so I assumed we were ready for this new stage. "Well, I mean, I hope you are."

"And you're my boyfriend?" she asked, neck still craned.

Great. I've made a mess of things. She's probably going to run off again. "I honestly should be asking you how this works, but yes."

She was silent.

"Maris?" Damn, I really had ruined our relationship.

She settled back down, her head against my chest again. "I'm just waiting for my boyfriend to sing to me."

Relief flooded my body. My girlfriend still loved me. "I'm not getting out of this song, huh?"

"Not as long as we're boyfriend and girlfriend."

"So, I guess that's a no?"

"Right on. Start singing, my little bird."

I wasn't escaping this, so I gathered my wits before I regretted it. I'd never sung for another human before, and especially not in front of the love of my life.

I began to sing the words that my mother had recited to me every night in childhood.

"Close your eyes, child.

Let the winds be and the stars shine.

In your dream, your hand will find mine.

The splendor we'll see.

Sleep, my boy, and fly free with me."

The song always made me feel connected to Ma, like she was listening to me somewhere out there. I hoped she was proud of me. Proud of the partner I was to Maris.

By the time I had finished the last verse, Maris had fallen asleep.

The hammock swayed gently in the breeze as I sang another round of the lullaby with my girlfriend asleep on top of me.

Chapter 32

First to Walk Away

Maris

"When you said a decent walk, you didn't mention that we'd be hiking Mt. Everest!" I huffed out.

We had been walking for what felt like hours in the dark, aiming to reach the caves before dawn. If we camped outside, we could catch the bats returning home to sleep during the day. However, if none showed up, we'd know they definitely weren't roosting there.

"It would have been an easier trip if we weren't carrying everything we own," Aleki replied as he led the way.

I was struggling to lug my two baskets, one on my hip and the other on my shoulder. Meanwhile, Aleki had four stacked on top of each other with the ease of a fancy waiter serving a tray of petit fours at high tea.

He glanced back to check that I was keeping up, but caught my wide grin instead.

"What's the smile for?" he asked.

"You said *we*."

Confusion marked his face in the light of the lantern he had fashioned out of an old jar with a candle stuffed inside and a wire handle wrapped around the opening. "We, what?"

"'Everything *we* own.' I like the sound of it."

He laughed. "I didn't realize I said it, but I like the sound of it, too."

"Good. Now carry me."

His eyes bounced from me to his full arms. "With which hand?"

I stomped my feet in a pouty tantrum. "You promised you'd carry me if I couldn't make the whole way."

"That was before you decided to pack like we were moving out of the hut."

"Ugh, fine. I'll walk. You know, of all the random things you've collected over the years, you would think there'd be a pair of shoes...or at least one shoe." One covered foot up a thorny hill would've been good enough. At least I could have switched off every so often.

"Walking on different types of terrain will strengthen your feet. Give it time. You'll develop calluses soon for protection."

"Ugh, gross. I had pretty feet once, you know." My feet had turned into a cesspool of blisters. Every day, something random would lodge itself in one of my soles and I'd have to dig it out with blunt rocks. Somewhere back home, a pedicurist in a fancy spa was crying at my shoddy work.

"You still have pretty feet." Aleki's voice carried a lustful tone. The man worshipped every part of me, including my ugly feet. "I would spend the whole night kissing them if we weren't pretending to be bat hunters."

"We're not hunting them!" I scolded. I wasn't a vegan or a vegetarian, but I didn't like harming animals unnecessarily. Though I had joked about cooking Poaka on occasion, I never meant it. It did bother me that Aleki had to hunt and fish for us, but it was how we managed to feed ourselves. It was part of the circle of life. As long as we didn't waste any of it, I could support hunting.

"No, we're *stalking* the bats."

"For their own good, of course," I added.

"Something tells me that's what all stalkers say." I could tell he was snickering without having a clear view of his face.

"What do you know about stalking, anyway? You live on an island with a population of one."

"Not anymore. It's at a population of two now." He dropped the baskets and planted a harsh kiss on my lips. His tongue dipped into my mouth, and

I melted into a puddle. He was a damn good kisser, and it was the only thing that could effectively quiet my busy brain. The American Psychological Association could stand to add it to their clinical practice guidelines for anxiety disorders.

I broke away, panting to catch the breath he had stolen. "We need to keep moving before the sun rises."

He pressed his lips to mine again, this time briefly, but still with the promise of dirtier things to come with his tongue later. "We're already here." He held the lantern up.

Around the curve, there was a small entrance in a patch of stone hidden between a pocket of trees.

"Only one cave?" I had anticipated there would have been many more based on the landscape.

"No, it leads to a network of them," he said.

"Have you ever seen bats inside of them before?"

"I haven't been up here in a while. The last time was a couple of years after the catamaran accident, when I was too young to understand where I was. It was far from any drinkable source of water to warrant staying, so I never came back."

"You hiked this when you were a kid?!" Jesus, I was out of shape. I did this kind of thing for a living, yet this place was seriously testing my physical health with its topography.

"Come on, let's go inside." He started moving, and I grabbed his arm just in time.

"We can't just waltz in there. If it's home to the bats, we could introduce disease into their colony."

He glanced down at his body. "I'm not sick."

"That you know of. We carry lots of bacteria, viruses, and fungi without realizing. Some of these can hurt the fragile organisms, especially if they're endangered."

"So then, we're not going in?" I loved the effort he put in to understand my madness.

"Only after first verifying that they use this space for roosting. Then we suit up."

"Suit up?"

I pulled out two large tarps.

"You're kidding," he said incredulously.

I shook the white sheeting gently, making a swishing sound. "I'd never joke about plastic."

The material was thick enough to serve as a barrier between us and our surroundings. I assumed that Aleki wasn't vaccinated against any pathogens the bats may carry, and it was important that he remained safe.

"How am I supposed to wear a plastic sheet?" he asked.

"Like a rain poncho!"

"A what?"

"Look, I cut out parts for our heads. And I even made booties to match out of old plastic bags."

It was dark, but I could hear his displeasure. "Okay, it just got worse." Aleki held his head in his hands.

"Babe, come on. You haven't been vaccinated against rabies or Ebola, so this is also for your safety. I'll be wearing one, too. Do it for me?" I begged.

"Say it again," he crooned.

"Say what again?" I asked.

"You called me *babe*."

"I did?" I hadn't realized it.

"You did."

"Oh." He was calling us *we*, and I was calling him *babe*, and neither of us was aware of the words coming out of our mouths.

"Say it again," he urged.

"Give me a minute. I'm trying to recollect what provoked me to say it."

"Don't think. You'll strip the magic," he teased.

"Babe," I said slowly, tone dripping with honey.

"Now say, 'Babe, I love you.'"

I rolled my eyes. "What are you, a ventriloquist?"

"Speak, sexy little puppet. Speak," he ordered. He had been hanging out with me too much because I could clearly hear my smart remarks on his lips.

"Babe, I love you." Surprisingly, I didn't cringe. I didn't hold my breath. No words had ever felt more natural to me.

"I love you, too, babe." He pressed into me for a soft kiss.

"You're so cheesy." I pushed my palms against his firm chest. "Oh my God, look!"

A shadow fluttered by, resembling a black orb. It was fleeting and moved through the cave's entrance. We'd found the roost!

I jumped up and down, clapping as quietly as I could, not wanting to spook the bats with my excitement.

"Should we go in?" Aleki asked.

"No, let's give them a chance to settle. It'll be easier to see the whole colony when they're asleep."

One by one, we watched the little creatures return. I couldn't decipher the species since we waited off to the side, too far to see them close up, especially in the low predawn light.

It was like waiting for the popping of popcorn kernels to slow in the microwave. After a few minutes had passed without another animal returning, I pulled out the ponchos. I slipped on my outfit first to show Aleki how to wear it. He wasn't a fan of the cloth masks I'd made to cover our mouths and noses, but at least everything had been sterilized. I wore the rubber gloves, and I had made some plastic "mittens" for Aleki out of two clear food storage bags.

I took the lantern from him, since my hand coverings weren't capable of melting as easily as his, and we entered quietly. The entrance was longer and darker than I'd anticipated. Aleki followed along behind me.

We moved without speaking, yet our garb was rather noisy. I slipped on the ground from the bags on my feet, and thankfully, Aleki was quick to catch me before I fell on my ass.

We traveled through the maze of stone. The entrance was tight but sturdy. The air was thicker inside, and our coverings added to the claustrophobia. I reminded myself it was a good sign that the air was warm enough to keep the bats comfortable through the day as they slept.

The entrance narrowed to the point that I didn't think we could go deeper. I could've squeezed through, but Aleki was too broad to fit.

I glanced back at him, silently asking how to proceed. He motioned for me to go alone.

It was impossible to know what lay ahead, but I trusted that Aleki wouldn't urge me if he believed it was dangerous.

I crouched down so as not to hit my head and advanced slowly.

The atmosphere condensed so much that I knew I was going to pass out. *It's all in my mind.* If I slowed my breathing, I could avoid the risk of fainting. Hyperventilating would make matters worse, and if I couldn't regain control, Aleki couldn't get to me.

Loose debris shuffled under my steps, and I lost balance and slid onto my back. My hand shot up, saving the lantern. I visually followed the upward bounce of my voice from the yelp that had escaped.

My eyes widened as I took in the sight. Tiny furry bodies. There must've been over a hundred of them snuggled together.

All Pacific sheath-tails!

A warm hand rested on my shoulder, and I jumped. *Aleki.* He had shoved his way through the narrow entrance.

His covered hands roamed my body, checking me for injury. I shook him off and gave him a thumbs up that I was okay.

I tapped his chest and pointed, drawing his attention upward.

There were so many bats, and the scientific community had no idea they were here.

From the corner of my eye, I noticed a fuzzy body huddling at the edge of the resting colony. It was smaller than the others. A baby? No, the wings were too developed to be a pup. Its face was hidden. I angled my light slightly, not enough to disturb it but so I could get a better view.

I gasped, my heart seizing painfully in my chest.

White. Its delicate muzzle was *white*.

His neighbor's muzzle was white, too.

Fuck. I counted about twenty individuals with white patches, each cuddled closely in such tight quarters. It was only a matter of time before the fungus spread to them all.

Aleki noticed my panic and quickly took the lantern from me. He led me back out, shoving through the tiny hole and pulling me along. I was in a daze the entire way.

As soon as we had cleared the entrance, he ripped off his mask and body covering. "What's wrong?"

I undressed slowly, still stunned. "They're infected. They have white-nose syndrome."

He didn't understand my diagnosis, but he knew it was serious from my tone. "All of them?"

"No, I counted twenty, but soon it'll deplete the entire colony unless they're treated." I wanted to help them right immediately.

"Medicine? What type of medicine?"

"We're not really sure. We use different therapies based on the species profile. We've never had a case documented in a Pacific sheath-tail before."

Aleki wanted to help, too. I could hear it in his voice. "How do you get this medication?"

"We have them in my lab back at the university, but I'd have to—"

I stopped, unable to finish the rest of my sentence, except Aleki already knew what I had been about to say.

"You'd have to go home to get them."

There it was, the inevitable end of our relationship. The culmination of our two different destinies placed on opposite poles.

I was a scientist who had devoted my life to caring for the welfare of animals with the help of the modern world, integrating science and technology to help the ecosystem. And Aleki was a man so intertwined with his ecosystem that he couldn't exist if he was removed from it.

Could I be happy here, knowing that I was unable to access tools from my old life to help these organisms?

I knew the answer.

And Aleki knew it, too, as he did what I had always feared a partner would do to me if I ever entered a relationship. He walked away first.

Chapter 33

Reality Check

Aleki

Have you ever had an impression that the universe was conspiring be-hind your back?

Like things had been set in motion without your knowledge as a means to punish you for something you didn't know you had done?

I had that notion now.

Maris had done nothing wrong, but I couldn't fight the sensation that my face was still covered by the cloth mask. Everything was wrong and I needed space.

The shell I had grown after I had landed on this island, the one that had hardened my emotions so much so that I couldn't feel anymore, had regenerated. The joy from our relationship was already like a distant memory.

If I retreated first, it would hurt me less when she physically left. Indifference was my protection against heartbreak. It was easier to harden my heart, to bury it with ice until my blood eventually ran cold again, than to face the reality of what her leaving would mean. What her coming into my life in the first place had meant.

Her footsteps followed behind at a distance as the sun woke up for another day and slowly stretched its rays like tired arms.

We walked the same route separately. We were slipping back into the people we had been before we had fallen in love: two souls who had randomly traveled the same path for a brief time. That was all. Nothing more.

We made it back to the hut, and Poaka jetted past me, heading straight for her. She knelt on the ground and hugged him.

There was a possibility that she would never be rescued, but I knew she was more driven than ever before. Humans could accomplish anything when they had purpose. It was the reason why I had never successfully left—my parents had died and there had been no one to return to in New Zealand.

Maris rubbed Poaka's belly and talked to him, the usual vibrancy in her voice now lacking. He wiggled as she rubbed his neck, soaking in every bit of the attention. Her absence would hurt him.

Not as much as it would hurt me, though.

She caught me staring and straightened up. "Can we talk?"

Daylight was now in full force, and our new reality was etched onto her face in the form of dark bags under her eyes and her pale complexion.

It was easier to hide our hearts in the darkness than in the light.

"I don't know what there is to say," I said.

"Anything would be better than silence. You barely spoke back there."

"I didn't think I had to. We both know what seeing those sick bats means." I wasn't a scientist, but I knew how serious the situation was. The bats were sick, and Maris had a calling to take care of them.

"We don't actually know if I can leave. I tried to be rescued before, but I failed miserably." She was attempting to lighten the mood by planting false hope inside me. Yet again, she was considering my emotions over hers.

"But, you're still going to try to leave?"

She was turning the knife in my chest, even if she didn't want to do it. "I am."

I sighed. "And I won't stop you, if it's what you want."

"I don't *want* to leave you. But I'm a scientist, and I have an obligation to the organisms that I study."

"And my obligation to you is always to never hold you back from your commitment."

She moved in as if to touch me, but I didn't have the heart to meet her the rest of the way. "Aleki, it doesn't have to be a final thing. I would come back to see about the bats. And to see you."

"To be with me? To stay?"

Her gaze fell from mine to her feet, speaking volumes about our future. "I don't know. I mean…I wouldn't know anything until I could get back to my lab and confer with my team."

"And bring them here?"

She caught my hostile glare. "What?"

"They'll want to come here and see the cave, see the land they've never heard of, see the freak who has been living here his whole life." I didn't want the public here, invading my space. They'd colonize this place, forever changing my home.

"Aleki, no. You're not a freak." She planted her delicate hands on my rough chest. I turned my face, suddenly self-conscious of how unrefined I was compared to her—how savage.

"You're the one who called me Cryptid before you knew my name. What do you think your city friends will think of me? They'll do what people from my old world always did, poke and prod at anything different."

Her touch was gentle when she cupped my face. "You're not weird. And they won't do that to you. I'll make sure of it."

"Will you be able to stop them from bringing more people? You and I both know it'll never happen that way. Initially, they'll be concerned with the bats. Then the island. Before you know it, dozens of people will want to study it, take things from it, completely disrupting my home. This is my home, Maris. The only life I've ever known for a long time. And you going back not

287

only takes away the one person that I love, but it puts my existence in danger. Life will never be the same once you leave."

"I can't just do nothing. An entire species is in danger. Your existence is already compromised if the bats die off. Your food supply, both plant and animal, would dwindle over time. This affects you, too."

I took a deep breath, willing my irritation to settle. "I'm not asking you to do nothing."

She crossed her arms over her chest, already withdrawing from me. "Then what are you asking me to do, Aleki?"

That was the question. What did I want her to do? I wouldn't make her do anything. The situation was frustrating and beyond my control. "I don't know. I wish that last night never happened."

She softened a little. "Me too. I'm really sorry. I love you with all my heart, and I promise I'll always be yours. I won't abandon you. If I ever get rescued, it'll be temporary. I'll be back soon, and we'll figure the rest out."

She buried herself in my chest, and I inhaled her spicy-sweet scent.

"I won't abandon you," she promised. "You could have left me on the beach as shark food instead of taking me in. I'll owe you forever for saving me."

"You don't owe me anything. I'd do it all over again if you showed up on my island. I'd keep you as mine in every life." That was the only truth I was sure of now, despite all of the uncertainty that faced us.

Her tears dripped down my chest. "Babe, I promise, I'll come back to you. Don't give up on me."

I kissed her head, wishing I could believe that our love was that simple and that the outside world wasn't waiting to complicate it.

***

Needing to clear my head, I had left Maris back at the hut while she caught up on sleep, and somehow found my way to the beach. I didn't remember making the trek, but here I was with my spear and basket in hand and my feet sinking into the sand.

I watched the sea. Its waves were active, matching the tempo of my mind.

Perhaps Maris was right. Would it be so crazy to believe that she could return home, seek treatment for the bats, and come back to me as if time apart had never happened? I wanted to think things would be that easy, except I had never been an optimist.

For a while after I had fallen for her, I could only see the good in my life, but that had vanished as quickly as it had come. The world wasn't that simple, and Maris knew it, too. Her childhood had been similar to mine since she had been deprived of what the average child experienced. I suspected that all the promises she had made to me were really to convince herself that things could be that easy. If she said the words, she could believe them.

Deep down, neither of us believed them.

I noticed a speck on the horizon grow larger.

Dread filled me as it barreled through the water, heading for the shore.

Twenty-four years here and a boat had never shown up…until now. This was how the world worked. As Maris would say: "Sick irony and twisted timing."

Multiple bodies moved inside, but only one jumped out, splashing into the water. A man.

His stride slowed as he took in the spear I held. He lifted his hands into the air as if to prove he was unarmed. He viewed me as I had anticipated anyone from the outside world would—as a threatening barbarian.

"I come in peace." His voice was weak, lacking any rigidity, just like his backbone as he stood before me.

I lowered my spear, aiming it at the sand instead.

He had pale skin, contrasted by the dark hair atop his head and the forest in the shape of eyebrows above his eyes. His nose was weak—that of a man who was meant to sit behind a desk.

"My name is Eli, and I'm looking for a woman," he shouted, as if unsure that I could understand English. It reminded me of Maris when she had first arrived, except not one bit as cute.

I knew exactly who he was. He was that asshole Maris had been seeing before washing ashore. I instantly hated him. He'd touched her, seen her naked, and I wanted nothing more than to skin him alive. I gripped my spear but aimed it downward to the sand.

"Do you understand me? I'm looking for a woman with brown hair who goes by the name of Maris."

I closed my eyes. *My Maris.* He had come for my Maris. To take her away from me. To rip my heart out of my chest.

Some would say that it was a stroke of luck that someone had arrived to rescue her right when she needed to find a cure for the bats.

I would say it was the biggest case of bad luck that I'd ever experienced.

"Please, if you understand anything I'm saying, can you respond? I'm desperate for help."

I could hide her. Pretend not to understand English. Go back to denying I could speak. Never tell Maris that I had seen this Eli.

But my conscience wouldn't let me. My love for Maris wouldn't let me.

Defeated, I replied. "F-follow me."

Chapter 34

The Past Always Catches Up with You

Maris

I couldn't sleep. I tossed and turned in bed, despite having been awake for more than twenty-four hours. The sheets were too cold even in the heat because the wall of muscle I had grown accustomed to curling up against was absent.

He had asked for space to clear his head. The same man who was so obsessed with me that he couldn't go long without touching me before he was compelled to throw me down and bury himself inside of me. Now, he couldn't get far enough away.

It all reminded me of how we were when I had first washed ashore, except we didn't hate each other. We were still very much in love—so much that it was now the wedge that drove us apart.

I didn't want to leave him, but I couldn't sit idly by to watch a dwindling bat population suffer. The scientific community needed to know about the sheath-tails' susceptibility to white-nose syndrome. If it was affecting non-hibernating bats here, it could most certainly affect them in other tropical locations, as well as other species, too. Many of the locations with sheath-tailed bats could suffer drastically if bat populations decreased. Food supply would dwindle and pests would overgrow. The consequences of this mysterious infection would be devastating to nations.

Just on this island, the fungus could affect all bat populations, and in about ten years, the ecosystem would be very different. Aleki's access to fruits and vegetables would be limited since there wouldn't be enough bats to pollinate the plants. Also, the surrounding wildlife who survived off those same foods would die off, and his hunting trips would become less successful. His life was in danger if I didn't seek treatment, and I wished he'd understand that.

I had to leave—for him. He was the love of my life, and he had said that he could never go back to the modern world. He was afraid of the world seeing him as some circus sideshow. *The boy who lived in the jungle.* So the only option was to ensure his survival in his home.

I would be back. I had promised him I would be. Unfortunately, I couldn't predict how long it would take for me to return, or what would happen after I returned to treat the bats. I might have to go back to Washington again for more medication if the first round didn't work.

I rubbed my eyes, weary and stressed. *Fuck sleep.* I kicked off the blankets and padded out of the hut. Poaka scampered behind me, eager to empty his bladder and search for food.

Our sterilized tarps and booties from the night's trip hung on low branches, airing out. I had made sure to at least bring back and clean everything we had worn inside of the cave. A few baskets of other random items I'd left needed fetching later.

Poaka squealed as he discovered a stash of mushrooms that Aleki had left for him near the empty fire pit. I patted his head and left him to his own devices.

While he was eating, I grabbed the towel next to the drying gear and stumbled to the shower.

The valve squeaked when I turned it, and cool water came dribbling down the spout, washing my body clean.

My mind flashed back to the colony. The masses of petite bodies clustered together, unaware that some of their friends could kill them. Then the image of a withdrawn Aleki, after I said I'd return to him, hogged my head.

He didn't believe me. I couldn't wholly believe myself, either. Our future was uncertain.

I was thinking too far ahead. First, I needed to be rescued, then I could worry about goodbyes. Aleki and I still had more time together, and I wasn't going to let anxiety ruin it.

I turned off the water and toweled dry. I applied some of the oil he'd made for me from pressed jasmine flowers to the side of my neck. The floral scent instantly lifted my mood and transported me to a better time.

I dressed in my T-shirt and set to drying my hair before heading to the beach to find Aleki. He'd said he was going fishing to clear his mind. I was still in this relationship, whether he wanted me or not. I wasn't going to shut him out for fear of rejection. No, I was going to prove to him that I was all in, despite the obstacles we faced.

Footsteps approached the camp. Not one set, but two. I recognized the heavy, unrefined ones. The other steps, I couldn't place. They were lighter and more hurried than Aleki's.

Poaka screeched uncontrollably, piercing my ears, and chills spread over the back of my neck, terrified that he was in danger. "Poaka!" I shouted.

I abandoned my towel and rounded the corner. I was stunned by what I found.

"Eli?"

Poaka lunged at him, baring his teeth. Eli snaked around him in time and rushed to me. His hug was suffocating.

"Maris. I've been looking for you for weeks." I withdrew, but he refused to let go and held onto my arms as he examined me. "Are you okay?" he asked, his forehead wrinkled. His fussing annoyed me. I was like an experiment he was studying.

"I'm fine." I shrugged away from his touch and met Aleki's gaze. He was standing behind Eli, his face solemn like he was attending a funeral—the funeral of us.

"Thank God! You have no idea how scared I was when you fell off the boat, and then we couldn't find your body in the water. The crew said there was no way you could've survived the impact. Everyone told me to give up hope of finding you, but I never did. I knew you were alive." He pulled me in for a hug again and kissed me, aiming for my mouth, but I turned before he could make contact, giving him my cheek.

Aleki tensed at the interaction, and I prayed he noticed how sorry I was. Eli was all over me, way more than he had been before the accident, and it was far too dramatic, even for me.

I stepped back, putting some much needed distance between us. "I'm okay, Eli. You didn't need to worry."

He shot Aleki a judgmental glance, then glared at Poaka, who was on high alert with his tail in the air, ready to pounce as soon as Aleki gave him the signal.

"Your safety is the most important thing to me," Eli said.

"I am safe—safer than I'd be anywhere in the world. Aleki took care of me." I focused on Aleki as I said the words. He was my protector.

"What are you wearing?" Eli grimaced at my T-shirt, wet hair, and bare feet, while he was dressed in premium hiking gear.

"I mean, it's all I had. My other clothes were wrecked."

"It's better than that, I suppose." Eli cast a disdainful glance at Aleki's loincloth, then grabbed my arm, urging me to follow him. "Let's go. I can get you clothes on the boat."

I wrenched away. "No. Let me go." This was all too sudden. Now that I'd been presented with the chance to leave, I didn't want it. I needed time to think. Time to breathe. Time to be held.

I ran to Aleki and wrapped my arms around his neck. His warmth encased me, and only then was it safe to inhale again. "Did you signal for rescue?" We had barely discussed it. I had never imagined he'd make the impossible happen so quickly.

"N-no," he whispered against my head. His stutter had returned, and it killed me inside to know he was hurting—that I was hurting him.

I looked up at him. "Then how?"

He shrugged. "B-bad luck."

Eli was eavesdropping. "I have been searching for you nonstop. I directed the search team here."

I ignored him, my attention on the only man I cared about. "Aleki, I don't want to leave. I want to stay with you. God, I love you." My voice broke sharply as the harsh reality of being separated from him and Poaka, my family, barreled into my heart. I sobbed hard, panicking. "What do I do? Tell me what to do," I begged. I was babbling and blurting words out faster than my brain could process.

Aleki leaned down and pressed his forehead to mine, holding me close. "Maris, I love you m-more than words can say. You'll be b-back. Remember? And I'll b-be here, waiting for you."

I nodded, committing his words to my mind. My heart. "I will be back," I echoed slowly. It was all going to be okay. We'd be together again.

"She will not be back," Eli barked, disrupting the sense of calm Aleki had blessed me with.

Aleki positioned himself in front of me, towering over Eli. "Shut. The. Fuck. Up." His voice was clear and unwavering, stunning both Eli and me.

I pulled his arm. "Please. Don't fight. Aleki, come with me back to Washington. We can be together forever."

Eli scoffed, his disbelieving glare darting from Aleki to me. "We're not bringing...this," he spat.

Poaka grunted, reminding Aleki that he was ready for war.

Eli's disgust burned my skin. "This is the reason you want to stay? Because you fell into his bed?"

"Shut up. Don't talk about him like that," I shouted, tears streaming down my face. I was angry and sad and anxious all at the same time, and his yelling was like a fist around my lungs.

"Why are you defending him?"

"Because I love him," I cried.

Eli gasped, horrified. For several seconds, he resembled a fish, opening and closing his mouth. "Maris, you're not well. You need to come home with me. You're clearly suffering from some form of Stockholm Syndrome. I need to get you medical care."

A hysterical laugh bubbled up from my throat. I wasn't well, but for none of the reasons he thought. "You have no idea what you're talking about."

"Your aunt is worried about you. I'm worried about you. I'm not leaving here without you, Maris."

"I need more time." I toyed with my fingers. I was desperate for silence. More time to think this through.

Eli grabbed my wrist hard to drag me away. Poaka scrambled forward, nipping at Eli's ankles. Aleki was fast and punched Eli in the face.

Eli howled, covering his nose. "Fucking bastard!"

I stood by in shock as I watched Eli writhe and Aleki rub his knuckles from the impact.

Aleki cupped my face gently and pressed a kiss to my lips, consuming every bit of me, and my body melted into his.

Intense brown eyes studied my face as if memorizing every detail.

"G-go with him, Maris."

Before I could argue, he sealed his lips to mine one last time. Without another word, he stormed off into the hut, the door slamming on our chapter together with finality.

Poaka crooked his head to me, his eyes wide and shiny, and I lost any bit of composure I'd been holding on to as I knelt on the ground and hugged him. Sobs racked my body while I kissed his head.

"Take care of him," I whispered into Poaka's ear. "Take care of him until I return to my family."

Chapter 35

Toe the Line

Maris

"What were you thinking, hugging that man? He's a stranger, Maris. God knows what weapons he's hiding there. He could have killed you!"

I listened to Eli rant like an idiot as I sat on the boat, huddled under a blanket, letting the waves sway my body. His voice was miles away, despite eating up my personal space with his presence. Everything was numb. Physically, I was here, but my soul was still on the island with Aleki.

How was he right now? Was Poaka with him so he had a friend to lean on?

I wished I could check in on him.

I wouldn't be seeing him tomorrow. Or the day after that. For how long, I didn't know—

No. Leaving was the right decision. It was the only way to help the bats.

Returning home was necessary. *Right?*

My stomach churned like the sea, both violent as if protesting my decision.

"What did I do?" I sobbed, throwing off the blanket, and effectively cutting off Eli's lecture on my carelessness.

"What are you doing?" he asked, startled.

"Stop the boat!" I shouted.

He grabbed my arms hard. "Maris, calm down."

"We need to stop this boat. I need to go back. Aleki is waiting for me."

"Maris, listen to me. We are not going back. Your home is not back there." He was speaking to me like I was a child, and it was making me more anxious.

I ran to the railing and clutched the smooth metal.

"Don't touch me. I want to go back to him." I planted my foot on the edge, but before I could jump to freedom, I was yanked down and fell flat on the deck.

Eli straddled my belly, weighing me down. I kicked and screamed at the top of my lungs, but I couldn't move. "Let me go!"

He shouted over me to someone out of my frame of view. "Radio the authorities and tell them we'll need an ambulance. We need to get her straight to the hospital when we make it to shore."

I sobbed hard, Eli's face blurring through hot tears.

"What did that savage do to you, you poor girl?"

Chapter 36

No Place Like Home

Maris

Three months later—Washington state, U.S.A.

My eyes burned as I clicked through peer-reviewed articles, scanning rows of text like a machine scanning barcodes. The information dumped into my wasteland of a brain, stored for use at a later time. My finger never left the scroll wheel on my mouse, not even to scratch my nose or fidget in my lap. Before, when I'd worked, I had always been in motion, and now I found myself, more often than not, frozen. Still. *Too still.*

And nothing around me seemed to move, either. Time never changed. No one aged. The university had remained untouched while I was away. My office was still the same, not a pen out of place from how I had left it.

The only difference was inside of me. The part of me that had finally come to life…had died. For years, I had believed I was broken beyond repair. Then I had realized how untrue that assumption had been, that I was capable of so much more than what my environment, the people around me, could give me. And when all of that had changed, I had become free to bloom.

Footsteps echoed outside in the hall, careful and controlled. Perfectly planned. Predictable.

Not to my surprise, they stopped in my doorway. I didn't look up. I already knew she was standing there and how the visit would go.

"Maris." No hello. No humor. Just homogeneous gray. I didn't bother answering because she'd invite herself inside anyway.

"You'll need glasses soon if you continue to stare at the screen like that."

My pupils betrayed my brain and flicked to her position as if summoned by the formidable woman standing properly in her charcoal-gray pantsuit. Her silver stud earrings were plain and peeking out from her gray hair. *Talk about a gray aura.*

I sat back in my chair. "Aunt Sherri. What brings you here?" *Nothing good.*

She entered without invitation and took a seat on the chair across from me. I saw much of myself in her: the thin and pointed nose, lips that turned down slightly at the corners, eyes with specks of gold. I had inherited more from her than my own mother. It also extended to our strong sense of obligation. Or maybe that had been forced on me by her.

"I came to check on you."

"That's very kind of you, yet very off-brand." She had never been a warm woman. I had always sought her approval, but nothing I'd ever done had earned the affection I so desperately needed as a child—and now as an adult.

"Are you taking your medication?"

"Ahh, that's it," I said, realization dawning on me.

"That's what?" Her nose wrinkled, much like mine did when I was confused.

"The real reason you're here. You took time from your busy day to play social worker, coming for a wellness check."

She let out an exasperated sigh that reminded me of when my mother used to do the same thing when I spoke back to her. "You need to take your medications. The doctor warned that they're important to your recovery."

After I had threatened to jump overboard, we'd stopped in Fiji and were met by an ambulance, which had rushed me to the emergency room for care. The doctors there wouldn't listen to my pleas to be let go and had instead sedated me enough to fly me back to the States on a private medical plane comped by the university.

Apparently, my face had been all over the news for months, and my missing case had become high profile as "The American Researcher Lost at Sea." Wild lore had developed that I had been snagged by mermen and brought to a secret island where I'd been kept as a sex slave. People were waiting for the sex-slave bat girl to do an interview or release a book, but I never fed the sensationalistic media beast. I ended up holing up in my office most of the time to avoid people at all costs.

"That man is a quack." The doctor who'd taken over my care when I arrived in Washington was completely incompetent. I had known it from the second I'd caught him Googling rabies symptoms after he had found out I was a chiropterologist and had been in contact with wild bats, even though I had relayed to him none had ever bitten me and I was up-to-date on my vaccinations. He'd assumed it was the cause of my mental state until blood panels—that I had demanded—had come back as proof of his stupidity.

Then he'd doped me up on a bunch of antipsychotics and anxiolytics, which had left me dazed and out of my body. After discharge, I had continued them for a while to numb the pain in my chest, but I hated how I felt on them, like I was moving through molasses, slow and tired. So, I had weaned myself off of them and hadn't taken one in weeks. I wanted to wallow in my heartache, not diminish it.

It was evident that, yet again, Aunt Sherri disapproved of my self-*un*-medicating. "Have you been meeting with your therapist?"

"Nope. Haven't had time." I was too busy with research on white-nose syndrome to talk about my feelings or be gaslit for leaving my heart on a deserted island. Plus, the therapist was friends with my aunt, so there was no way I was confiding in her.

"Maris, you had a mental breakdown and suffered trauma."

I slammed my laptop shut and shoved it into my bag. Those familiar phantom ants crawled on my skin, begging me to get away from this intervention. "We're done here." I hurried to the door to leave.

"Don't walk away while I'm speaking to you." She remained seated, as if expecting me to obey.

I turned to her. "Then respect my boundaries. I told you never to talk about the island."

She approached me like I was some curiosity for her to study. "What happened to you there? You haven't told me anything. Eli told me you were raving about how you had fallen in love with some beastly man who paraded you around some sick bats."

I shut my lids, and my life on the island, from start to finish, played in fast-forward motion, stopping on the last time I had seen Aleki. *My Aleki.*

My heart ached as if I was going to die right on the spot.

"His name is Aleki. He isn't a beast, he is a good man. One who took care of me when I needed him most. One who I fell in love with." I glared at her. "But you wouldn't know anything about that, would you?"

"There's no need to be condescending." The woman was cold as ice. Her niece was clearly in pain, and she wouldn't break her tough exterior to *feel* with me.

"For my entire life, you've been a pillar. When I was younger, I idolized you as this larger-than-life-being because you were so strong, especially at a time when I felt so small and vulnerable. I had somehow tricked myself into thinking that I should be like you. *Work hard, fulfill my duty, and never waste time on human relationships.* I learned to bargain with my body to seek the comfort and security I needed but had never received as a child. I pushed away anyone who dared to ask me for more because I was afraid they'd leave me first. A circle my parents started but you continued with your emotional neglect when you took responsibility of me."

Silently, she swallowed the words I pressed upon her—everything I had wanted to say for far too long.

It had been acceptable for her generation to raise children by any means necessary, even if it denied them basic needs like expressing emotions. Nowadays, that was considered a form of abuse based on how negatively it could impact kids. I was proof of that.

Sure, I had made the choice to sleep around to search for safety and had lived to tell my tale. What if it had taken a turn? What if I slept with the wrong man? Ended up in a physically abusive relationship or with a sexually transmitted disease? I could've really harmed myself, and while I would've been partly responsible, Aunt Sherri and my parents would have had to share the responsibility, too.

"After I washed ashore, I was forced to deal with the emotional neglect of my childhood for the first time. To truly be solitary and not feed the addiction I had learned…sleeping with men for the comfort I was starving for. But Aleki understood my loneliness. I had been alone in a world filled with people, while he had been completely alone.

"The experience showed me that no matter where I lived, I couldn't escape the hurt inside. I learned I didn't need to use sex as a bandage. Aleki gave me everything I needed to heal those wounds without expecting anything in return. And together, I think we cured each other. We fell in love, and I left him out of obligation. Obligation that you taught me. That I had to place duty above human emotion, like I was a machine. That education and work were more important than my heart."

Aunt Sherri's bland exterior morphed and her cheeks reddened. It was like watching a black-and-white TV show converted to Technicolor for the first time.

She threw her hands up, finally losing control. "You think I wanted this? To raise a child when I never had any interest in having one of my own?"

Her words cut me deep, but I was already numb. I had always known that I'd never been wanted—not by the people who had made me and not by my guardian.

"Sometimes you have to put your personal regards aside and fulfill your duty. My sister died, and I had an obligation to her. If I hadn't stepped in, I shudder to think on what street corner you'd have been on by now. I sacrificed a hell of a lot for you, and you're ungrateful for all the good things you received because of it, like a roof over your head and an excellent education."

"I didn't receive a childhood. I'm so thankful that you did take me in, but you couldn't give me what a kid grieving her parents needed, and it festered. You can't expect a kid to understand sacrifice and emotional repression. I needed warmth and happiness, but you weren't capable of giving me those things. And now that you see how that affected me, you expect me to continue to fulfill obligations and repress my emotions, instead of allowing me to mourn another death in my life. This time, I won't let you. I'm not taking the medication. I want to feel it. I want to feel the heartache of the loss of the love of my life."

Aunt Sherri sighed, and I was suddenly greatly aware of how tired she seemed.

"I don't know what to say, Maris. I tried with you. I was never cut out to be a mother."

I approached her, lowering my voice.

"I know. Some women aren't, and that's as valid as some women ador-
ing motherhood. We were both dealt shitty deals when Mom and Dad died.
We burdened each other unintentionally. Now, we're older." I pulled at my
cheeks so the skin was taut, as if giving myself a face lift.

She chuckled. I had never heard her laugh, and it was a nice sound.

"And hopefully wise enough to stop these behaviors that don't bring
us joy."

My aunt stood before me, for the first time, a defeated woman. She
could conquer any task she set her mind to, except her niece.

"I really wanted to do right by you. To make you into a successful person," she admitted.

"You have. I have a career because of your influence, but my path is
different than yours. I am not you."

Her head hung loosely above her sagging shoulders.

"I'm sorry, Maris. I wish I could have been the guardian you needed."

"And I wish I could've just been your niece. We were forced onto each
other in a way that neither of us wanted."

She did something she'd only ever done once before. She pulled me in
for a hug. I closed my eyes, feeling as I had at eight years old, at my parents'
funeral—like I had family.

"You have my support in anything you decide," she whispered.

And I was finally grateful for that.

***

Aunt Sherri and I said our goodbyes, and she left my office just before I packed up for the day. I took the long way out of the building, needing to clear my head.

She had said she'd support me in everything I did from now on. I couldn't tell if it had been a loaded message, or if that was how I had received it.

"Hey, Maris." Malcom waved to me as I was passing his office.

I entered. "You're back."

"Just landed a few hours ago," he said from behind his computer, his fingers moving over the keyboard, rapidly tapping keys.

"And you're here working, when the workday is nearly over? Did you even stop home to shower off the airplane stink?"

"No rest for science," he said without glancing up from his screen. That was Malcom, always preferring work over human interaction. Aunt Sherri would have loved to raise him.

I sat down in the chair across from his desk. "Isn't that the truth."

"Didn't expect to see you back to work yet."

"Yeah, I don't do well playing patient." My medical leave hadn't yet expired, but it didn't matter to me. I'd rather be at the university than haunted by thoughts in my empty townhome.

"We're lucky that Eli found you. You were in the middle of nowhere. No one knew there was land there until he picked it up on the radar."

I needed to reexamine the definition of this luck that everyone kept saying I had so much of, because I sure didn't feel *lucky* at the moment.

"Yeah, that Eli is a leprechaun with a shit ton of gold coins."

That distracted Malcom from his screen. "Still haven't made up with him?"

"I'd prefer to ignore that he ever existed."

Eli's clinginess was a reminder of how destructive my past actions had been, and being around him only brought me back to that time in my life. After we had made it back to the States and I had regained my wits, I'd told him to fuck off. His attention had been suffocating and overstimulating. He hadn't taken my request well and had berated me again for my relationship with Aleki and how I'd lost my standards when I'd fallen off the boat.

Eli was angry and he was allowed to be. But I couldn't deal with him when I was hurting so badly, so I had never made contact again. He still worked for the university, and I avoided him at all costs.

"Are you okay?" Malcom asked. He knew all about my hospital stays and mental breakdown because he was the one who had urged the university to comp my travel expenses coming back to the States. It was also because of him that I still had my job despite questions about my competency to remain on the team.

I wasn't okay, but it was too sticky a topic to dive into with Malcom.

"You know, just reminding myself to breathe. And to lift one foot off the ground at a time while walking. And to not eat glue."

His gaze softened. "Make sure to pace yourself."

"So, how was your trip?" I broached the topic gently. While I had been in treatment, Malcom had been the one to facilitate the study of the bats. He'd organized a team, since I had been incapacitated, and they'd leaped into action quickly, using the coordinates that Eli had found on the radar.

For now, we had exclusive rights to study the island since the bat population was suffering from disease. That helped to limit the number of visitors to just employees of the university.

"That place is wild as fuck. How did you possibly survive there for that long? Jesus."

"Yeah, it was pretty unruly." My feet were still healing from the blisters.

"We found the colony you discovered and were able to administer the loading dose and the maintenance dose of the antifungal."

"Oh, good, how did they handle it?"

"Pretty well, from what we can tell."

"And what about the other species?"

"There are so many varieties that it's been difficult to track all the roosts down. We've tagged as many as we could to monitor them, but it's turned into a bigger job than I had expected. Identifying all of them could take months before we're able to ensure that no other species are infected. I tapped in a few graduate interns to stay back with Keats and Mahoney until I can make it back out there next month."

My head swam with what an enormous undertaking this had turned into. "God, that's a really big project."

"No kidding."

"You know, I've been researching the use of beneficial bacteria topically, and I think that could be helpful as an adjunct to maintenance treatment. Perhaps introducing it into their water supply. When I was there, I observed a large number of individuals drinking from a specific water source. Maybe we could lace the water so it's introduced into their gut biome?"

Malcom tapped his lower lip. "That's not a bad idea at all, especially if we can protect the ecosystem in the water source from the bacterial treatment."

I paused, bracing myself for what I was about to ask—what I *wanted* to ask. "How is he?"

Malcom leaned back in his chair and folded his hands in his lap. "Are you sure you want to know?"

Oh God, was it that bad?

My heart fell into my stomach as I nodded. "I want to know."

"He told us where we could shove our nets."

I laughed so hard that I snorted. It was impolite, but the image of Aleki—the grumpy, half-naked jungle-dweller—telling a group of reserved scientists that they could shove their mist nets up their asses was hilarious. "That sounds like him."

"How did you live with him for that long? He's a scary dude. He made Keats cry."

My mouth fell open. "Oh no, what happened?"

"Keats asked him if he knew where the waterfall was, and Aleki growled at him. Never seen Keats so ghostly pale before—not even when a jaguar almost attacked him."

I giggled. "He is pretty disagreeable at first meeting…*was.* You know what I mean." I sometimes forgot I wasn't still with Aleki, and when the realization hit, it was like the floor had fallen from under me.

"I know exactly what you mean," Malcom said, pretending not to notice my stammering. "And his pig is worse."

My eyes widened. "Poaka?"

Malcom rubbed his head. "Shit, it has a name?"

"What did he do?"

"He tried to eat me."

"What?!" I couldn't help the volume of my voice. Poaka was intimidating in size, but his temperament was softer than a puppy's. "I don't believe it."

Malcom flashed his wrist, showing off a two-inch scab below his watch.

"Damn. Are you okay? Poaka was always a bit rough, but he never attacked me."

He adjusted his cuff over the healing wound. "Okay, maybe I embellished. He tried to eat my watch."

I settled back, the story now making sense. "That sounds more like the Poaka I know. Always hungry."

"He misses you," Malcom said.

"Poaka? I miss him, too." He was the sweetest companion a girl could have.

Malcom's voice turned serious. "No, Aleki."

"Oh." I blinked rapidly to fight away the tears. The wound was open and threatened to bleed all over Malcom's desk if I didn't get a hold of myself. "He said that?"

Malcom shook his head. "But he kept asking if I'd gotten permission from you to do anything with the bats."

A smile broke through my sadness. I missed him so much.

"He smiles the same way whenever he hears your name. Never fully, like something heavy is weighing down the corners of his mouth, keeping him from doing it freely."

"He does?" It pained me to know that Aleki was hurting like I was.

"Yeah, then it fades quickly the way yours did, as if he realized it had all just been a dream or something."

My heart ached for him—to be with him.

Malcom closed a file to the left of his keyboard and placed it at the corner of his desk. "I wanted to talk to you about something, though."

I pressed my hand on my chest to numb my broken heart. "Shoot."

"This project is going to take God knows how long. And I'll have to rework my schedule to fly out there every few months. It'll blow a large portion of the budget, since I have to staff interns and team members out there. There's also the matter of how much of the terrain we've yet to map."

I nodded, but wasn't quite following the direction of the conversation yet. "That sounds like a lot."

"It is. It would be easier if we had someone who knows the geography. Who knows the wildlife, and the wild human, who lives there."

I held my breath. "Malcom? Are you asking me what I think you're asking me?"

His gaze narrowed at me. "Only if you're up to it."

I took a deep breath, and instantly, I smelled the fresh air and felt the tropical sun's warmth kiss my skin like a fond memory.

"Plus, I think Aleki is planning to steal our boats."

My brows pinched together so hard that my forehead tugged on my hairline. "Huh?"

"Yeah, he lurks on the beach often, examining them. Once, I even caught him inside of one, messing with the gears. If I hadn't shown up in time, he would've jetted away like James Bond."

I giggled, humor finally finding me after it had abandoned my body months ago. "Why would he want to drive a boat?"

"Maybe to go find something he lost? Or someone?"

My breath hitched. Aleki was planning to leave the safety of his island...for me.

"So, can I count on you to man the field?" Malcom tapped his finger on his desk, waiting for my answer.

I nodded furiously. "I'm in."

He clapped his hands, settling the deal. "Good, because you're scaring the rest of the staff with your zombie-like demeanor."

I laughed again, my heart beating giddily. "Why is everyone who works for you so weak?"

Malcom offered me a smile. Not as my boss, but as my friend. "Funny, your boyfriend asked me the same question."

Chapter 37

Boat Klepto

Aleki

People were on my island. I hated people.

People were intrusive and demanding, and these infiltrators were no exception.

They were scientists who asked too many questions and disturbed everything.

I had intimidated them enough, at least, that they had stopped visiting my hut to ask me to be their tour guide.

Poaka despised them, too, and charged at the leader after his wrist-watch had reflected sunlight into his eyes one too many times.

He was testier than ever before, existing in only two modes: agitated or depressed. The visitors didn't help.

I wanted my privacy back.

But a part of me didn't want them to leave since they were connected to Maris.

My Maris.

Life could never be as it had been before, when I had been alone, because she had changed me. Every smart comment, every smile, every kiss... She had awakened the parts of me that had gone dormant after my parents had died.

I didn't have photos or home videos of her. The scientists were my only link, and as long as they remained, I had a pathway to her.

She had been surprised when Eli had shown up for her, despite demonstrating her desire to seek treatment for the bats. It was like she hadn't been convinced she could ever leave. However, I never had a doubt. A person could accomplish anything as long as they found a purpose.

It happened sooner than I had anticipated, though. And I'd never imagined that her ex-lover would be the one to carry her home.

I spent nights wrapped in bed sheets that were still perfumed with her scent, convinced she had forgotten her promise to return once she had realized how much easier a life with Eli was. I didn't blame her for choosing him and the amenities that a man of the outside world could offer. What more did I have to give her than a bushel of bananas and some salted fish?

Maris was a special woman—too special to conceal. She needed to be shown off, taken to nice places, and showered with gifts. She deserved much more than I could give her. And while I hated Eli with every fiber of my being, I hoped that he treated her well.

That didn't stop my heartache, though. I missed her like a drowning man missed air. Days blurred into nights, and I moved through time like an apparition, not quite alive but not fully dead. I had stopped marking the days on the trees. It didn't matter how many years had passed when I would eventually meet the same fate my parents had. I hoped it would come soon.

I wished that Maris was happy. Maybe one day she'd get married and have babies of her own. She'd be a wonderful mother, so enthusiastic and caring. I wanted her life to be fulfilling, allowing her to flourish.

I studied the contents of my basket. The fish were finished curing. These would last me several days until I could figure out a way to find more food. I remembered that food could be bought from stores, but I didn't have any money. Perhaps I could set out traps for smaller prey like birds and rodents when I got to my destination.

Poaka shoved his nose into my stash, and I pulled away my goods in time. "Nope. Sorry, buddy. These are for me."

He protested with a high-pitched squeal.

"I wish I could take you with me, but you'd hate the modern world. It's covered in concrete, and it's so hard that it'll scrape your knees if you're not careful."

His eyes dimmed, and his head lowered. Leaving him would be as hard as when Maris had left us. I rubbed his ear and kissed his head. "Don't worry. I promise to be back soon and bring Maris with me."

He shuffled energetically when he heard her name. He loved her. We both did.

"Want to come wish me farewell?"

He grunted, and we set off together. The coast would be clear this time of day. I had made a mental note of the scientists' daily schedule, and this was when they were by the pond.

We reached the beach in no time, and just as I had thought, no one was around the boat.

There had been two boats when the leader of the scientists had been here. But he had taken one of them to return to his university—to return to Maris.

He had caught me lurking around them one day. I had just figured out how to turn the damn thing on when he'd suddenly appeared from nowhere and asked me what I was doing. I hadn't responded and instead stormed off. He was a nosy jerk, and I couldn't make a move without him stalking me.

Fortunately, he was out of the picture, and I could set my plan in motion. Well, I didn't have much more thought out than stealing the boat. I figured I could sail until I found land and then ask to be taken to wherever it was that Maris lived.

I crouched to the ground, eye level with Poaka. "Be a good boy. I'll be back very soon."

He let out a whine.

"I know. You're not used to being left behind, since you're in the habit of leaving me. I swear, I'll be back before you know it, just like when you disappear."

Poaka grunted when I rubbed his fur. I had to do this. It was the only way to salvage our family.

I boarded the boat, swaying with it as it rocked on the waves. I tucked the salted fish beneath the seat and set to turning on the engine. I had no idea what all the other controls did, but I would soon figure it out.

I closed my eyes, inhaling the fresh scent of my home for a final time. I was already homesick for my hut. *I need to leave. This is the only way to get Maris back.*

Suddenly, a buzzing sounded in the distance. I looked up to see another boat sailing to shore, this new one with tinted windows I couldn't see inside.

Fuck. The scientist leader had come back to check up on me again. I had thought he'd left for good.

The boat stopped, and I prepared for another inquisition.

"Going somewhere, sailor?"

My heart seized in my chest. My ears were playing tricks on me. I had heard her voice many times before, and each time, it had been my imagination. But…this time had sounded different. More real.

I couldn't believe my sight when she hopped into the water and peered up at me. She shined like an angel, or some other worldly being in a green dress, like she had been born amongst the trees.

Poaka jetted up to her, splashing through the water that he hated very much, and she ran to greet him, her brown hair falling delicately over his fur.

I jumped down from the boat. "Maris?" I was unable to shake the disbelief.

"You remembered my name," she joked, twisting her fingers as she always did when she was nervous. The redness on her face from the days of constant sunshine had disappeared, and her lean physique had softened slightly, giving her more noticeable curves. She had been beautiful before, but now she had a magnificent glow about her.

I approached her slowly, afraid she'd vanish as soon as I reached her. I wanted whatever this was to stay—this mirage, this dream—for as long as possible.

I reached my hand out, yet didn't touch her, worried it would break the spell.

She took my hand in hers and pressed it to her cheek. I soaked in her warmth. "This is real."

Her eyes glistened with tears. "It is."

Mine grew wet, too. "You came back."

She pressed a kiss to my palm. "I would never break a promise to you."

"You didn't stay with Eli?"

"Eli who?" She smiled. "There's no one but you."

I hugged her tightly, and she wrapped her arms around me and dug her fingers into my skin. It was as if we had been away from each other for a lifetime, but my heart mended immediately as I pressed her to it.

I pulled away, cradling her beautiful face. "How did you get here?"

"The university sent me. I worked out a deal with my boss. I will be permanently stationed here and head the bat treatment project. He will deliver medication and supplies by boat, and I will administer them."

"Does that mean more scientists will be coming?"

She giggled, and my ears devoured the heavenly sound. "I heard how much you love them. On the contrary, they'll go back in a month or two after we get a good handle on the roost locations, and I'll manage here on my own. Every once and again, a few may come to help with treatment or set up new technology, but they'll be mostly invisible."

Her eyes twinkled as brightly as her smile, but I could see a light murkiness behind her shine.

"How are you?" I whispered. I had wished for her wellness and safety every night.

She shrugged as if she didn't want to relive the details. "It was a rough few months away, but I made it out alive."

I knew exactly how she felt. Both of us had experienced similar starts to life, and though we had been forced down different paths, our trauma had left us both orphaned enough to bring us together—to complete each other.

"And how long will you stay here?" Now that I had her back, I couldn't imagine losing her again.

She bit her bottom lip, as if expecting rejection. "As long as you'll have me, babe. I'm yours."

I grinned, my heart ready to burst. "Forever, then."

I lifted her up, and she wrapped her legs around me. My lips found hers, and we kissed each other hungrily, picking up as if no time had ever been lost between us.

Fabric rubbed against my abdomen. "Three months away, and you started wearing panties again?"

"I couldn't flash the captain of the boat my vagina when I was getting on and off. Plus, I brought more with me."

I drew my neck back in disbelief. "You brought underwear?"

"Oh, yeah," she answered excitedly. "And clothes, pots and pans, dishware, toys for Poaka, and more books for you!"

I searched around, not seeing any bags. "Where are they?"

"They're still on the boat with the crew." She waved back at the ship, still in my arms, and was greeted by a series of whistles from the men aboard.

I immediately pulled her dress down to cover her panties. "They've been watching us the whole time?"

She nodded, a wide smirk on her lips.

I let out a possessive growl and carried her far away from the audience. She was my woman and for my eyes only.

"Where are you taking me?" she asked, bouncing in my arms while I ran through the jungle at top speed. I was a man on a mission.

"To the hut."

"But my bags!"

"Fuck the bags. They can wait."

"Why?"

"Because I have plans to ruin this underwear first…in private."

She giggled as I carried her into the hut and threw her onto the bed. The hem of her skirt slid high on her thighs, and her breasts heaved as I lifted the fabric, exposing red lace.

I hummed thoughtfully, tracing my finger along the edges.

"Like them?" she asked shyly.

"*Love* them."

She raised her head and whispered, "Good, because I packed some more lingerie for us to enjoy."

Excitement bubbled in my chest. I had read about them in novels and seen them in magazines, but seeing them firsthand was more exhilarating, especially when Maris was the one wearing them.

I pressed my nose to the apex between her legs, inhaling the scent I'd missed so much. She gripped my hair, and I couldn't wait any longer for her. I pulled down her panties and slid them off her legs.

"I thought you were going to rip them off like a caveman."

"I'm saving them. They're sexy on you, and I want to see you in them when I tie you up later and fuck your mouth." I ran my finger down her drenched slit.

A seductive hiss escaped her lips. "I don't remember you being this slutty. I'm impressed."

"What can I say? You drive me wild." I plunged into her, sheathing my pulsing cock inside her warm walls.

Her back arched as I pumped into her, reaching so deep inside that I could feel her heart pounding only for me. Our breathing grew ragged.

She cupped my face. "I love you so much."

"There will never exist a day when I will stop loving you, even after I leave this earth."

We moved in unison, our souls joined and chasing our destiny together again, and finally, this wild life felt like home.

Content Warning

Reader discretion is advised.

The following epilogue chapters contain subject matter involving childbirth, death of a beloved pet/animal, and reincarnation. The second epilogue chapter concludes with a happy ending.

If you are sensitive to any of these topics, it is recommended to end your reading experience of *Wild Life* now.

Epilogue

Six Years Later

Poaka

A sharp scream rang in my ears. Lately, they couldn't pick up as much sound as they used to, but this sound was harsh enough to wake me up from my third nap of the day. Or maybe it was my fourth. I couldn't keep track anymore, as I now spent more time sleeping than awake.

The screaming continued, accompanied by a bunch of other familiar voices. I stretched my legs and wobbled onto my hooves. My balance was unsteady, and it always took me a little while to stabilize before I could move.

I walked up the ramp that my humans had built onto the porch stairs. Aleki was good with his hands and could make almost anything with some wood and time.

I trotted through the open front door to find myself in the center of the commotion. My view was partially obstructed from the ground, but I could make out Maris on the bed. She didn't look well. I had seen her like this once before. Within a few hours, she'd regain her color, and by tomorrow, she'd be up on her feet like she always was, scurrying around and taking care of everyone. She was kind to me. Always sharing her snacks and rubbing my belly.

She was in pain, and her legs were spread open. Aleki held one of her ankles, and a strange woman who had come by boat a few sunrises ago held the other.

Another woman was at the end of the bed, calling out orders to everyone. The two strangers visited often whenever Maris's belly grew. And then, when it was about to explode, they stayed for longer.

"You're doing a great job," Aleki said to Maris. I understood human language very well since Aleki had taught me when we had found each other. He had read books with large words to me over and over until I understood each one.

Maris didn't pay much attention to his encouragement. She was too sweaty and uncomfortable to speak.

"Okay, the baby's head is almost out," the woman between her legs said. Her voice was loud and clear. She was smart. "I need you to push as hard as you can with the next contraction."

Maris nodded. She was normally very talkative, and I always worried when she was quiet.

Suddenly, Maris yelled again, scaring me enough to skitter backward.

"NOW!" the woman between her legs shouted. "Push!"

Maris groaned deeply, like she was angry.

"Keep going," Aleki encouraged her. "It's almost out!"

Maris's groan continued, until finally, the woman between her legs pulled something out with her hands. It was covered in a slop that didn't smell good like mud. Then the *thing* belted out a loud screech.

Maris let out a cry of her own, her face wet with tears. Aleki let go of her foot and rushed to her side to kiss her head. "It's a girl! I'm so proud of you, my love. Thank you for making me a father again."

The other woman took the crying thing and put it on Maris's chest. Maris and Aleki were smiling now and showered it with enough attention that it stopped crying.

"Do you have a name for her?" the woman at the end of the bed asked.

Aleki looked at Maris. "Marina," Maris said.

"Oh, that's a beautiful name. Perfect for an island girl," the woman who had held her foot crooned.

"I can't wait for Forrest to see his baby sister," Maris said softly, grinning down at the now quiet thing.

Baby sister. My family had grown bigger with this new baby. Aleki and Maris were great parents to Forrest, and Marina was lucky to have them, too.

"Are you ready for Forrest to come in?" Aleki asked Maris.

"Yes, poor thing must be lonely playing outside for so long. I feel guilty excluding him, but I didn't want to scare him with the visual of childbirth. He's only five years old."

"That was a good call," said the woman at the end of the bed. She moved around quickly, using various shiny instruments to cut the long rope that hung from the baby and then massaged Maris's belly.

"Thank you again, Dr. June. We're so grateful that you and Heather were able to come out here again to deliver Marina." Maris smiled at the two strangers.

"It's no problem. We'll stay for a few more days to make sure you're okay."

"Thank you," Aleki said. He noticed me standing by the bed. "Hey, buddy. Have you been here this whole time?" He scratched my head. "Did you see your new sister? Her name is Marina."

Maris held the baby up for me to see. She was asleep now and seemed so little that it was hard to believe that only moments ago she had been screaming loudly. She looked a lot like Forrest.

"Do you think you can go fetch Forrest for me so he can meet Marina?"

I let out a grunt, but it came out more like a honk. My voice didn't work like it used to.

"That's a good boy," Aleki said. "And, Poaka, we love you."

His affection was as good as an ear rub. I loved him, too. I loved all of them very much. I just wished I could tell them in their language. Instead, I nudged his hand with my nose and then made my way back outside.

I couldn't move very quickly and did my best to make it to the back of the hut, where I saw a figure huddled on the ground, stacking rocks in a pile. Forrest greeted me.

"Poaka, is Mommy okay?" His mouth tipped downward. He loved Maris a lot and didn't like spending any time away from her. He loved Aleki, too, but not as much as he loved his mother.

He had the same color hair and green eyes as her, yet his skin was dark like Aleki's, especially since he only wore fabric around his waist, which allowed his skin to tan in the sun.

I let out a honk.

"Can I go inside?"

I honked again.

He stood up and followed me to the front of the hut. Except, he didn't go in immediately.

I looked up at him.

"I'm scared," he said, his voice shaking as it did whenever he was afraid.

I rubbed my side against his legs, and he dropped to the ground and buried his face in my fur. Liquid seeped into my skin, and his body trembled.

I loved Forrest. He had been a good friend to play with and always included me in whatever he was doing.

Forrest finally pulled away from me. "Thank you for hugging me," he said. "You're my best friend."

He was my best friend, too.

"Forrest, come and see your new sister." Aleki came to the bottom of the porch ramp and brought his son inside.

I watched from the open door as my family gathered together. There was so much love inside the hut. Love that I was lucky to have been a part of for many years.

I had overheard Aleki and Maris saying they had lonely childhoods and had longed for affection. I wouldn't have guessed it from how well they showered us all with it.

My humans were special, and I would always be around to protect them with my soul, but my body was tired.

I took one last look at them all huddled together on the bed, bathing each other with kisses and smiles. This would always be my favorite image of my family. All of them happy.

I turned away and walked slowly into the thicket of trees that I used to fly through at top speed. My hooves hurt from the journey, but when I passed the trees with the gashes, I knew I was close.

I found my spot next to the two beds of dirt where Aleki's parents were buried. I had never met them, but from what he had told me, they had been good humans, too.

I lay down on the wet dirt and blinked my old eyes. In my mind, I held the picture of my human family, full of life, as I took in my last breaths of warm jungle air in this body that had served me well.

Through my blurred vision, I saw the distorted image of the one I'd always find in every life.

His deep voice called out to me. "Poaka, is it time again, buddy?"

Epilogue II

Three Hours Later

Aleki

I watched Marina suckle lazily at her mother's breast. "She's asleep," Maris said softly, her finger tracing the baby's smooth skin. I had never been more in love with Maris than I was right now. She was the strongest woman in the world for tolerating that much pain and never giving up.

The doctor from the hospital at the university that still employed Maris had left us alone, followed out by her assistant. They were staying on the boat docked at the beach, so it was just us in the hut for the next few hours until they came to check on Maris again.

"How long is she going to sleep for, Mommy?" Forrest was nestled in my arms, watching his little sister with curiosity. He reminded me of Maris in his appearance, but he had my need for understanding how things worked.

"At first, she'll be very sleepy, then the newborn tiredness will go away and she'll want to drink milk all the time."

"Maybe she'll want to eat my food, too? I can share some bananas with her."

Maris let out a chuckle. "She can't eat bananas yet. Before you know it, she'll grow up and you'll be able to feed her anything you eat."

I could tell from her voice that she was exhausted and trying to stay awake to give Forrest attention so he didn't feel left out. That was Maris—an excellent mother, even when she had very little of herself to give.

She was the busiest of all of us, wearing multiple hats during the day. Not only was she a mother, but a scientist. She still worked for the university, even after she had fully eradicated white-nose syndrome on the island. Because of her research, her colleagues in Washington had been able to publish the results of her treatment, helping other bat species suffering from the fun-gus around the world.

She facilitated research for other scientists to study the wildlife on the island since she lived here full time. When teams arrived, she served as their guide, helping them to acclimatize to the environment.

We had very little use for her salary out here, so she had arranged to have it deposited into a savings account in Washington in the event we ever needed to relocate to the modern world. She had decided it would be great to leave the money for our children if they wanted to study at university or start their own company one day. I agreed that our children should have op-tions available to pursue their dreams.

"Okay, Forrest," I said, taking over so my love could have a little peace while Marina slept. "Let's give Mommy a little break. She needs to get some rest."

"Ahh, but I want to stay with Marina."

"You can while I hold her, and let Mommy sleep."

"You don't have to do that, babe," Maris said. "I'm enjoying this quiet time with all of you."

She was going to sleep. I'd make sure of it. "It's important that you rest when she's resting."

She laughed softly. "You sound like a parenting book."
"I should. I reread the one we used when you were pregnant with For-rest."

She rolled her eyes. "You're obsessive."

"Protective. There's a difference. And you really should rest. I can feed Forrest too, so he has something to occupy himself with."

"Can I eat mangoes?" Forrest asked excitedly.

"No mangoes for dinner," I said. "You'll be bouncing off the walls when it's time to go to sleep."

"Sugar doesn't make kids hyper," Maris said. "They've proven that."

"I don't believe it." My mother used to always say that sugar made kids hyperactive, and it had been ingrained into my head as fact.

"Don't make me eat salted fish," Forrest whined.

"It's good for you," I countered.

Forrest stuck out his tongue. "It tastes bad."

"Then don't eat dinner." I crossed my arms over my chest.

"Ugh, fine."

"He's your kid," I said, casting Maris a judgmental glance.

"I'm totally fine with that." She kissed Forrest's head. "How was Poaka when you went to check on him?"

I treaded carefully with my answer so as not to stress her out. Her recovery was important, and it was my job not to worry her with things out of her control, so I lied to the love of my life. "He was fine."

How could I tell the woman I loved that our beloved animal had died...but then would come back to life...again?

Of the many things on this island that were strange, Poaka was the most curious case. I had met him when I was a child and had thought that he was just a pig. When he had died the first time, I had been heartbroken. My only companion had been ripped away, further deepening the wounds left by my deceased parents. Living by myself had seemed impossible—until Poaka had returned to me.

I hadn't realized it was him at the time, since he had arrived outside my tent as an energetic piglet who soon pulled me out of my depression. Except, then I had started noticing signs, like the same configuration of spots in his fur, and how he seemed to know exactly where he was going to find water, or his favorite patch of mushrooms, or how excited he behaved when I named him Poaka, too.

My suspicions had only strengthened when I had lost the new Poaka. And like clockwork, he had reappeared again as a piglet, as if just waiting for me to let him in.

Poaka was not just my buddy, but my guardian angel. In every iteration of life, he found me. And it was only a matter of time before he found me again. The island truly had a way of taking care of me.

I had never shared the truth about him with Maris, because I had thought I'd have more time. This cycle had already lasted longer than past ones.

It was time to tell my family Poaka's secret. I would share it with Maris later tonight when Forrest was asleep, then we could explain it to him together in the morning, before he interrogated me about where his best friend was.

343

As had happened before, I heard a faint screech outside.

I opened the front door, and on the doorstep was a little creature.

Forrest gasped. "Is that a baby pig?" He ran to the threshold and sat on his haunches, sticking his finger out for the visitor.

Maris poked her head up from the bed to see the little guy. "Where did it come from?"

I shrugged. "No idea."

"Maybe it's lost," Maris said. "Poor little guy must be hungry. Wait, is it a boy?"

I glanced down quickly to check. Poaka had always come back as male, but there was a first time for everything.

"It's a boy."

Forrest jumped up and down. "Dad, can we keep him?"

I looked over to Maris, as if asking her opinion.

She nodded.

"Yay! Poaka is going to love him. It kind of looks like him, too, right?"

I grinned knowingly at the familiar arrangement of spots on cream fur. "Ready for another round of trouble together?" I whispered into Baby Poaka's ear.

He let out a tiny squeak in agreement. Forrest and Marina were so fortunate to be able to grow up with Poaka just as I had.

"Welcome to our family, little guy," I said loudly, scratching his head. "We're a little chaotic, but we have a lot of love to give."

Poaka would always find me, and I had a feeling that when it was my time, I would find him, too, because this island had a way of providing for those it loved.

The End

Afterword

I cannot begin to express how much it means to me that you've chosen *Wild Life* to read, review, and post about. I write these stories to connect with you, and I am forever grateful for our bond. Let's continue to keep in touch through my newsletter on my website: *www.victoriawoodsauthor.com*

This story came to me years ago when I was battling postpartum depression. In 2022, I was admitted to the hospital at 28 weeks pregnant because my water broke. It was perhaps one of the most traumatizing experiences of my adult life. I worried for the health of my baby. At the time, the hospital still had strict protocols in place post-COVID and I wasn't allowed to have my two children visit, or any other visitors for that matter. I felt my sanity slipping away with each of the thirty days I spent inside of my tiny hospital room.

Then at 32 weeks, my beautiful son was born. Although healthy, he was still a preemie and was immediately whisked way to the NICU minutes after delivery. For the next month, I split my days between making up for lost time with my older babies and getting to know my new one in the NICU.

I was emotionally spent. My muscles had wasted away from weeks of bed rest. The trauma had finally caught up to me and I spiraled hard.

I was so deep in my depression that I hadn't even realized I was in it until one day I outlined a plan to my husband to move out of our house and take the baby. I assumed that this new arrangement would be best for the entire family. I was prepared to walk away from my husband and older children without feeling any sort of sorrow. I was sick and my husband was the only one who could see it.

As we reworked our life to prioritize my mental health, I leaned into moving slower. To take my time and honor my recovery. Because of this, the gray fog cleared just enough to infuse my brain with images of a couple in a hut. The woman was on the table and a man was applying honey to her wounds. It was the turning point in the relationship for this couple. I was obsessed with the scene. Over the next few days, I built their backstory, plotting a man who had been stranded and a scientist who landed on his island and disrupted his peace. Maris was my psyche reincarnated, complete with intrusive thoughts and insecurities. And Aleki was the blanket of safety I was so desperately seeking in my postpartum state.

These two characters gave me a reprieve from my struggle, but it would take another year before I started writing their story and two years before completing it. Finishing this book will always be my reminder of how strong a person can be when they find their purpose.

Wild Life isn't just about Aleki, Maris, and Poaka. No. It's my love letter to the fourth, invisible character: the island.

As the child of a Caribbean parent, I am proud of my heritage. As small as the ecosystem and population can be, there is something special about being connected to an island. A person can't help but feel tied to their land, like in a mutual loving relationship. The island and you.

In this story, I wanted to recreate that relationship especially from Aleki's point-of-view.

Aleki is such a part of the island that he no longer yearns to be rescued. And the island will forever take care of him as evident by Poaka's secret. I also wanted to give the island a life of its own to reassure all of us (myself included) that although Aleki and Maris would live their entire life on the island, they would be taken care of. It was important for us that they remain cared for in our minds long after the story ended.

So once again, thank you for reading *Wild Life*. This book wouldn't be possible without you or my team.

To Carolyne and Sam, thank you for your constant support and amazing feedback on my book baby. *Wild Life* would not be the same without you.

To my wonderful ARC readers, you have no idea how grateful I am that you took a chance on my book. Thank you!

To Nisha's Books and Coffee PR, Luna Literary Management, and Swipe the Book PR, thank you for all of your hard work to bring my book into the hands of readers.

To Paisley, another one for the books! Thank you for tolerating my chaotic mind and caring for my manuscript.

To Chinah, I don't really know how to thank you for all of your hard work. I am so lucky to have randomly met you at AC'24 and now to be one of your clients. You were my calm within the storm throughout this process. Thank you for inspiring me to be a better writer.

To Nisha, whenever I need help, you're always ready for battle. I cannot thank you enough for all of the hats you wear for me. Thank you for talking me off ledges, for holding my hand, for lightening my plate, and most importantly, for being my sister. I love you.

To Brian, the creative genius who understands my madness. I honestly don't know how you do it, but you always seem to know just what my book needs to shine. Thank you for everything.

To Sam, your cover designs constantly impress me. I am deeply attached to every design you make for my books. Thank you for always tapping into my vibe.

To A, you are that friend who listens to everything I say and commits it to memory as if they were your own thoughts. You've taught me the importance and value of being a *safe friend*. Your friendship has changed my life forever. I love you, my sister. Thank you.

To V and our babies (human and fur), you are the most important *animals* in my life. Thank you for always cheering me on and holding space for me when I'm writing. Your love makes me feel invincible. Without you, I am nothing. My *forever* loves.

About The Author

Victoria Woods is an *Amazon Bestselling Author* who enjoys crafting stories filled with sexy alpha-males, brilliant female leads, and love worth wandering the globe for. Inclusion and diversity are important themes in her books because of her mixed Indo-Caribbean and Bangladeshi roots.

A native Floridian, she now lives in Seattle, Washington. She's inspired by full moons, underdogs, and her amazing husband, three kids, and two feisty Pomeranians.

www.VictoriaWoodsAuthor.com

Other Works

The Power Series:

Power

(Available in English and Spanish Editions)

Empowered

(Available in English and Spanish Editions)

Control

Uncontrolled

The Numinous Series:

Songbird *(Prequel)*

Numinous

The STEAM-y Series:

A Discovery: Love and Other Things

(Available in English and Spanish Editions)

Wild Life

Scan to see entire backlist

www.ingramcontent.com/pod-product-compliance
Lightning Source LLC
Chambersburg PA
CBHW030351120726
47901CB00007B/1979